Also by Diane Leslie

Fleur de Leigh's Life of Crime

BEVERLY HILLS LITERARY SOCIETY

Diane Leslie

Sponsored by Northern Trust

Fleur de Leigh in Exile

A NOVEL

Diane Leslie

Simon & Schuster

New York   London   Toronto   Sydney   Singapore

SIMON & SCHUSTER
Rockefeller Center
1230 Avenue of the Americas
New York, NY 10020

This book is a work of fiction. Names, characters,
places, and incidents either are products of the
author's imagination or are used fictitiously. Any
resemblance to actual events or locales or persons,
living or dead, is entirely coincidental.

SIMON & SCHUSTER and colophon are registered
trademarks of Simon & Schuster, Inc.

For information regarding special discounts for bulk purchases,
please contact Simon & Schuster Special Sales at
1-800-456-6798 or business@simonandschuster.com

Designed by Lauren Simonetti

Manufactured in the United States of America

10 9 8 7 6 5 4 3 2 1

Library of Congress Cataloging-in-Publication Data
Leslie, Diane
Fleur de Leigh in exile : a novel / Diane Leslie.
p. cm.
Sequel to: Fleur de Leigh's life of crime.
1. Girls—Fiction.   2. Boarding schools—Fiction.   3. Children of celebrities—Fiction.
I. Title.

PS3562.E8173 F57 2003
813´.54—dc21
2002030660

ISBN 0-7432-2608-9

For

Doug Dutton
Lise Friedman
and Ed Conklin

founder, cornerstone, and mainstay of
Dutton's Brentwood Books

Guardians of literature, benefactors of the humanities,
champions of customers, employees, aspiring writers,
writers, itinerant authors, students, babies, very old
ladies, dogs, hummingbirds, and drifters. Avid readers,
upholders of the first amendment, tech support, example-
setters, do-gooders, patrons of music and the arts,
mentors, confidantes, researchers. A colonnade of the
community, an exaltation of booksellers.

ACKNOWLEDGMENTS

A large cast of characters moiled behind the scenes while this novel took center stage. I wish to thank:

Joan Friedman, a marvel of memory, intelligence, insight, imagination, humor, and empathy.

Marilyn Grossman Berg, for bringing her own sunshine to Tucson and to me all those years ago.

Yetive, Pepita, Miriam, Gretchen, Christine, Kristin, Meg, Cheryl, Jay, Cathy, Nancy, Janyce, Billy, Idalia, Suzanne, Liz, Jennifer, Hammurabi, Rebecca, Eileen, Mignon, Josh, Paige, Christine, Dan, Marcela, Andy, Nancy, Gladys, Karen, Scott, Rebecca, Tony, and Aurora—my magnanimous confreres at Dutton's Brentwood Books.

The belle and e-belletrists: Susan Chehak, Tim Farrington, Nancy Hardin, Linda Phillips, and Ellen Slezak.

The perpetually gracious and generous Jonathan Kirsch.

Eileen Lynch, my brave-hearted friend and shrewd critic.

The members of Jim Krusoe's workshop, who so thoughtfully critiqued a troublesome chapter.

Laurie Fox, my cast-against-type, compassionate, creative, and witty agent, and her wise partner Linda Chester.

Wayne Wershow, Julie Ballentine, Jacqueline Green, Jim Schneeweis, Aminta Rivera, Carmen Vialda, Lily Echeverria, Barry Rubin, Celine Emadian, and Ken Anderson, who perpetually macadamize life's bumpy roads—whew!

Laurie Chittenden, for being an all-time good sport.

The exceptional Simon & Schuster production team: Victoria Meyer, Laura Webb, David Rosenthal, Michael Accordino, Mara Lurie, Lauren Simonetti, Elizabeth Hayes, Leah Wasielewski, and especially my brilliant, talented, and stunning editor Denise Roy.

Technical advisers were required: Gregg Hurwitz volunteered his sister Melissa Hurwitz, M.D., who so kindly explained the pathology of tuberculosis. Sharon Lannan fielded veterinary questions. Musical score by Peter Elbling. Cuyler Huffman and Madeline Conroy freely shared their knowledge of infant behavior.

My mother, Aleen Leslie, hardly lets a day go by without bestowing on me material for future books, and Brendan Huffman, Dana Hufftone, Tamar Galatzan, and Patricia Saphier are sublime kin. So is Fred Huffman, my handsome, resilient, humorous, and supportive husband.

All interest in disease and death is only another expres-sion of interest in life.

—Thomas Mann, *The Magic Mountain*

Contents

Fleur de Leigh in Exile

I

The Invalid Invalids

A Rorschach of teardrops stained the lap of my dress. Weary of my sob story, I peered out the window of the bruised station wagon in which I was riding. If there had been a town, I'd missed it. A dusty, sun-seared landscape appeared before me wherein grimy beer cans, french-fry wrappers, crumpled paper cups and straws had been impaled on the spines of innumerable saguaro cacti. From the fleeting vehicle, it seemed to me, I was looking at a petrified forest of shish kebabs.

My parents, Charmian and Maurice Leigh, who considered cactus so hideous they wanted the entire phylum banned from Beverly Hills, were responsible for slapping me down in this alien collage.

"Think of yourself as a . . . conquistador," Charmian had suggested on the way to the airport. "I'm speaking metaphorically, *tu comprends*, about what you'll discover at the boarding school to which you're bound."

"There's no better antidote for your health than Arizona," Maurice had chimed in. He had hypochondriacal tendencies, so I paid little heed to his statement.

"Did I ever tell you about Junior Laemmle going off to war?" my mother asked. She believed in neutralizing distress with a story.

"Many times," I grumped, because I could have repeated this one word for word.

"Junior, the only son of Carl Laemmle, the founder of Universal Studios, was delivered to the train by limousine," Charmian said. "While Junior's mother sobbed and his father quivered, the chauffeur stowed fourteen Louis Vuitton trunks, not to mention the dozen wicker baskets puckering with the young man's favorite viands, into a small, albeit first-class, compartment. Mr. and Mrs. Laemmle the First had furthermore arranged for the chauffeur, livery et al. to accompany Junior to the battlefield. They owned a studio, so why not?"

"Would you send someone with *me*? If *I* had to go to war?" I asked.

"Women don't go to war. They stay home and . . . rivet."

"But if they did? If women were soldiers?"

"Your father and I don't have the wherewithal of a mogul. You'd have to go it alone," Charmian said. "And possibly, if Junior had served in the military without assistance, he would have developed a backbone."

"Please, please, don't make me go," I'd appealed to my parents one last time.

"A movie star's daughter's got no cause to cry," the driver of the car informed me. At the Tucson airport, he'd introduced himself as Dirk Swiggert. His pronunciation belonged, as Charmian would have noted, strictly to horse operas. A Milquetoast dressed in emulation of the Marlboro Man, Dirk had to be the school's jack-of-all-trades.

"I'm not a movie star's daughter," I felt compelled to let him know. "I'm really not."

"The scuttlebutt says different."

"What scuttlebutt?"

"What they're sayin' around school."

"My mother *had* a show—*The Charmian Leigh Radio Mystery Half Hour*. When it went on television, it didn't last long."

"Never heard of it," Dirk said. "She's a movie star in these parts."

"She'll be glad to know." I sighed. "But please remember, I personally have *no connection* to Hollywood."

"Well then there now, better mop up them tears," Dirk instructed me. "We're a hop, skip, and a jump from the premises."

Before us sat a squat, crumbling adobe wall that, since it spanned only six or seven feet, had the sole function of holding up a sign. RANCHO CAMBRIDGE WEST, it said. A bovine skull, pale as a ghost's sheet, had been tacked beneath it—by a disgruntled student, I surmised.

Twenty feet beyond it, where Dirk parked on gravel, I viewed a small compound—definitely not an oasis—of five single-story buildings that had seemingly been dropped on random patches of crabgrass. A narrow, cracked cement path connected them. Crudely stuccoed in white with green tar-paper roofs, the bland, unimposing structures were meant, evidently, to billet an entire academy of learning.

"Go on now, hon, git out," Dirk said as he leaned across me to open my door. "Jest walk on down that pathway past the classroom buildin' on your left till you come to the first residence. That'll be the girls' dorm. I'll bring your suit-case on over on my next round. Gotta git back to the air-port before supper. Got another gal comin' in all the way from the Eur-o-pe-an continent."

I was fifteen years old, exiled from the only home I'd known, and starting a new school midsemester. Feeling sophomoric in all senses of the word, I didn't want to be left alone, not even by a handyman. But being an obedient girl, I acquiesced.

Sans suitcase, I found my way to the dorm, opened the front door, and stepped into what I would soon learn was called the rec hall, appropriately spelled *wreck* by the Ran-cho Cambridge West pupils. The large room could easily have housed a Ping-Pong or pool table, but the earthen tile floor hosted nothing more than a frazzled vinyl couch. I studied the sparsely stained pinewood doors spaced at intervals around the halls' spackled, putty-colored walls. Those doors led to the dorm rooms, I had no doubt, but all of them were closed.

Why hadn't my parents sent me to the first-rate finish-ing school in Switzerland where I could have been reunited with my best friend? True, I hadn't seen Daisy in five years, but the memory of her amused savoir faire always kept me company. Capricious, wily, and beautiful, Daisy never would have allowed an abrupt expulsion from home to dampen *her* spirits. *She* had internal fortitude.

At least I'd escaped Hollywood, I consoled myself. Here in Arizona I would fulfill the all-embracing desire that I'd nurtured for most of my fifteen years: to live with normal, amicable people from America's heartland. And so, like a lone actress on the stage as the curtain rises, I crossed over to one of the doors and knocked.

"Oh hey, yoo-hoo," a ponytailed girl yodeled at me as she flounced into the hall, nudged me out of her way, and closed the door behind her. I took several steps back as she ogled me from head to toe. "Fee, fi, no lie, it's you, and wouldn't you know, you're wearing a costume right out of an old movie," the curious person commented.

To create the illusion that I was off to somewhere *"beau monde,"* my mother had required me to wear a long-sleeve purple sheath designed for her by "Irene." Shirred shearling trimmed the hem, collar, and cuffs. In its day—before Jackie Kennedy transformed fashion—Charmian had looked truly precious in it. I did not. The purse that *made* the outfit an *ensemble,* or so said Charmian, was fabricated from plucked ostrich skin. I felt blessed that my feet were smaller than Charmian's or I would have been wearing a dead bird's shoes, too.

"Hi, I'm Fleur Leigh," I said, wondering if I should try to explain my apparel. "My name is hard to remember unless you know it means *flower* in French."

"At RCW it means baloney," the girl said, puffing out her cheeks and crossing her eyes.

"And what's your name?" I asked, deciding to ignore her discourteous jibe.

"Oh, how now brown cow? Let's get this straight: we *know* who you are, Blossom. And we're not impressed. But me? I'm Reba Rand."

The appellation surprised me. It sounded like a Hollywood creation, the kind a studio would pin on a ravishing actress born Gertrude Schneck. Alas, due to the circumference of her stomach, Reba had not one iota of a starlet's appeal. "My, that's a melodic name," I said, attempting to pay her a compliment.

"Right, and there's nothing wrong with me, either, that won't be cured in exactly three more months," Reba said. She rubbed her protruding stomach in case I didn't catch on. "Say hello to Wozzums."

Trying to disguise my shock, I complied with her request. "Hello, Wozzums," I said. I didn't know that a girl Reba's age could be pregnant and still attend school. In the history of the Beverly Hills school district there had been only one pregnancy, so far as anyone I knew knew. As soon as the administration had received intelligence on her fecundity, the offending mother-to-be had been expelled.

"So, Blossom. Wanna meet the other girls?"

Maybe pregnancy impeded memory. "You're on the right track," I said gently, "as to my name."

Reba cackled and motioned toward the door. "We talk soft in this room. The sickest ones're all in here."

"Sickest?"

"Oh, hey, what did you expect? Everybody knows that Arizona is the health capital of the world," she said as though huckstering for the Tucson chamber of commerce. "Perfect climate for what ails you. This town is one big super-duper hospital, didn't you know?"

My father *had* associated the state of Arizona with remedial medicine, I remembered. "You mean all the kids at this school are sick?" I asked.

"Right you are with Eversharp. So what's wrong with *you*? Be honest now—no fakers allowed." Reba fingered the doorknob. "No movie-star brat would be hustled to this boneyard if she wasn't ready to kick the bucket."

My teeth began dancing a flamenco in my mouth. My father had been sending me to doctors as often as most girls have their hair cut. Did my parents know something about me I didn't?

"So, okay, keep your ailment to yourself. Who cares? Who gives a baby tooth? Anyway, everyone's dying to meet you. Oops." Reba clucked her tongue. "Guess I shouldn't say *die*. Just be sure you don't excite Sparky or her heart will go kapluie. I kid you not." With that warning, Reba threw open the door.

Charmian could uproot a bedroom while dressing for a cocktail party, but even her discards looked orderly compared to what I encountered. The blinds were drawn against the late afternoon sun, but in the dim light I could see at least eight girls, two to each of the room's four beds. Swathed as they were in hospital gowns, the patients were hardly distinguishable, and an armamentarium of medical equipment further obstructed my view. An IV appliance dripped liquid into some poor, prone girl's arm. The ladder back of the one viable chair in the room had an enema bag jauntily woven through it. A wheelchair, canisters of oxygen, a traction contraption were in evidence. The bedpans outnumbered the beds.

I wondered now if the multitude of tablets and capsules Maurice foisted on me daily were harbingers of a fatal disease. My favorite nanny had departed from our house when I was an impressionable four-year-old. "C'est fait. I had to let her go," Charmian had tsked at the time. "Miss Nora is chronically ill. Your father has witnessed her germs jitterbugging all over our plates and silverware. Really, she's a regular Typhoid Mary."

At the time I'd thought *typhoid* and *typhoon* were one and the same: the blowing of wind, sand, leaves, and noses.

"But I love Miss Nora," I'd beseeched my mother.

"She probably infected you, but she'll do it no more."

Could it be that Miss Nora's microbes were still vagabonding through my veins?

A vision of Cocteau, our purebred Saint Bernard, flickered through my optic nerves. When Cocteau had contracted mange, he, too, had been exiled, along with his disenfranchised hairs and scabs. His bed had been incinerated. Were my mattress, sheets, and four posters being trucked to the Department of Sanitation at this very moment? I considered the probability, then let out a scream, a feeble one that I doubted could be heard above the susurrus of coughing, wheezing, and moaning.

"SHUSH."

"SHUT UP."

Reba clamped her hand over my mouth. "What did I tell you? YOU WANT TO GIVE SPARKY A HEART AT-TACK?" she shouted as I struggled to extricate myself from her grasp.

"She's new. She knows not what she does." A rasping, unsteady voice coming from the bed nearest the window took up my defense. A face whose pallor approximated a paste of flour and water captured everyone's attention.

My attendant abandoned me and rushed over to the papier-mâché girl, evidently the one called Sparky, a nick-name doubtlessly attributable to her red hair. "DON'T GET EXCITED. YOU'VE GOT TO DO WHAT THE DOCTOR SAID."

Directing a flaccid smile in my direction, Sparky fell back on her pillow.

"DON'T SMILE. DON'T GET EMOTIONAL," other girls said.

"ARE YOU LISTENING TO THEM, SPARKY?" Reba added, her voice abrasively shrill. "If you aren't, let me remind you, you're gonna be a dead duck."

"You can fuck your duck," Sparky retorted.

Among the teenagers I knew, profanity was still taboo. Even my father reserved his basest ejaculations for the company of men. Aghast, I took Sparky's foul language as another sign of Rancho Cambridge West's inferiority. Echoing my confusion, a gangly girl in the corner piped up, "Eah, eah, what's she saying? What's going on?"

"That's Deaf Dena." Reba introduced a skinny yet bosomy girl. "Shout hello at her, will you, Blossom?"

"HELLO, DENA!" I cried, not bothering to correct Reba about my name.

"Eah?" Dena responded.

A girl named Melly—short for Melinda, I soon learned—struggled out from under her sheets. Atop her child's body shone the sunny face of a cherub and a halo of Hershey-colored hair. Her mischievous smile won my instant affection. If only her hands and bare feet weren't so grotesquely swollen and ulcerated.

"Melly, you know if you walk on them, your feet will fall off," my guide through this hellish ward told her.

Melly let out a groan.

"Leprosy," Reba enlightened me.

How can that be? I wanted to ask. But because I'd been taught by several nannies that courtesy and civility would see me through the grimmest of times, I automatically said, "It's nice to meet you."

"Gosh! Wow! You *aren't* a snob!" Melly remarked, sounding genuinely surprised. Her warm, expressive voice carried with it a trace of a giggle.

A tall, broad-shouldered, manly girl wearing dark glasses and tapping a red-tipped white cane bumbled too close to Melly, knocking her onto her bed. The floor was so cluttered that the girl had to wave her cane a foot above ground level in order to advance. In the process she thwacked my shins.

"This is Lizzie," Reba announced. "She'll be your roomie, and she wants to get acquainted *now*." Reba spoke louder than she had for Deaf Dena, as though all of Lizzie's faculties were on the fritz. "Mind if she feels you?"

Before I could protest, Lizzie ran her sticky fingers over my eyes and nose and cheeks and mouth. She smelled of horse manure.

"Stop scrunching up your face," Lizzie growled while I gazed into her blank stare. "You *are* scrunching it, aren't you? If you're not, you're really homely."

"How's the great desert air of Tucson supposed to cure blindness?" I asked in retaliation.

"It's not," Lizzie answered. Her impenetrable glasses were aimed at my ear. "My parents booted me out. The tap-tap-tapping of my cane was driving them out of their gourds."

I would have commiserated—after all, I'd been booted out, too—but just then someone began coughing. The deep, phlegm-filled hack might have emanated from a large, ailing dog. *I'd* been vaccinated for whooping cough, but had *she*?

"Is there a doctor on the premises? Is there a school nurse?" I asked, as much for myself as for the hacker.

"Forget it," Sparky weakly advised me. "Still, *I* can't stand the sound of Babs's lungs turning inside out. It makes my heart skyrocket."

"You mean your *pulse*, Sparky," Miss Know-It-All Reba corrected her.

"Babs'll be silenced in a jiffy," a tall, stringy-haired girl volunteered. "Hot compresses coming up."

"Who's she? What's wrong with *her*?" I asked Reba over the sound of discharging phlegm.

"Meet Tammy. She's got allergies. They're nothing."

Not only were my teeth chattering in spite of the heat, I couldn't stop shivering.

After Tammy slopped a hot, wet towel on Babs's chest, she hurried to Sparky's side. "What can we do you for?" she asked. She seemed unusually devoted.

"I need peace. I need a place to call my own," Sparky answered plaintively.

"You mean heaven? Oh, Sparky, not yet!" Melly pleaded.

"Help me. Please. I need Dino," Sparky whined.

A record player, its chunky spindle suitable only for 45-rpm records, was immediately hauled from under her bed and the needle placed in the desired groove. Dean Martin, a singer who had been the brunt of my friends' jokes—Wolfman Jack *never* spun his discs—now served the noble purpose of drowning out Babs's barking. But Martin's singing may have caused—and most certainly didn't prevent—an asthmatic girl to have an attack and an epileptic girl to have a fit. The latter writhed on the dorm-room floor.

If this was an act, why were they performing it for me? What had I done?

Melly, leprous feet and all, and Lizzie, holding her cane like a partner, began to dance clumsily. To the tune of "Volare (Nel Blu Dipinto Di Blu)," Sparky performed a levitation. She jacked herself up on her elbows and struggled to sit up. Slow as a sloth, she dislodged the blanket from her legs. Seeing their misaligned position, I could have sworn they were atrophied. Gradually Sparky inched her feet to the floor and rose to achieve a shaky balance.

A new record fell into place on the turntable, and Bobbie Vee's "Take Good Care of My Baby" aptly began to play. While the other girls subdued the writhing epileptic, Sparky danced. In slow motion she wiggled her shoulders, ground her hips, and rubbered her legs à la Elvis.

Though skeptical, I felt afraid, so much so that I yearned to be excused and exit this room, this school, this vortex of diseases, this new, loathsome life. "How can you stand this?" I demanded of Reba.

"That's the way the cookie crumbles," the smart aleck said.

Groaning and panting, Sparky danced on. "Really, you should get back in bed," I pleaded with her.

"What for?"

"To give your heart a rest," I said in earnest.

Sparky stared at me gravely. Her eyes held mine until, with a quick motion, she embedded her top teeth in her bottom lip and began to shake. Was this the onset of a heart attack? I reached over to her, hoping to guide her into bed, but my touch triggered a series of strangulated noises. First came hisses, a balloon expelling air, then a few muted chokes, but very quickly the sounds intensified and proliferated into a hearty roar. Sparky was in the throes of a laughing jag!

When Sparky laughed, I discovered, the world laughed with her. One by one, be they deaf, dumb, blind, gimpy, ulcerated, epileptic, asthmatic, or pregnant, they laughed. A cacophony not unlike the bellowing of sea lions packed the room. Had one of the canisters I'd spied contained laughing gas? Had it exploded? If it had, wouldn't I be laughing, too?

II

A One-Dish School

"**Y**ou might as well sit at our table," Melly generously suggested, pulling out a chair for me soon after I'd entered the mess hall. Only minutes before I'd watched this pixie of a girl peel away gauze soaked in calamine lotion and dotted with lumps of clay, the ulcers of her leprosy. All the while she'd chanted, "Out, damn spot. Out, out, out," portraying the only Brooklyn-accented (or so I assumed) Lady Macbeth I would ever encounter. Though the other girls—after they'd removed their death-mask makeup and hospital gowns—favored jeans and short-sleeve blouses, Melly had slipped into black tights and a long-sleeve black shirt like a Beat poet's moll.

Over the din in the dining room, I began to express my gratitude for Melly's invitation, when Sparky, one of our tablemates, spoke up. "You mean the movie star's daughter stoops to sit with us yokels?"

To countermand the sting of her sarcasm, I adopted Charmian's modus operandi and focused on the premises. The mess hall evidently doubled as a library. Bookshelves, with cutouts for doors and a pass-through from the kitchen, lined three sides of the room. They seemed to constitute a convalescent home for books. Doddering encyclopedias, weathered atlases with eroded bindings, and mildewed volumes of the Hardy Boys series sprawled and sloped on the shelves. The fourth wall consisted entirely of glass, though it offered no panorama, only a reflection of the unworthy interior. The door, also glass, trembled tumultuously whenever anyone went in or out, adding insult to the injury of the overwhelming racket.

"Don't mind Sparky. She likes to mouth off, but really, she's harmless, aren't you, Sparks?" Melly asked with facetious ferocity.

Sparky glowered. I would have sought alternate seating arrangements had not the other occupants of Melly's table nabbed my curiosity. I remained in situ.

Charmian had assured me that my new school would be co-ed. "I would never coop you up with a bevy of brainless females," she'd remarked. "Boys supply the . . . joy, the *oom-pah-pah* of life."

"Oh, I almost forgot," Melly said, indicating the two boys seated at either end of our table. "Meet Bri and Lionel."

"An," Bri muttered with annoyance. "Bri . . . *an.*"

"Nice to meet you," I said, disarmed by his buff physique and wavy nutmeg-colored hair. Even though his ears were sprinkled with what appeared to be frost but must have been an uncommon form of dandruff, I found his face oh-so-compelling.

"Makeup will conceal that minor defect," Charmian might have remarked while flirtatiously lolling in the glow of Brian's "ideal cinematic features." Had she been positioned to do so, my mother would have cast him as a young lieutenant on a battleship captained by Gregory Peck. She would have given the boy one epic scene in which to flaunt his courage, talent, and muscles before torpedoes crushed his hull. Charmian wanted to direct.

Though I could mimic my mother with accuracy, I didn't have it in me that day to loll or flirt. Instead, politesse directed me toward Lionel. "Nice to meet you, too," I said, not wanting to slight this less distinguished member of his gender.

But Lionel only gazed plaintively at Melly. He seemed to have been struck dumb.

"Don't mind Lionel," Melly said. "He's in love with me, or so he says. You see how he shows it—he stares. I hate it. Really, Lionel, I do."

"Lionel Laird Lawrence the Third," he intoned without shifting his gaze from Melly. "How do you do?"

I'd never met anyone who looked anything like Lionel. His flapjack face repudiated the third dimension. On that flat surface, his small eyes pushed toward each other over a too thin nose. But his mouth was oversize, as though custom-built for someone of excessive verbiage, while his jumbo ears, antithetically, indicated an attentive listener.

"How did it go, my Mellykins?" Lionel asked. "Tell me about your afternoon of sick-lickal stardom."

Melly offered Lionel a glance of great charity. "Lionel talks nonstop," she complained. "The trick is, don't let him get started."

"I'm too much in love to talk now," Lionel said, his scrawny chest heaving with emotion.

"Or eat?" Both boys and Sparky and Melly disregarded the plates that had been set before us.

Melly sighed. "It's healthier not to."

"You mean you know what's in this . . . casserole? You're allowed to go into the kitchen here?" At home that particular room—my favorite in our house—remained off limits to me. My parents feared their only progeny might someday discredit them by assuming a menial cooking job.

Aside from Dirk the handyman, I had not yet met an adult at Rancho Cambridge West. It therefore seemed ill-omened when two frigid, veiny hands pressed down on my shoulders with glacial force. In my peripheral vision I discerned a bony, graying woman.

In a hesitant, unstrung voice, the woman behind me inquired, "Are you the new . . . ?"

"Meet Mrs. Prail, the headmaster's wife," Melly said. Then, whispering just loud enough to be heard above the clatter, she added, "You could say she's also his albatross."

Lionel stood up and, with a bow and a flourish of his wrist, presented me. "Mrs. Prail, allow me to introduce, um, Blossom."

"Oh . . . Blossom. I should have known," Mrs. Prail said. "It's just that . . . *two* girls arrive today."

"I'm the one called Fleur," I said, trying to slither out from under her grasp.

"Well . . . is everything . . . all right?" she stammered.

"Fine and dandy," Sparky responded.

"Actually, Mrs. Prail, the dinner looks delicious," I said in all honesty, because the gooey gallimaufry certainly would not have been permitted on the No Whites Inside Diet my father had designed for me. "But I'm not very hungry tonight. What I'd like instead is a bowl of consommé."

"Oh," the woman responded in a very hurt voice. Her frosty fingers melted away from my frame. "That's not what I meant. I wanted to know . . . if you're feeling . . . at home. Are you going to be happy here?"

"I don't know," I replied.

"Well, well then . . . well," the headmaster's wife answered and meandered away.

"Did I commit a faux pas? Asking for consommé?" I asked my tablemates.

"Too bad, Miss Snobola. You better get it straight— this is strictly a one-dish school," Sparky announced. "If they're serving shit on a shingle or adobe melt, like tonight, that's the meal. They aren't about to pluck a chicken just for you."

"So it's just like home," I answered.

"Yeah, right," Sparky said. "Every night poor little Blossom has to stuff down all her filet mignon and caviar before she can leave the dining room."

"We *never* have caviar," I snapped back. "My parents were children during the Depression."

"What's that supposed to mean?" Sparky asked gruffly.

I would have patronizingly explained, just as it had been explained to me, the stock-market crash of 1929 and its myriad repercussions if I hadn't noticed a figure, both familiar and foreign, standing outside the glass entrance door. She had paused to consider her reflection and smooth her hair. Cut short when I last saw her five years before, her hair now flowed like maple syrup down to her shoulders from either side of an off-center part.

So much had gone awry in the last several hours that it seemed plausible I was now only conjuring the fulfillment of a long-held wish. Yet some finer-tuned element in my brain sent me scurrying outside. A smile of jack-o'-lantern proportions must have illuminated my face as I hollered, "Daisy, Daisy, Daisy."

She threw her arms around me. We squeezed and kissed until tears deluged our four eyes. "You better not cry. Crying makes you look like Rudolph the red-nosed reinqueer," Daisy recited an old line of ours.

"And crying intensifies *your* beauty, I happen to remember."

"It does heighten the color of my forest-green irises," Daisy agreed. "I've been observing myself in the mirror for the last two weeks while I cried out my heart, liver, kidney, and spleen."

"Why? What's happened?" I asked, concerned.

"Right now I'm too exhausted to belt out my chanson of woe. I'll sound off as soon as we're alone. Meanwhile, did your mother forget to tell you not to call me Daisy?" My old friend had a European accent now and, despite her furtive manner, exuded self-possession. "This is of utmost importance, Fleur. No one must know my old name. I'm Twyla now. Twyla Flint. Three short syllables. Say it, please."

"Twyla Flint," I repeated.

"Good," she said and relaxed a little. "So! Don't you think Twyla is a gorgeous name? It has a classical ring. And Flint is the most resilient stone there is. I looked it up. I like the recurrence of T and L sounds, don't you?" She spoke in the breathy strains of an artist at a gallery admiring her own best work. Her manner of speech, phrasing, diction, and vocabulary—the reward of a Swiss education, I assumed—affirmed her refinement, erudition, and adulthood.

"Just tell me how you happened to come here, Daisy," I urged.

"Fleur, you *must* call me Twyla. *No one* must discover I'm LaGiana Belmont's daughter."

"Okay . . . Twyla, but please, what brought you to this gruesome place?"

"Is it gruesome? I hadn't noticed in the dark. But how could it be? Your mother picked it out," Twyla said.

"*My* mother? For both of us?"

Mrs. Prail suspended our reunion by stepping between us and scrutinizing Twyla. "*Now* I know . . . who's who. You look just like your mother, the way she was in *The Lady Is Lucky*," she told Twyla with an awestruck purr. "Why, it's plain as . . . the nose on your face."

An odd choice of characteristics, I thought, because Twyla's nose appeared to be the result of recent renovation.

"I don't know what you're talking about," Twyla responded.

"Oh dear . . . have I said something wrong? It's just that I've seen every movie LaGiana Belmont ever made. Well, maybe not the ones she makes in Europe now. I didn't mean . . . Please, come inside and eat your dinner," Mrs. Prail said apologetically. She held open the door for Twyla but seemed to forget about me. Behind them I observed Twyla's mesmerizing effect on the student body. Elizabeth Taylor in her princess-of-Hollywood years made no grander impression when entering Romanoff's.

"Oh, for Christ's sake," I heard Sparky groan. "Do you see what I see? We did our whole darn act for the wrong girl."

Twyla, as if at a soiree, appeared to be searching for a place card, so I shepherded her to my table, where Lionel had already squeezed another chair between Melly's and his. For the first time he'd allowed his eyes to wander away from Melly. Once Twyla was seated, Lionel knelt on one knee, bowed his head, and tried to kiss her hand.

"Lionel's taking the direct approach," Brian commented, and I became unhappily aware that he, too, had been captivated by my friend's pulchritude. "Melly, you're losing your boyfriend."

"I hereby grant you permission to switch your allegiance to this new, more worthy woman," Melly told Lionel.

"I'd like to introduce my dearest friend, Dais—*Twyla*
Flint," I told my tablemates. In the newly hushed dining
hall everyone could hear what I said.

"Don't forget, there has been a lapse in our friendship
during which I have changed a great deal," Twyla murmured just as Mrs. Prail set down a steaming plate before
her. Twyla glanced at what Sparky had called adobe melt
and pushed the dish away. "I'd like a salad, please, with
olive oil and vinegar and a fresh lemon quarter on the side.
I sent a telegram with that specific request yesterday. If
you didn't receive it, Mrs. Prail, tell me immediately. I've
lately become a stockholder of American Telephone and
Telegraph."

The headmaster's wife wordlessly withdrew, staring
glumly at the spurned supper in her hands.

I didn't remember my friend being so eloquent, but I
thoroughly admired the new, improved, mature version.
Her demeanor, the now faultless oval of her face, her perfectly proportioned body, even her flawlessly polished fingernails bespoke the daughter of a movie star, if not a
starlet herself. All eyes and ears in the room, including
Brian's and Lionel's, remained fixed on her.

To my amazement and more to Sparky's, Mrs. Prail
soon returned to our table with a large dish of greens.

"Why, thank you," Twyla said appreciatively. "You
understand that no European can endure a meal that
lacks fresh fruits and vegetables. I trust these were picked
today? For dessert a mango would be sublime. But if you
haven't got one, I'll understand. Any tropical fruit will do."

When Mrs. Prail stepped away, Sparky applauded Twyla. "Yup, you're the real thing and playing it to the hilt," she said.

"I beg your pardon?" Twyla responded.

"You beg for nothing," Sparky answered. "But pray tell: what is wrong with you, and why the heck did you come here?"

"Whatever do you mean?" Twyla inquired.

"I'm sure you know that almost every kid who comes here has something wrong—a disease the desert air's supposed to cure—or why else would they be at this rinky-dink ranch school?"

"Oh no you don't," I interrupted. "Twyla, they already pulled this huge practical joke on me, pretending they were deaf and dumb and dying. They were fairly convincing, too. So don't believe a word they say."

"But it's true," Melly said. "Not that we're dying, but we all *are* sick to one degree or another. Why else would anyone come here? Didn't you ever hear about the lung camps of Tucson?"

Sparky and Brian and Lionel concurred, though I refused to believe them.

Twyla placed her hand over her mouth, making a show of yawning politely. Then she stood up. "My morning began in Switzerland at four A.M. Greenwich Mean Time. I probably passed the international date line, which would add a whole twenty-four hours to my journey. It's imperative I get some rest."

"What? And miss your mango?" Sparky asked.

"My gift to you," Twyla replied, blowing the girl a kiss as she left the table.

Twyla and I stepped into the rec hall. "I haven't been to my room yet," I told Twyla. "I have no idea where you or I are supposed to go."

Twyla began opening doors to the bedrooms and turning on lights. "*What* goes on in *there?*" she asked about the "sickroom," which hadn't yet been tidied. While I tried to produce a succinct description of the afternoon's escapade, she continued searching the lodgings until she spied three upright trunks commanding most of the space in the rearmost room. "Here I am," Twyla said.

The walls of Twyla's room had been painted a forbidding tannic-acid brown, and the flat, low beds—cots, really—were covered with common Navaho blankets. Just after I beheld my own solitary suitcase roosting on the unadorned floor, I also noticed a horse-head clock, several snapshots of ponies, and a few sloppily folded clothes cluttering an otherwise barren set of shelves. "I guess you and I are sharing this room with someone else," I said.

Twyla roughly snapped open the locks on one of the trunks. "If I weren't so depleted, mentally and physically, I'd march to the administration building, wherever it is, and raise Cain. I *told* your mother I would accept nothing less than a room of my own." As she pulled nightclothes and toiletries out of the trunk, she said, "I believe, just this once, I'm going to let myself fall into bed without creaming my face."

Thus, she unzipped and let drop her custom-tailored white gabardine slacks and draped her pale yellow silk blouse over her trunk. Once she'd slithered into a peach satin night-gown, she lay down on one of the cots and closed her eyes.

"I know you're really tired," I said, "but please tell me—what made you leave Switzerland? And what does Charmian have to do with it?"

"*Merde*," she said sleepily. "I was frantic, verging on hysteria, when I phoned. You'd think, if only for gossip's sake, your mother would have mentioned our conversation. I called for you, actually. She should have told you."

"If only I had known I would find you here, my elation alone would have kept the plane in the air," I said.

"In brief, I had to leave Switzerland post-haste, and I needed a place to live with a guardian of some kind until my eighteenth birthday. Which, you'll remember, is March fifteenth, five months from now. The idea of moving back to Beverly Hills appealed to me, and thereupon I thought of you. As luck—or ill luck—would have it, charming Charmian intercepted my call. Your mother made it clear that one teenager was already more than she could abide in her household. So she rustled up—isn't *that* the apt word—this little old private school for the both of us."

"But I've been such a *good* teenager," I protested.

"Mothers like ours aren't thrilled to have younger, prettier, peppier daughters sparring with them on the domestic front," Twyla said through a yawn.

"I'm not prettier than my mother, but you are. So, okay, what happened with your mother and father?"

But Twyla had fallen asleep. It shouldn't have surprised me; when we were younger and spent nights together, she regularly dozed off in midsentence.

I heard a tapping at the door and was pleased to see Melly stroll in. Peeking around the trunks, she said, "Wow! Is Twyla asleep already?"

"I'm afraid so. She's like the heroine in the Edna Ferber novel *Saratoga Trunk*. Her biggest talent is sleeping. I read that book a few years ago—it was on my mother's shelf—and I loved it. While everyone else went crazy, the main character slept. It's highly unlikely Twyla will wake up before tomorrow."

"Oh well. It's probably for the best. Lizzie's going to have a hard enough time accepting you as her roommate," Melly said with an apologetic smile. "In fact, Lizzie's asking me to move in here to act as a buffer between her and Twyla. I'll try to do it tomorrow. Not because I'm Miss Altruism of 1962—I've had my fill of Reba and *Sparky*."

"Which one is Lizzie?"

"The blind-as-a-bat girl who felt your face. Try to remember, it was just a joke," Melly said, stepping back toward the door. "Lizzie, you can come in now."

Lizzie's cowboy boots clacked across the room, and she bumped herself down on the bed nearest the horse-head clock. At least she tipped her hat.

"Say hi to Blossom. But say it softly, because you'll notice that Twyla is asleep," Melly coaxed her.

"Wait a minute. Excuse me. Could we start over? My name is Fleur, and that's what I'd like to be called." In fact, I wished my name were Phoebe or Imogene or Pepper.

"Oh, sorry," Melly said.

"Hi," Lizzie responded without enthusiasm.

"Listen, I didn't know I was going to like you, and I'm truly sorry I can't stay while you two get acquainted," Melly said breathily. "My assistance is required in . . . the sickroom. A cleanup operation is under way."

"By the way, where did you get all that medical . . . malarkey?" I asked. "It looked so real."

"It *is* real," Melly said. "A pharmacy lent us the whole kit and caboodle. We have to take it back in the morning. All packaged up like new."

"You mean they're going to sell those things! After they've been used? Don't you realize that's unsanitary?" I sounded like my father, but I couldn't help thinking of the diseases, counterfeit and real, that had been in contact with the goods.

"Don't worry, we're spritzing everything with Lysol and Listerine the way our, um, friend at the pharmacy told us to. He's in inventory control, so he'll make sure everything's decontaminated before it's reshelved. We're paying him twenty dollars for his trouble. Plus tip," Melly said with a mischievous grin. "Anyway, just so you know, there's a compulsory study hall from seven to nine. In the mess hall."

"What'll I study?" I asked.

"On second thought, you should probably ditch it. I'll

tell the Adjudicator, if I can, that you had a lot to unpack," Melly said.

"The Adjudicator?"

"That's what he calls himself. To see him is to believe."

"Unfortunately I don't have anything essential to unpack, just a few souvenirs," I said, pointing to my lone suitcase. "We left the house in quite a rush."

"Oh, I thought one of these trunks . . . Is that all you brought?" Melly asked with dismay. "How odd."

"My mother's sending my clothes parcel post."

"Okay then, if you come to study hall, I'll show you the ropes. See you then," Melly said and backed out of the room.

Lizzie stared at me silently, so I sat down and stared back, contemplating her cowboy attire.

"Don't bother to get comfortable. And tell your friend, too," Lizzie said, indicating Twyla's sleeping form. "Nobody rooms with me for long. Everyone thinks I'm a goon."

"Why?" I asked. Good manners prevented me from asking, *Do you snore or slobber or fart?*

"The kids just hate me, that's all I know. They call me Lizzie Borden. They call me Gila Monster and Squid Dirt. They mean it, too."

"But they let you be part of this afternoon's—what should I call it?—masquerade. You were very convincing, by the way," I added. "The point is, you were included."

"Yeah, so I wouldn't spill the beans. I probably would've, too," Lizzie said earnestly. "I'm going crazy here.

I'd be in the nuthouse already if I didn't have my horse."

I scanned our room, half expecting to see a fluffy stuffed equine. "Where is it?" I asked.

"Gwendolyn lives in the stable, naturally. She thinks I'm the greatest person on earth. She's got more brains than anybody at RCW, teacher or student. I mean it." At this Lizzie laughed a dull-noted half-cackle.

"Do other kids keep their own horses here?" I asked.

"Nope, just me. But if another kid wanted his horse here, there's room in the stable," Lizzie said. Then she clomped into the bathroom and closed the door.

Charmian would have dismissed Lizzie as a horse girl. "It's always girls, never boys, who fall in love with horses. They do it, unconsciously of course, to sublimate their sexual desires. Horseback riding is a mode of masturbation, and they can do it—unmolested—for as long as they like, until, I suppose, their bottoms ache from the bouncing," Charmian once told me. "But if you *must* go riding, an unyielding brassiere is indispensable. I learned that vital information when I took on the role of Miss Misty in *Saddle Tramp*."

But ever since the day during my sixth or seventh year as a Leigh, when my nanny Florence had incorrectly assumed my mother was retrieving me from the Hitching Post, I had my own aversion to horses. To *anything* western in fact.

The Hitching Post was a movie theater on Cañon Drive in Beverly Hills that featured only westerns. Lariats, saddles, steer skulls, whips, and ten-gallon hats overlaid every inch of the walls. Children, who often arrived in cowboy regalia, were required to remove the guns from their holsters and turn them in at the ticket booth before passing through the fabled saloon doors into the theater itself.

In my early, impressionable years, *The Charmian Leigh Radio Mystery Half Hour* had convinced me that behind every friendly countenance lurked a kidnapper. That day, as the hours passed and the movie replayed and no one came for me, I'd been too frightened to tell an usher or the theater manager that I'd been left under their auspices to molder. Eyestrain and the nine Almond Joys I ate while tearfully viewing *Westward Ho, Hell-Bent Horse and Rider* five times gave me excruciating head- and stomachaches.

"Most children—any normal child—would delight in spending *toute d'une jour au cinema* munching popcorn and candy and Coke," Charmian said by way of apology when, six hours after the pickup time, she made her entrance at the movie palace. "Not only that, watching a picture over and over gives you insight into filmmaking technique."

How curiously fate had contorted my life, I couldn't help thinking, by placing me at a horse school with a cowgirl and a movie princess as roommates.

"Would you answer one question?" I asked Lizzie when she emerged from the bathroom. "Are you here because you have some kind of disease?"

"Yeah, sure, like everyone else. But me? I get asthma pretty bad. The air in Tucson is s'posed to make it go 'way. But there's somethin' I know that the doctors, and my parents, neither, don't believe. Long as I sleep with

Gwendolyn—and it doesn't matter if it's here or at home—I don't have asthma."

"You're saying there's no reason for you to be here?"

"I'm sayin' Gwendolyn's the best medicine in the world."

III

The Adjudication

Though the aroma of adobe melt and several prior slumgullions remained in the air, the mess hall had ostensibly become a room for rumination. Unlike our seating arrangement at dinner, the students scattered now, sitting two or three at a table. Melly and I, being the only occupants of ours, sat at either end.

Distressingly, my appetite returned full tilt, but I saw no hint of a snack, not even a pitcher of water. Since I had no assignment and felt too baffled to contemplate my current circumstances, I snatched a book off a shelf, opened it, and used it as a shield. Peering over the mildewed copy of *Noblesse Oblige*, edited by Nancy Mitford in 1956, a book whose title intrigued me, I panned the room, surreptitiously watching Brian.

"Look over there," Melly whispered and pointed. "You

haven't met Cuyler Jackson or Eddie Conklin. They're pretty cute, too, don't you think?" The girl could read my mind.

"They're tall and have no pimples," I softly concurred.

"Because they're seniors," Melly elucidated.

To my astonishment, my fellow students, who had not struck me as scholarly, busied themselves with textbooks. They appeared engrossed, but on closer inspection I realized they were tracking the study-hall monitor, otherwise known as the Adjudicator or Mr. St. Cyr. He strode about the room in measured steps, first circumnavigating the periphery, then corkscrewing around the tables, then reversing his route.

The Adjudicator might have been younger than my father and older than my mother, whose age I had never determined with certitude. He had a long, dramatic nose through which he inhaled and exhaled obstreperously, keeping time with his stride. His chin seemed to form its own hairless goatee, and his trenchant eyes glared as from out of a deep freeze. Below them pouches drained into secondary and even tertiary puddles. As each of his rounds brought him into my proximity, I caught a whiff of whiskey and cologne. Already I could hear Charmian commenting on his decadent demeanor: "Casting directors need look no further for their Fagins, their Shylocks, their Long John Silvers." No wonder the students kept their noses only millimeters from their books.

Afraid of being caught in his gaze, I didn't immediately notice his conspicuous velveteen cape. Russet with a lining of amber satin, the cloak might have been de rigueur for certain gentlemen in nineteenth-century Berlin or in another, even darker world. At the time I didn't make a connection between the Adjudicator's moniker and his cape; he was a far cry from any superman.

Each time the Adjudicator's circuit brought him near my chair, his pace slowed—of that I was certain. And midway during his thirty-first orbit, he came to a halt. With a swoop of his cape, he alighted like an osprey, wings momentarily spread, on the chair next to mine. "What's that you're reading?" he asked as though making an accusation.

I knew many more adults than children, and it had been my function at my mother's parties to, as she put it, entertain the rude, lewd, and diffident guests. So, pretending Mr. St. Cyr was one of Charmian's between-roles actor friends or a producer who abhorred actors or a writer who held producers in contempt, I bravely responded, "So far I've read only the title."

He removed the book from my hands and glowered. *"Noblesse Oblige,"* he read aloud, enunciating each syllable, each vowel and consonant for that matter, in precise, confident tones. *"Noblesse oblige:* the phrase refers to the obligation of persons of high birth and rank to behave benevolently and honorably in all manner of society. I find this book of essays a most intriguing selection for *you* to have made."

At some time in his life the Adjudicator must have studied elocution. I relished the fluctuations and tidal flows of his voice and wished to hear more of it. "Why?" I asked.

"Surely you've already seen for yourself that the very circumstances of your birth have set you in a different stratum than most of the, ahem, scholars here."

"To be honest, I chose *Noblesse Oblige* because it was the least battered book on the shelves. And let me just say that I think you have me mixed up with . . . the other new girl. Everyone here has mistaken me for her."

"Nevertheless, this slim volume should stand you in good stead. Pay it heed," he advised me.

I had an inkling that the Adjudicator knew nothing of Twyla's arrival. And though everyone who had met her, even Mrs. Prail, had intuited Twyla's background, the study-hall monitor hadn't seen her yet.

For myself I needed information. I had not received any instruction, any orientation, any connection to someone with authority. Who would look after me? "May I ask you a serious question?"

The Adjudicator giggled through the vibrissa in his nose and said, "Not in here. Follow me. We'll speak privately."

I waved to Melly and, for no conscious reason, tucked *Noblesse Oblige* under my arm. Mr. St. Cyr and I trudged fifty feet away from the mess hall, and without warning I found myself standing on desert sand. The moon illuminated some very menacing cacti, but Mr. St. Cyr made a point of gazing heavenward. I followed his stare. Evidently he thought I'd be so struck by the lunar exhibit that I wouldn't notice him slide a small flat bottle from his back pocket. It was not the elegantly engraved silver flask

Charmian slipped into in her purse on days at the track—
his had a label. After the Adjudicator quaffed some of the
contents, he whisked his bottle from view. Only then did he
ask, "Now, what is the nature of your inquiry, my dear?"

"This afternoon when I arrived, the kids put me
through the kind of initiation rite that I thought happened
only on college campuses. They made me believe—well,
sort of—that most of them were quite sick. It was a little
scary, but I'm not complaining about that. It's just now
that the prank is over, they still contend that they're ill.
That's why they've come to Arizona, they say."

"So they tried to terrorize you with recitations of ail-
ments, surgical procedures, and suffering, did they?" the
Adjudicator said. He curled his fingers into a semblance of
predaceous talons. "We won't let them get away with that."

"Oh, no, please don't mention it to them," I pleaded.
"That isn't my point. I just want to know the state of their
health."

"You've come to me seeking truth because you sensed I
wouldn't prevaricate. They *are* sick. So am I. You must be,
too. For our various reasons, we come here to dry out. Tucson is the last gasp, the last locale on earth one would
choose if one didn't have to. If I leave"—he threw his hands
upward as if to the gods—"it will be to cross the River Styx
in Charon's dinghy." Again he pulled the vulgar flask from
his pocket, this time not caring whether I glimpsed it.

His self-imprecation frightened me. "Mr. St. Cyr, is
there a telephone around here?" I asked in an attempt to
escape.

* * *

The school's telephone booth, the one place to make outgoing calls, leaned unsteadily against an outer mess-hall wall. I stepped inside it, but no light came on when I closed the door. So, by moonlight and with fingers trembling, I trolled through the single pocket in my mother's dress and used one of five dimes I'd found there earlier—the only money I had—to place a call home.

"Leigh residence," our cook, Lois, answered just as she'd been instructed to. When my dime chinked back into the return slot, I felt genuine relief.

"Lois, this is Fleur. I need to talk to my parents."

"Oh, good glory! How was your flight? How's the weather? I hear the climate is superb. My niece moved out there for her neuralgia years ago, and she's never come back."

"Lois, would you please ask my mother or my father to come to the phone? Please. Please."

I heard thick orthopedic shoes thud across the hard floor in the butler's pantry, the squeak of the swinging door, and a muffled voice. Very soon high heels tapped toward the phone.

"I can only talk for a soupçon," Charmian said. "Your father is having an important meeting. But I've got good news—he may be producing a picture very soon. There's a juicy part in it for me, so—"

"Please listen to me. Just for a minute. Do you have any idea where I am?" I asked, trying not to convey anxiety or malice.

There was a pause. I heard Charmian suck on her ciga-rette. "Well . . . we put you on a plane for Tucson this after-noon. Don't tell me you didn't arrive!"

"Why did you send Daisy and me here? Why couldn't Daisy live with us until she turned eighteen?"

"We don't have a guest room. You know that. As it is, I'm sleeping in a bathroom," Charmian reminded me. She wasn't exaggerating—a carpenter had recently con-structed a cozy berth for her over my parents' bathtub.

"I would have shared my room with Daisy. I would have slept on a cot if need be," I complained. "Which, for your information, is what I'll be sleeping on here."

"I just couldn't bear the responsibility of two adoles-cents. Not now, with my career in flux," Charmian said.

"All right, then—granted. But why did you pick Tuc-son? Have you ever been here?"

"It's supposed to be beautiful."

"Says who?"

"Mmmm . . . many people."

"How many people did you ask?"

"Fleur, *chérie*, I don't have time for repartee."

"And did you ask anyone about this school? Did you get references? Did you talk to a single parent who ever had a kid enrolled here?"

"Don't say *kid* when you mean *child*. It sounds so gauche."

"Charmian, tell me honestly—am I sick? Do I have some disease that demands desert air?"

"Of course not."

"Does Daisy—or Twyla, as she wants to be called—
though you forgot to tell me—have something physically
wrong with her?"

"Not that I know of. Why? Has she lost her looks?"

"Charmian, what ever possessed you to send us here?
How could you do this to us? Please, please, let us come
home. What have we done to deserve this?"

"I'm sure Daisy isn't behaving like the bad sport you
are. Take a look around—the ad was beautiful. Spruce up
your tan in that glorious sun. Go for a swim in the sumptuous swimming pool. Ride one of the thoroughbred
horses," Charmian advised me.

"What thoroughbreds? Besides, not even Robinson Jef-
fers could make me love horses, and you know that. You've
always congratulated me for not being a horse girl."

"All right, I forgot. But so what? *Ça se vaut.*"

"Charmian, the kids, the students, abhor me. And they
aren't going to like Daisy—I mean Twyla—any better.
They're rude and miserable and dopey."

"Don't be a prig, Fleur. You need to acquire the skills to
get along with people from all walks of life. Even in Hollywood one has to work with occasional barbarians. One
must learn how to handle and charm them. That's the
most worthwhile education I could possibly give you."

"Teenagers don't want to be charmed. They want you
to be just like them. And I'm not."

"Fleur, unstuff your shirt! In my teens I had nothing but
fun. The boys, the clothes, the parties. Stop trying to ana-
lyze all the . . . ephemera of youth. Just enjoy it. As I did."

* * *

The only sign of authority or guiding principle at the school became apparent at exactly ten P.M.—some master switch was thrown to shut off all the lights in the dorm. More awake than I'd been all day, I considered rummaging through the sleeping Twyla's trunks to find a pair of pajamas or a toothbrush. But feeling too abashed to ask Lizzie for the use of her flashlight, I climbed under the covers in the same, now sweaty, dress I'd been wearing since awakening in Beverly Hills. Lizzie's presence prevented me from sleeping naked, but I doubted I would be sleeping, anyway. I was far too apprehensive about my future, and Twyla's, to relax. And how could I possibly even catnap with Lizzie shooting daggers at me—I could feel them in the dark—from her corner of the room? "Is something wrong?" I finally asked.

She yawned loudly.

"I thought you'd be the kind of person who falls asleep the minute her head hits the pillow," I said.

"Uh, yeah. That's me. If I'm in the right place. If I'm with Gwendolyn, I do," Lizzie said as she blinded me with the beam of her flashlight. "But I'm not with Gwendolyn because I have this lousy paper to write."

I had no real interest in her assignments, but it seemed only civil to ask.

"Remember when you went out of study hall with the Adjudicator? And then he came back alone? Well, he assigned us to write an essay. About you."

"You're kidding!" I said. No wonder no one, not even

Melly, had said one word to me after study hall. "Why would he do such a crazy thing?"

"Because he's the Adjudicator," she said.

"What about me do you have to write?"

"Why we're jealous of you. Something like that. Why *we assume*"—she tried to imitate the Adjudicator for a second or two—"you think you own the world just because of your mother's a famous movie star."

"But she isn't a movie star."

"Yeah, we know. Once we saw the beauty over there"— Lizzie aimed her flashlight at Twyla's inert form—"we knew we got it wrong. She's LaGiana Belmont's daughter, even *I* could see that. We tried to tell Mr. St. Cyr, but he wouldn't let us explain."

"I'll talk to him in the morning," I said.

"The paper's due in the morning," Lizzie snarled. "If I don't write it, he'll take away my horse time."

"That doesn't sound fair."

"I stink at writing. I can hardly write my name. Here, you try it. If you hadn't of come here, I would be snuggling with Gwendolyn right now." With that Lizzie tossed her notebook at me, then a flashlight, two pencils, and an eraser.

I pitied Lizzie, facing such a futile exercise. She hadn't been jealous of me and wouldn't envy Twyla, either— Lizzie had everything she wanted in Gwendolyn. "You don't happen to have anything to eat in here, do you? I don't write so well myself on an empty stomach," I said, not above extortion.

"Yeah, maybe. I had some Hershey bars, if I didn't give 'em all to Gwendolyn."

Switching on her flashlight, I took the Hershey squares and let them soak on my tongue while I contemplated the assignment.

Dear Mr. St. Cyr, I printed slowly and thoughtfully. I reasoned that Lizzie, lacking familiarity with essays, would favor the epistolary form. *I don't see why you think I'd be jealous of anyone getting stuck at this hellhole. Especially not Fleur Leigh. Or whatever you want to call her. It doesn't matter where she came from, she's here now in this (I repeat) hellhole, pretty much alone. Not only that, she doesn't have pajamas or a toothbrush or anything appropriate to wear on her first day of classes.* (I considered whether the word *appropriate* hovered above Lizzie's vocabulary reach, but with no thesaurus at my disposal, it was the best I could muster.) *Not only that, Fleur got too nervous to eat dinner, and now she's hungry! All I got to give her is the hay I keep for my horse.*

To prove how unjealous I am, I'll tell you about Gwendolyn. See, she's my best friend. She knows everything there is ever to know about me. She loves me, and best of all, she lives here. Fleur doesn't have a pet, and her old friend—the real *movie star's daughter—acts plenty snooty. So, summing up, I'll just say that I wouldn't trade places with either of the new girls, whether they grew up in Beverly Hills or any other fancy hills on God's planet. Yours truly, Lizzie.*

Had my name been placed at the end of the page, I confess, I would have avoided the clichés, sentence fragments, misplaced modifiers, dangling participles and other grammatical misdemeanors that appeared above it. But without proofreading or scanning for spelling errors, I handed my penciled version and the flashlight to Lizzie.

Her woolly eyebrows converged in the flashlight's gleam as she studied the text. "Hey, this is swell," Lizzie finally allowed. "I couldn't never of said it, but this is just how I feel."

"Thanks," I answered, hiding my pleasure at the compliment.

"Are you still hungry?"

"Well, yes, I am."

Lizzie pulled herself off her bed. I was surprised to see that she hadn't undressed. She hadn't even removed her hat and boots. Darting through the space between the trunks, she left the room.

In a minute or two Reba tiptoed in with a pad of notebook paper and two high-power flashlights on full beam. Their shafts of light fell on Twyla before they found me. "Oh, hi," she said casually, as though she hadn't expected to find me there. "Um, I brought you this flashlight. You can have it for keeps. And listen, Lizzie says you're hungry."

"She's right."

"Well, hey, me and the Wozzums had this great idea. We're going to hightail it out of here and get you a shake. There's a Foster's Freeze about half a mile from here, sittin' by its lonesome on the desert. So, are you chocolate or vanilla?"

"Chocolate, but either will do."

"It'll take about half an hour round-trip. That's a long time when you're waiting for something real tasty. You're going to need something to keep your mind off your stomach. So. I'll buy your shake; you write my paper. And if it's something really good where, say, I get an A, I'll give you this nightie I got from my folks." She held it too close to my eyes for me to focus on the pattern. "I never wore it, honest."

"I'll write your essay if you promise not to treat Twyla the way you treated me. I think she's going through a very rough time," I said.

"The sleeping princess? She's too beautiful and famous and rich to have rough times."

"Just promise you won't hold what little you know about her against her," I said sternly.

No sooner had Reba left than Sparky arrived. Her red hair gleamed in my flashlight beam. She had brought a sandwich wrapped in a towel and spread it out on my lap.

"Where did you get this?" I asked, assuming she'd broken into the kitchen.

"I always keep something nutritious on hand. This is Velveeta, mayo, and Weber's best," Sparky told me. "Sorry, I'm out of baloney."

Mayonnaise and white bread were verboten on my No Whites Inside Diet. (Velveeta hadn't been cataloged one way or another.) I happily transgressed under Sparky's scrutiny.

"Do you like it?" she asked.

"It hits the spot."

"I can make you another. Maybe your friend's going to want one, too, when she wakes up. I'd be glad to make it if only I had more time," Sparky said, and I took it as a hint.

"Didn't you write your paper yet?" I asked, speaking and chomping at the same time.

"Well, I've been waiting for inspiration. But none's come. Lizzie showed me the paper you wrote for her. I'll pay you a cupcake a paragraph to do one for me."

"I'll do it," I said. "Just promise to be kind to me and Twyla from now on. We are not the spoiled brats you think we are."

Sparky glanced over at Twyla. "She's sure a good sleeper. I'll give her that."

I enjoyed ghostwriting the first ten or so papers. Each student had her unique voice, her individual mode of expression, and I attempted to capture, even accentuate it, on paper. Eventually, however, the operation became tedious.

"I've already written my essay. I had fun doing it, actually. And it's not bad," Melly reported when she dropped by. "And listen, I happen to have an extra, unused and completely sanitary"—she emphasized the word—"toothbrush and some paste. They're for you."

"Thank you, thank you." I repeated it several more times, but my gratitude derived more from the fact that I didn't have to write her essay than the notion that my teeth wouldn't grow mossy.

That night I amassed a stick of beef jerky, a bag of Chips Ahoy! cookies, seven cupcakes, a package of Kraft

American cheese slices, a bottle of Brown Derby beer ("It's nutritious," Babs assured me), five Cokes, the flashlight, a bag of raisins, Milk Duds, a box of Kotex, a T-shirt, the nightgown, a pair of jeans, a pair of mukluks, and best of all, a pair of moccasins. I also drank the shake.

Similar gifts were delivered by the boys after they darted between the trunks and filed past the sleeping princess. Appearing at our windows rather than stumbling through the darkened rec hall, they resembled magi in their tattered robes. I accepted their offerings and their notebook paper while eagerly awaiting Brian's arrival. His failure to appear both disappointed and gratified me. The two people I had adored at first sight had written their own papers!

There were forty boarding students including Twyla and me, and I had written thirty-six brief essays. (They had become increasingly uninspired as the night wore on.) When at last the line of pilgrims dwindled to none, I changed into sleeping attire, ate a cupcake, switched off the flashlight, and ensconced myself under the covers.

"Guess I'll take off now," Lizzie said. "It's why I took this back room, see. I just climb out the window and lickety-split, I'm at the stable. No one knows. I'm telling you so you don't go forming no search parties."

"I promise I won't."

"Gwendolyn probably didn't miss me much yet. There's this big old stallion been comin' around she's in love with."

"Where does he come from?" I asked idly.

"It's kind of mysterious, but there's this tall hunk of a

guy who rides him into the stable. He ties him up next to Gwendolyn, then disappears for most of the night. They always leave before I get up in the morning. That stallion must tiptoe, or else I'd wake up."

"What's he doing here?" I asked.

"Seeing Mr. St. Cyr, I s'pose," she said as she undulated across the windowsill.

Being a night creeper, as Charmian called people who couldn't sleep until the wee hours, I was far too alert to rest. Switching on the flashlight again, I opened my suitcase. Gnawing beef jerky, I surveyed the belongings I'd carried to Tucson, the ones I most feared my mother would toss out or give to charity in my absence. I'd brought six books I owned in the *Wizard of Oz* series, a sack of my favorite buttons, a shoe box of shells, my choicest postcards, and a heavy-duty envelope of baby teeth, precious pieces of myself that I couldn't bear to lose. Opening a manila folder of fading pressed flowers, I reached in and lifted one of the fragile pompons on my fingertips. I held it close to my nose, hoping to recapture the scent of home.

IV

Learning Curves

On receiving word that the headmaster wished to see Twyla and me, I couldn't indulge to my stomach's content in the breakfast of what the students called "Miracle Powdered-Scramble Whip." They spoke to me now as an ally, a presumable accomplice in future essays. Still sucking eggy threads from between my teeth, I returned to our dorm room.

"Time to get up now," I said, giving Twyla's shoulder a gentle shake. "Time to greet the Tucson sun."

Only Twyla could wake up looking as though a makeup magician had just waved his wand over her face. Even her tresses appeared disarranged by a top-notch hairdresser. Nevertheless, her expression advertised grumpiness.

"I saved a cupcake for you," I coaxed.

"I don't touch that stuff," Twyla mumbled.

"As soon as you're dressed, I'll give you some cheese and raisins," I tried to bribe her. "We have an appointment with the headmaster in fifteen minutes."

"Bring me a café au lait, a croissant, and some prunes," Twyla commanded with a subtle tinkle of mockery. She yawned, stretched, abandoned her bed, jumbled through the drawers of an upright trunk, and finally carried three silken satchels of toiletries and a mound of clothing into the bathroom. Reappearing within twelve minutes—according to Lizzie's horse-head clock—she was unquestionably the daughter of LaGiana Belmont. "She who looks best leads the rest," Twyla announced.

We hastened to the classroom building that, to my jaded eyes, could have been assembled overnight on the Twentieth Century Fox back lot. Vermiculated metal and fiberglass desks, pitted blackboards, and a few pull-down maps were the extent of the decor. I'd paid little attention to the dignified revival architecture of Beverly Hills High School during my year and a month there, but suddenly I yearned to walk through its wide, solidly built, arched halls. Consequently, I greeted the headmaster unhappily. Twyla did no better. Her "good morning" sounded sour.

Mr. Prail's height alone could have accounted for the impression he gave of having his head in the clouds, but after a few minutes I concluded that his loftiness, his inattention to Twyla and me, added to the illusion. "Giant's syndrome," Melly would later diagnose. "The height—the unnatural elongation of the bones—shortens the life span." In addition, Mr. Prail's appearance and demeanor duplicated every schoolchild's concept of Abraham Lincoln. "You may sit down," he told us in an outlandish baritone. "And so shall I."

"Have you been headmaster here for long?" I asked.

"Long enough." Mr. Prail sighed. After a protracted pause, during which he stared at some paper lying on his desk and Twyla rolled her eyes heavenward for my benefit, he said, "Photographs were supposed to have accompanied your applications. But your documents came to us so, eh, pell-mell, I can't find them. You'll have to tell me, which one of you is which?"

For a moment or two Twyla and I grinned at each other. As in the old days, our thoughts coincided. But there was something pitiable about Mr. Prail, over and above his choice of a wife, so I quickly said, "May I introduce my friend Twyla Flint? She's just flown in from Switzerland. And I'm Fleur Leigh, from Los Angeles."

"So be it," he said as he wrote our names on the papers. When he glanced up again, he looked squarely at me and asked, "How did you happen to be living on the Continent?"

"You're mixing us up," I patiently told him.

"If I am, it's probably of little consequence," he said. Turning to the task at hand, he asked perfunctorily, "What language have you been studying, Twyla?"

"French, German, Italian, and always English," Twyla answered, impersonating an egghead.

I had often wished to study Spanish because California belonged to Spain before it became a united state, and I believed that if I could just translate the mountains, canyons, and street names, I'd know practically the whole language. But Charmian had required me to learn French so I could appreciate her *"bijoux de sagesse."*

"Sign me up for Spanish," I told Mr. Prail.

"Fine, then." He nodded, jotting a note on one of the papers that I hoped had my name on it. "And which elective do you prefer, Fleur?" he asked.

"Do you offer cooking classes?" I inquired.

"Not at all."

"Hmmm. What about mythology?"

"And you?" Mr. Prail asked Twyla.

"French for my language requirement, *s'il vous plaît.* And I suppose it's not considered an elective per se, but I'd like to continue with my German studies. I've been wanting to read Goethe and Mann," Twyla added slyly.

Mr. Prail's long face grew longer. "If only we had a teacher who could guide you, but we do not. Would you be capable of doing an independent study? None of our other students could, but you may have what it takes." He said this without making it a compliment.

"Natürlich," Twyla answered.

Again Mr. Prail made a note and then slid our class schedules across the desk. "Good luck," he said in an ominous tone. Unfurling the ribbon of his body, he stood up. With his ramrod posture, he might have been a general dismissing a fractious honor guard, though it was he who left the room.

"He's a tall drink of water," Twyla said, quoting a phrase we'd heard from our parents numerous times.

"The most important thing is, when are we going to talk?" I asked. Since Twyla was a senior and I a mere sophomore, our classes would take us to different rooms.

"Let's cut classes right now," Twyla suggested. "We could take a cab into town and find some decent coffee. With café au lait in my gullet, I'll talk to your heart's content."

"We haven't *been* to classes yet. How can we cut them?"

"That's just it. Our teachers won't expect us, so they won't miss us, either," Twyla responded in an it's-only-common-sense tone. "And really, I should unpack."

"I think we should attend our classes, get the lay of the land. Then we can act accordingly," I said, holding my ground.

"You always were a goody-goody, weren't you?"

"I was not. I am not."

"Don't expect, um, scholarship," Melly cautioned me just before the first-period gong. "Don't expect wisdom to be disseminated by the teachers. Don't expect much."

It took only a moment to discover that hopelessly thin partitions separated the history lesson from the chemistry lab. On the other side the English teacher was reciting "Elegy Written in a Country Churchyard" as though broadcasting from the grave. The monotonous drone of flies competed with the metallic scrapings of desks on the cement floor as fidgety students shifted, subconsciously edging toward the door.

During the day I attended five forgettable classes taught by teachers more apathetic than the students. When I arrived for the last class, my first session of mythology, Melly gave me the news: "No class today. We have an absentee instructor."

"Absentee or tardy? The other kids aren't here yet, either."

"Until today I've been the Adjudicator's only student, so sometimes he forgets little old me."

"You're the only student in the class?" I asked.

"Who else here knows what mythology is?" Melly said.

"Oh dear. Well, it must be demoralizing for Mr. St. Cyr, so why don't we give him a little more time," I suggested, but I had an ulterior motive. "While we're waiting, you could tell me what you kids meant last night when you said you really are sick."

Melly turned her desk to face mine. "It's peculiar that you didn't know this beforehand, but all this school is is a place to breathe and ease your joints. It's a drop-off for kids who get sick outside an arid climate. Nothing grows, much less pollinates, in Tucson, so even allergy sufferers get off scot-free. There are several such 'schools' in the area—this one just happens to be the cheapest. I looked it up at the library in *The Crespin's Guide to Preparatory Day and Boarding Schools*. Rancho Cambridge West has the third lowest academic rating and is the cheapest boarding school in the whole United States. My parents can just barely afford it. But what about your parents?" she asked. "You live in Beverly Hills. Why didn't they send you someplace nice?"

"I'm going to ask," I said. *Unless,* I thought, *they're paying Twyla's tuition, too.* But that didn't seem probable—my parents weren't all that philanthropic. "Well, anyway, did you come here all the way from Brooklyn?"

"New Jersey," Melly corrected me. "I suppose to you it's a second-rate state, but to me it's beautiful."

"I don't know anything about New Jersey," I admitted. "I don't even know where *old* Jersey is. So what do your parents do?"

"They're in the garment business, helped by my four sisters," she said, her eyes moistening. "I miss them so much. Really, I have the most wonderful family on earth. We live in a tiny house, but it's cute. Homey. Can you imagine six females and one poor man sharing a bathroom? My father sticks out like a sore thumb." Melly laughed at her own double entendre. "My sisters work in my parents' shop, sewing four hours a day, and still they're A-plus students. They have to be—me, too—or our parents would murder us. They weren't able to go to university because of Hitler and immigrating here. So it's really really important to them that we do. If my sisters and I hadn't been born, our parents would have become professors."

"Professors of what?" I asked, squeezing in a question while she took a breath.

"Everything. Anything. They're tremendously smart. And that makes them all the more determined that the five Weisdorfler daughters get through college. Three of my sisters are at Columbia now on scholarships. I'm planning on scholarships to take me all the way through medical school."

Perhaps because Melly's words flowed freely, I felt at ease with her. And we had time to kill. "Since you don't have leprosy," I gently chastised her, "what *do* you have? If you don't mind my asking."

"Rheumatoid arthritis," she said with a grimace.

I had heard of rheumatism, and I'd heard of arthritis, but not the two together, so I asked, "Aren't those old people's diseases?"

"When you put the two together, it's a kid's affliction. But it never goes away. The joints swell up—it's very painful. I got to the point where I was taking twenty-five aspirins a day just to be able to move. Finally a doctor told my parents that I was going to die if I kept on like that." If Melly hadn't stated this fact without a hint of self-pity, tears would have filled *my* eyes. "The doctor offered me only one ray of hope—Tucson."

"So this *is* the health capital of the world!"

Melly giggled. "Yeah, we got Reba to say it, but it's true."

"So how did you find Rancho Cambridge West?"

"My parents bought plane tickets right after we left the doctor. The three of us flew out here the next day," Melly continued. "We went to Jewish services because my parents assumed some nice family would be willing to take me in. Well, there aren't that many Jews in Tucson, and most of them are here because they're sick themselves. After about two weeks of futile searching—this was a year ago—my parents found this boarding school. They kept apologizing, trying to explain, but I broke down completely when it finally hit me: they were going to abandon me here."

"I'm so sorry," I told Melly.

"But I'm doing okay—the climate really does help—and I went home for a month last summer. That was great. You might have guessed that all you have to do to get A's at this joint is be polite. And, of course, every Saturday we all get to go to town. While the other kids shop and go to the movies, I camp out at the library. First I study what little is required at RCW. Then I work on vocabulary and math for the SATs. I also borrow any books I can find on medicine. They're in my room, by the way, if you want to look something up. Because of my health, I'll have to attend the University of Arizona. But maybe in the next six years someone will find a cure so I can go to a great medical school."

"I'm rooting for you," I said. Then, remembering where we were and why, I asked, "What do you think has happened to the Adjudicator?"

"I think he's probably . . . indisposed," Melly said.

"But surely he would have sent a substitute."

"He wouldn't have thought of it," Melly said, shaking her head. "RCW doesn't have substitutes, anyway."

"Should we let the headmaster know?"

"Oh, no! We'd get Mr. St. Cyr canned."

"But isn't it inexcusable for a teacher to—"

"Okay, okay, if you're so big on regulations, we'll go roust him. If you're sure that's what you want."

I followed Melly out of the classroom into the deliques-
cent sun. Looking south, away from the boys' dorm, I
noticed something unbefitting even this school's desert
setting. "What is *that*?" I asked Melly.

"You mean Ye Olde Car Wrecke? It's been here forever.
Maybe old Mr. Swiggert, Dirk's uncle, once offered an
auto-mechanics class, or maybe some students crashed it
there. No one really knows."

"But it's an eyesore. It makes the school look like a
slum."

"The carcasses of cars in various stages of decay can be
found in half of Tucson's front yards," Melly said. "I try to
think of them as the dinosaurs of the modern era. At some
future date after they're unearthed, anthropologists will
write articles about them. *National Geographic* will send
photographers."

In another moment I found myself assaulted by the
gummy chill, common in adobe buildings, of the boys'
dorm. A foul odor lingered. It took several sniffs to make
an identification—someone (or possibly all of the boys)
had forgotten to wash his socks. "Are girls allowed in
here?" I asked.

"Only if no one finds out," Melly said.

"But the Adjudicator must be the biggest stickler for
rules on the planet."

"Not necessarily," Melly said.

The boys' dorm twinned the girls' dorm in layout,
though where we had an ample storage closet, their dorm
housed the resident boys' dean. Melly didn't shilly-shally.

With an air of jaded déjà vu, she smacked her knuckles against Mr. St. Cyr's door. Then she turned the doorknob roughly and pushed. "Heck, it's locked," she said. "I'll be right back."

Melly must have climbed through the Adjudicator's window. In mere seconds, she unlatched the door from the inside. A stench even stronger than the socks assaulted my nose. Stepping inside, I beheld the image of Mr. St. Cyr's body—bare feet in the foreground, much like Andrea Mantegna's *Dead Christ*—lying insensate on a tousled bed. The fact that his few tufts of chest hair were coated with vomit shocked me far more than the sight of him in his birthday suit.

"_____ ead?" I asked.

"____ he was dead, most likely," Melly said, pointing ____ ing of Lucky Strike stubs and discarded Johnny ____ tles at our feet. "That's why he was so anxious ____ ur time in study hall last night. So we wouldn't ____ rrival of . . . his friend. If I know the Adjudica- ____ 't until his friend left that he did most of the drinking."

"He has a girlfriend?" I asked, unable to imagine the teacher tenderly caressing even the most exquisite of women.

Melly shrugged. "Most of his friends are men."

"Oh, right, Lizzie mentioned one of them. He rides a stallion."

A faint moan sent Melly into action. She stepped into the tiny bathroom adjoining the room, found a stiff, rumpled hand towel, and ran cold water on it. She wiped away as much vomit as she could and then rinsed the icky towel. "Fold this and put it on his forehead," she instructed me. "I'll get some aspirin and ice. This is as bad as I've ever seen Mr. St. Cyr. I'm going to call his doctor friend."

"Can't you just ask the school nurse for help? Wouldn't it be expedient if she took over his case?"

"You mean Jo Ella? The she-bitch? She'd give Mr. St. Cyr an enema and then get him fired."

"You're not going to leave me alone with him?" I pleaded.

"He won't bite. Not when he's like this," she said, making a quick exit.

My mother would have enjoyed the Adjudicator's attempts to brighten a dreary room. Gathered around a small but elaborate filigree chandelier, red velvet material draped across the ceiling and then curtained down the walls. It gave the impression, I supposed, of a Moroccan tent. The dimness of the light prevented me from appreciating the subjects of his many gilt-framed figurative drawings. Only the crucifix hanging over the bed, with a fairly cheery Jesus, would have given Charmian pause.

When Mr. St. Cyr finally hoisted an eyelid over a mullet-colored eye and took in my image, he groggily asked, "Who the hell are you?"

"It's Fleur Leigh speaking, Mr. St. Cyr," I said, imagining that he saw me through the wrong end of a telescope. "I'm the new girl, remember? Well, one of them. You had the other students write essays about me."

"Yankee, go home," he said gruffly. Then he moaned, coughed, and choked.

"Okay, Mr. St. Cyr, if you say so." I backed halfway out the door, only too glad to comply.

"Ho, uh, halt." His tone changed to one of desperation. "The dresser . . . Bottom drawer. Dog of the hair. Urgent care."

"All right." *Keep your pants on or, better yet, put them on,* I wanted to add. "Just tell me what I'm looking for."

"Behind cuff links. Rosary box. Wrapped in a shirt." He moaned.

When I found the bottle, I didn't pick it up, though he railed at me as forcefully as he could. On *The Charmian Leigh Radio Mystery Half Hour,* as well as at home, my mother sent dipsomaniacs off in a taxi before they reached the state of no return. "You mustn't let them tarry," she said, "or they throw up on your divan. And they never pay the cleaning bills."

Proving Charmian right, the Adjudicator launched a new swirl of vomit. I pressed myself against the door.

Melly finally returned with what she considered first aid and assessed the situation. "You're never going to keep aspirin down, are you, Mr. St. Cyr?"

"Bottle. Bottom drawer," he muttered.

"I'll have to get one of the guys to help until your doctor friend gets here," Melly told the drunkard.

How she extricated Brian from his class, I didn't ask. I was greatly relieved to see his princely face, even though, after taking one step into Mr. St. Cyr's room, he quickly pinched his nose and covered his mouth. "This is nasty," he said, sounding as if he had a terrible cold.

"Can you lift him?" Melly asked.

"Why didn't you tell me to bring my raincoat?" Brian grumbled. But with a few proficient movements, he wrapped the teacher in the soiled bedding, lifted the weighty sack of misery, and hobbled into the bathroom. Then, not all that gently, he lowered his cargo into the bathtub. Melly leaned over the tub rim, turned on the water—I assumed it was cold—and the three of us peered down at the vomit-streaked, sodden clump of a man. As much as I longed to remain in Brian's proximity, I decamped.

Though I had kept my distance from the sullied Adjudicator, I noticed that my new jeans and moccasins had been defiled and hurried to my room to set about washing them. But before I reached the bathroom and Lizzie's Lava soap, I spotted a small woman sprawled beneath Lizzie's bed noisily swabbing the floor. By means of grunts and groans or, for all I knew, the Inca language, she commented nonstop on the drawbacks of her job.

I wished she hadn't chosen this particular moment to invade our room with alkalis and acids, putrid cleaning rags, and a clattery bucket.

"*Ay, muchacha,*" she said from beneath the bed, "jou got *puercos* libeen here?"

"Hello," I answered. "My name is Fleur. I just moved in."

"*Mucho gusto.*"

"*Gracias*," I said. "And look, I hope you don't mind a suggestion, but wouldn't it be easier to use a mop?"

"Jou got?" she asked, punctuating her question with a series of muffled sneezes.

"Well, no. I'm just thinking of a way for you not to have to . . . lie down with the dust. What's your name, by the way?"

"Conchita," she said. "Jou wan buy mop for me?"

"Doesn't the school provide your equipment?" I asked. After all, every new maid at home demanded entirely fresh cleaning gear. Whatever brand of cleansers, dust cloths, carpet sweepers, vacuums, toilet brushes the last maid used, the new one routinely rejected.

"Ha ha ha," Conchita said in plain English. "Thees school don't probide notheen. They make me a messenger boy, too." With that she emerged, wiped her hands on her pants, and nabbed an envelope with my name on it from her cleaning caddy.

I opened the envelope carefully, trying not to tear the Rancho Cambridge logo, a saguaro cactus holding out its two branches as though luring innocents into its spines. The antithesis of the Statue of Liberty, it begged for a motto.

You are cordially invited for tea in Mrs. Prail's personal living quarters. Today at five P.M. sharp, the invitation read in the fastidious handwriting of a person who had learned penmanship before the advent of the typewriter. I looked for a solicitous *Répondez S'il Vous Plaît* or *Regrets Only.* Their absence meant I had no way out.

V

The Deluge

The transformation of our bathroom startled me. Its utilitarian surfaces glinted in the light of aromatic, carved-wax candles. Two lace-trimmed satin slips—fanciful substitutes for curtains—replaced the venetian blinds. Numerous soaps, jars of cream, hairbrushes, combs, curlers for hair and eyelashes, kaleidoscopic cosmetic bags of all sizes, and a pumice stone competed for space on the small counter.

Twyla, wrapped in a mauve silk dressing gown that I'd seen her mother wear when she played Lady Bijou in *Beguiling Lady*, was running water into the tub. "I'm invited to tea," she said in an affected English accent. "The headmaster's mouse—oops, meant to say *spouse*—wants to get acquainted. So I thought I'd just gussy up, as they no doubt say out here in the West."

"I received an invitation, too," I said. "For all we know, the whole girls' dorm is invited. So don't worry about pressing your cocktail dress. Probably come-as-you-are will do. I'll have to wear what I wore yesterday."

"You're right, of course. This bath is just a means of attempting to recover some weensy component of my emotional equilibrium. After all I've been through—and now faced with this horse school—I have to do *something* to calm myself," Twyla said, sprinkling bubble-bath powder under the nozzle.

"I'm a little, um, unstrung myself," I said, not wishing to allow Twyla sole claim to all the drama. I proceeded to describe Melly's rescue of Mr. St. Cyr.

"Melly? That little squirt who sat at our table last night?"

"Don't call her *squirt*. She's a very good person. Plus, she's competent. Melly really took charge of Mr. St. Cyr. I wouldn't have known what to do," I said.

"You would have let the man sleep it off, with the same end result."

My discomfort and curiosity about Twyla encouraged a subject change. "There's something I'm dying to know. What caused you, after all these years of silence, to phone me and then allow Charmian—of all people—to entirely redirect your life, if that's what she did?"

Twyla twisted her hair into a towel and reached for a jar. "As soon as I cream my face—it works better with steam—I'm all yours."

I watched as Twyla puttied her skin with a spumoni of

vanishing creams. "You may not know it. Nobody did," she said, concentrating on her beauty regimen. "My parents moved to Switzerland and placed me in boarding school there to parry the meddlesome tongues of gossip columnists here. The marriage of the world's most beloved couple, according to Walter, Louella, and Hedda, was coming unglued. My parents were very good-natured about it because, as my father told me later, they believed that if they could stay out of the klieg lights for a time, if they could get out from under Jack Warner's thumb, they would work things out."

Twyla's plastered countenance began to craze like old china as she switched to a confessional tone. "I do admit to writing to you during the time I attended a—shall we say—substandard school. I was only there a couple of months, and maybe I exaggerated my unhappiness a tad. For the most part, I missed my life in Beverly Hills. I've always been ashamed of penning that letter."

"Dais—Twyla, I was so afraid for you. It sounded like a suicide note. And then I couldn't reach you. The caretaker in the Beverly Hills house wouldn't give me your parents' Switzerland number," I whined. "My then-nanny said you'd probably died, that your parents must be using their clout to keep it out of the papers."

"Did you forget what a zealous writer I am, Fleur? I've *always* gone in for aggrandizement and hyperbole, you knew that," Twyla chastised me. "Fortunately, soon after I wrote that letter, Mother heard about a splendid school. A school so super, so top-drawer and exclusive, that only royalty and the children of ambassadors attend. Written into the charter is an admonition against admitting the children of movie people or Jews. Who, as you know, are often one and the same."

"Uh-oh," I said.

"With good reason, as it later turned out," she added, lifting her leg over the bathtub bulwark to test the water with pedicured toes. Then Twyla leaned over, adjusted the faucets, and gave the water a swish. "Mother had to petition the headmaster for a personal consultation. Supplication is what it was, and she pestered him for weeks before he gave in. Oh, I wish you could have seen the outfit she wore. A drab brown suit hemmed at the ankles, hair in a knot, no lipstick, no cleavage—she split the difference between a nun and a spinster! But Mother is a superb actress, and even without makeup, she's beautiful—well, I don't have to tell you. She speaks so eloquently that she proved, at least, she wasn't a Jew."

"What an accomplishment," I groused.

"When I was eventually accepted, I experienced an unpleasant period of adjustment. It was tough sledding at first with that European set, coming as I did from California, the Nature Boy state. But once I picked up some French and Italian, and shook the Americanisms out of my English, I became one of the school's upper-echelon girls.

"I wish you could have seen me, Fleur. Weekending in palaces and on yachts. I had clothes and jewelry—though mostly Mother's old baubles—and boyfriends galore. One little baron showed up with an engagement ring. I was even invited to be a debutante—in London, where only the crème de la crème come out. That event will take place this spring, just after my eighteenth birthday. But they're going to muddle through without me," Twyla said bitterly.

The tub had filled. Bubbles covered the spigot. Twyla stepped out of her dressing gown. I wondered how some bodies, like hers, could be so perfectly formed while others, like mine, so undershot the mark. Most likely the European crowd had judged Twyla by her splendor in a bathing suit rather than by her language skills.

"Come on. Get in with me, like we did in the old days," she urged.

"I *am* a little soiled," I said. I felt bashful about allowing Twyla to find out how little growth my body had undergone. But she refused to continue her story until I joined her. Ever so sheepishly, I removed my clothes only to hear her say, "Oh, Fleur, you have the most petite, feminine body."

"Is that just another way of saying I'm a shrimp?"

"It's a shame your hair isn't as blonde as it used to be—of course, that can easily be rectified—but you're small boned and you have a China doll's face. No wonder Charmian had to get rid of you."

I lowered myself into the warm, bubble-bedecked bathwater. As in the old days, Twyla had left me the faucet end of the tub.

"Okay, I'm in. Please continue your European saga," I said while I tried to pad the plumbing fixtures with a towel.

Holding a small jar in one hand, Twyla leaned over and smeared some of its contents on my face. Then, leaning back against an inflatable pillow at the smooth, slanted end of the tub, she began: "It's Mother who ruined every-thing—my whole life and Father's, too—by falling in love with a ridiculous runty Jewish director. Trust me, you've never heard of him—he's Polish—and I refuse to speak his name. My mother left my father for the little twerp."

"That's awful," I said, "but the fact that he's Jewish shouldn't enter into the mix. If he were Episcopalian, you'd hate him just as much."

"He convinced my mother to break up what we used to call our 'trinity,' meaning the three of us, though Father called us the 'triumvirate' because we commanded atten-tion wherever we went," Twyla said.

"Your parents had some pretty beautiful features to pass on to you," I agreed. But I couldn't let Twyla think I hadn't noticed her one facial alteration. In Daisy's younger years, her nose had accommodated a slight but unfortunate bulge that, in profile, insinuated a bird of prey, if only a hatchling. Now no sign of the baby beak remained; instead a delicate, faultless nose had been aligned on her face. While girls who attended Beverly Hills High School usu-ally chose a pug or a Roman, the *spécialités* of Dr. Isadore Birnbaum, Twyla had obviously enlisted an artiste. "Except the nose. Your nose outshines both of theirs."

Twyla laughed. "Do you like it?"

"It makes you look even more like a Belmont."

"Thanks," Twyla said rather sadly as she made herself

more comfortable by pushing my legs out of her way. "But there is one fly in the ointment of your hypothesis. Just before Mother ran off to Assisi with the ratty little Polish pipsqueak Jew, she told my school that Father had full responsibility, that he would be paying the bills. But when the first of the month came around, Father refused to pay. He told the school he wasn't my father—he claimed that he and I had no blood relationship at all."

"You mean because your mother hurt *him*, he took it out on *you*? That's so cruel . . . and immature and . . . deceitful," I sympathized.

"Fleur, he didn't lie," Twyla said, splashing me for emphasis.

"What do you mean?"

"The headmaster had the unpleasant duty of explaining to me that Father hadn't met Mother until she was already pregnant with me, that when Roland and LaGiana fell in love, she refused to marry him unless he agreed to raise me as his own. And he did it, very convincingly I might add, for seventeen years. But I guess once Mother ran off with the bohunk, Father felt he'd fulfilled his obligation."

I wanted to ask for the definition of *bohunk*, but empathy seemed more appropriate. "What a blow that must have been."

"You may not know that although Father had once been a matinee idol, his recent career was predicated on Mother's success. She would accept a role in a picture only if they found something for Roland. So guess what? Roland is suing my mother for alimony!"

"What a horrible mess."

"Can you imagine anything more humiliating than having the headmaster tell me all this? At least he saved me from reading about it in the papers." Twyla kicked her feet so vehemently, she could have drowned me.

"Gosh, I'm so sorry. What did you do?"

"What *could* I do? I locked myself in my room. With no food and only tap water to drink. Europeans, you see, don't use tap water even for brushing their teeth. It took the school ten days to figure how to get me out."

"How did they?" I asked.

"I was just this much shy of death," Twyla said, indicating about a sixteenth of an inch between her finger and thumb, "when they removed my door from its hinges!"

"Was your mother there? Was . . . Roland?"

"Of course not. Mother was ensconced in her love nest in Assisi, and Father—I mean Roland—had moved to Hong Kong. He's always been a star there. But I have to say, Roland did do me a tremendous favor. To get even with Mother, or possibly because he loved me a little, he wrote a letter telling me about my—listen to this—trust fund."

It was my turn to splash. "A trust fund! You have a trust fund?"

"Turn on the hot water. The tub is getting cold," she directed me. I had to move away from the faucet and sit on my knees so I didn't get scalded.

"Yes, I have a trust fund, and along with it, I have a guardian, Mr. Wolfgang Quincy, at the Credit Suisse

Banque Internationale. He's such a dear. And he adores me. He says I'm witty and terribly smart. I love the way he says *terribly* like an Englishman. We've had a few lunches and, once, cocktails. Mr. Quincy has assisted me in borrowing money from the *banque* in order to hire a private detective to find my true father. On account of Mr. Quincy's regard for me, the *banque* is charging only four and three quarters percent interest."

My estimation of Twyla's worldliness ascended to Mt. Olympian heights. I had never known anyone under forty years of age to speak of rates of interest. The little I knew about banking I'd learned from Charles Dickens. And yet I suspected that I had an endowment, too, because every so often Maurice would thrust a thick sheaf of legal papers, documents, or exquisitely designed stock certificates into my hands and demand that I sign them. "But wait," I would say, "let me look at them. Who is the artist for IBM? Who designs these beautiful documents for General Electric?"

"This isn't art appreciation—it's business," Maurice would growl back. "Let's get this over with."

"But what am I signing? Am I buying or selling? What am I agreeing to?"

"For Chrissake, I can't possibly explain it so you'd understand. I haven't the time," Maurice would bark. "Stop wasting it. Just sign your name wherever there's an X."

Twyla went on, "So I've hired a private detective named Al Mandell. We haven't met face-to-face, but Fleur, I'm half in love with him. We have great conversations about

criminology. For example, Al never drinks on the job.
If he's in a bar, he orders white gloves—so-named on
account of their low alcohol content."

"What's in them?" I asked.

"The point is that as you and I are speaking," Twyla continued, "my very own private eye is in hot pursuit of my
true father. That's why I'm taking such good care of myself.
It's possible the man doesn't even know I exist. If I can
make myself positively stunning, it will soften the blow."

"But Twyla, you *are* stunning. Even with creamed face
and turbaned hair."

"Thank you," she said modestly, rising from the tub.

"Twyla, don't you want to rinse off?"

"Oh no, never. I'd lose my body oils. That's why I use
this special bubble bath—it won't hurt my skin."

Who was I to argue? Her skin glowed. "I'm just not a
bath person, I guess," I told her. I wasn't a cosmetics person, either, I thought, as I held still so she could wipe off
the cream she'd applied to my face. I did luxuriate in our
intimacy, our friendship resumed.

"The Greeks and Romans knew the healing powers of
baths," Twyla reminded me.

"In all this, you haven't told me why you changed your
name," I reminded Twyla.

"Didn't I? Oh. Hmmm. When all this happened, when I
found out I wasn't who I thought I was, I realized all the
elements that made me Daisy were fraudulent. Even in my
early years, I wasn't really a Daisy. If anything, I was an
Orchid, don't you think?"

I did.

"So what else would you suggest? I had to discard my . . . daisyhood."

"But it's your name. Why would you want to hang on to your body oils but exfoliate your name?" I asked.

"I'll give you a practical reason. Mother is suing me! How do you like that? My trust fund was set up by my grandmother, my mother's mother. Fleur, she left me a fortune, six hundred thousand dollars. Mr. Quincy says if we continue to invest it conservatively and spend sparingly, I'll be set for life. But Mother thinks the money is hers. She's dying to get me into court with her battery of lawyers. Changing my name is part of concealing my whereabouts. Plus, I like the name Twyla."

"I loved Daisy Belmont."

"Then you can learn to love Twyla Flint."

"Okay. Twyla, if you have the money, why didn't you just stay at your school? You could have had your debutante ball, too, couldn't you?"

"For one thing, Mother would have known where to find me. For another, the school kicked me out! We proved that *movie people* are just as sleazy as they believed."

"But that's so narrow-minded. Weren't they concerned about what was best for you?"

"Apparently not. Now remember," Twyla said in a furtive tone, "if you see a stranger hanging around, come and tell me at once. More than likely he's serving a subpoena."

"I'll go along with anything you want, Twyla. Just tell me one thing."

"And what would that be?"

"What is a *bohunk*?"

Twyla laughed heartily. "You haven't changed an iota."

To reach the Prails' apartment, Twyla and I passed the pool in which I had hoped to swim some refreshing laps before dinner. On first glance, I thought I beheld a desert mirage. But no, the watery site didn't waver and move away as we walked—it insisted on remaining right where it was. Murky and rife with unidentifiable organisms, some of them jumping like minnows above the oleaginous surface, the pool looked like a mammoth bowl of watery black-bean soup. A germ factory, Maurice would have called it before ordering it to be drained, scoured, and steam-cleaned.

"Melly warned me about this pool, but I didn't believe her," I told Twyla.

"You're getting awfully chummy with this Melly character, aren't you? She's riffraff, Fleur," Twyla warned me.

"You're wrong."

If it hadn't been cluttered with bric-a-brac, highboys and lowboys and shin-chipping coffee tables, a stiff couch, and a half-dozen spiny chairs—a bricolage of recent periods from some former and presumably larger abode—the Prails' living room might have reasonably accommodated a single immutable, upright adult.

Poor Mrs. Prail, I thought as she honored us with a pained little smile. She gestured to a padded bench embellished with actual antimacassars to protect its narrow arms from ours. Imagining all nine feet of Mr. Prail sitting here took cerebral exertion. "Thank you for coming," his wife said gravely. "You don't mind? You weren't . . . were you? What I mean is . . . are you?"

"We're not," I said, hoping to intercept her oral misfires.

"Actually, the timing of your tea is a bit awkward," Twyla said, cranking up her cosmopolitan accent. "I have not as yet unpacked."

"Nevertheless, we're very grateful you invited us. We thank you," I said, observing the hurt expression on Mrs. Prail's already tormented face.

We waited wordlessly for her to pour tea, but she appeared to be as inert as the furniture.

"I guess this is part of the Rancho Cambridge West tradition, right?" I asked.

"Yes. No. What?" she responded.

"Having the newcomers to tea," I said, already scouting for scones or macaroons or the extravagant pink-dyed crustless watercress sandwiches popular at Beverly Hills sweet-sixteen teas.

"Is it? Oh . . . as a rule, I find the children here ill-mannered. But you are respectful. You wear suitable clothes," Mrs. Prail said in a high, off-key pitch. She poured tea into two of the cups. "Sugar? One lump? Two? Cream?"

"Speaking of clothes, Fleur," Twyla said, gesturing toward mine, "I've been wondering about your dress. You had it on last night and now here it is again. Only your best friend would tell you, it doesn't do a thing for you."

"Three lumps," I told Mrs. Prail, pointedly ignoring Twyla's remark. How could Twyla not recognize the despicable dress as belonging to my mother?

"Lemon for me, please," Twyla requested.

"Lemon!" Mrs. Prail looked startled, as though Twyla had asked for artichokes or avocados, which, according to Charmian, remained unheard-of outside California. No dainty dish of translucent citrus slices graced the table, I now noticed, nor any morsel of food. The woman wouldn't risk spoiling our appetites.

"Twyla will be content with sugar and milk," I reassured Mrs. Prail.

"Sugar and *cream*," Twyla corrected me.

The headmaster's wife plunked the cubes into our cups and stirred them herself, as though she feared *we* might crack her china with our spoons.

The china clunked, proving its inferior quality, and the napkins were made of paper. "The teas I prefer are Kalimpong, Darjeeling, or Lapsang Souchong," Twyla commented. But the tags dangling from the teapot belonged to Lipton, *my* favorite.

"Is it . . . grand? Where you live?" Mrs. Prail inquired while we sipped. "You both must know dozens of . . . important people."

I didn't think of myself as a cynic, but I suspected that

Mrs. Prail was about to solicit our aid in procuring auto-graphs of celebrities. Avoidance of such requests being my policy, I quickly asked, "May I use the powder room?"

The urinal in the corner of the bathroom indicated that it had once been attached to the mess hall; the fixture evidently embarrassed Mrs. Prail, because she'd endeavored to fashion it into a philodendron planter.

When I returned to the living room and my tepid Lipton, Mrs. Prail asked, "Have you two . . . met Mr. Prail, my husband? He's the . . . headmaster here."

"We met him this morning," Twyla responded. "He didn't have much to say."

"Then you didn't have a chance to find out what a brilliant man he is?" Mrs. Prail asked.

"Not by a long shot," Twyla responded.

"My husband is *educated*. He has a *Ph.D.* And yet we live like laboratory mice. We came out here for his lungs! But now that he's recovered, Tucson is getting us down. My husband, more than I, because I . . . am able to adjust . . . to anything," Mrs. Prail said with gritted teeth. "So I want you to do something for Mr. Prail and me." Now that she'd arrived at the kernel of her enterprise, her stammer fell by the wayside. "I want you girls to ask your illustrious parents if they can get work for an actor who strongly resembles the most important president this country has ever known."

"Mr. Prail is an actor?" I asked.

"He has acting experience. He has played Abraham Lincoln in pageants, plays, and parades."

"Fleur, you must mention him to your parents," Twyla

said wickedly. "I'll surely tell mine about Mr. Prail. I have no doubt he should be in Hollywood."

I looked beyond Mrs. Prail's frizzed graying hair to see the face of our Civil War president. "I didn't mean to interrupt. Are you entertaining?" Mr. Prail asked his wife.

"No, no . . . not . . . entertaining . . . no . . . I . . . wanted to befriend the . . . new students," she said with a gasp.

"Yes, I should have guessed, kindly, God-fearing woman that you are," Mr. Prail said soberly. I didn't know whether he was speaking some kind of Quakerese or the language of derision.

Evening found me in the telephone booth again. "I won't ask you about the weather tonight," our cook Lois said. "There's no point, is there? It never changes in Tucson. It's always hot and dry. A cold-cream climate, I call it."

"I'm too young for cold cream." I had no wish to discuss Twyla's lotions and emollients.

"Oh, use it. Use it. Take care of what you've got," Lois said.

As I waited for one of my parents to come to the phone, I positioned myself to see the moonbeams striking the algae that padded the pool's surface. In the dark it reminded me of the La Brea Tar Pits in Los Angeles, where the bones of prehistoric animals, who had tarried once to lap water from what they thought was a pond, were still being dredged from the deadly trap.

Charmian had, on numerous occasions, interviewed the tar-splattered paleontologists who hovered around the pits as she endeavored to concoct a plot for a feature film of *The Charmian Leigh Mystery Half Hour*. Her first scene would reveal a sticky human corpse of recent vintage, dredged up in the belly of a fully intact skeleton of a triceratops. The chief anthropologist, afraid of losing his dinosaur to police bureaucracy, would consult Charmian Leigh, PI. How the body got where it did, and why, would stump an audience, but it had stumped Charmian, too. Nevertheless, she planned to direct and star in the movie as soon as she licked the plot.

"I'm surprised you miss us so much," Maurice's voice grated through the receiver. "But don't make a habit of calling every night."

"If you let me come home, I won't call you ever again. Not from here, at any rate."

"How long have you been there? A day and a half? Well, I've paid for the first semester! So you'll have to grin and endure it," my father ranted. "That's all I have time to say. Groucho Marx just stopped by."

"He did? Why?"

"I don't know," Maurice mused. "He was out for a walk. He needed a laugh, he said. But I've got to get him out of here. A couple of agents are due in twenty minutes. No room for humor when you're making a deal."

"Maurice, I promise. I'll get a job and pay you back for the school. I'd be deliriously happy as a waitress at Delores's Drive-In. Even the teachers at this school are off their rockers. The headmaster wants you to set him up as an actor in Hollywood. Well, he *is* a dead ringer for Abraham Lincoln. His wife says he gets raves whenever he puts on the stovepipe hat."

"This town uses Raymond Massey when they need an old Abe," my father said. "What kind of actor plays only one role? No, I take that back—there are lots of actors and actresses who do that. Look at Joan Crawford. Look at Jane Russell! But Abraham Lincoln could never play a cop or a murderer or a cowboy. See what I mean?"

"The point I'm making is that he's cheeky and out of line, asking his wife to ask me to ask you for an acting job," I rambled.

"Nothing wrong with ambition," Maurice replied. "Add to that perspicacity and—"

"My ambition is to come home," I answered. "It's Daisy's, too. She's on the verge of a breakdown. We're miserable. And everyone's sick here. Did you know that? Is there something you're not telling me? Do I have a disease? Does Daisy? Be honest. Is that why we're here? Is it? Is there something wrong with us, too?"

If I sounded overwrought, Maurice ignored it. "Look at Tucson as heliotherapy," he said. "It's good for everyone."

"How about heliotherapy in Beverly Hills?"

I would have sworn I'd stay outdoors from dawn until sunset if Maurice hadn't interrupted with "All right, Fleur, I have to go. Groucho's calling. Do you hear him? Can you smell his goddamn cigar?"

"If you could just fly down here for a day . . . or Maurice, you could send your secretary. Mrs. Bodine would give you a fair, unbiased assessment."

"Mrs. Bodine's gone. Gladys is my secretary now. And by the way, she mailed you a checkbook. For your laundry and personal items. Make a list of the checks you write in the register," he said. "I'll be talking to you. *I'll* call *you.* Not the other way around."

I looked out of the phone booth in the direction the sun had sunk and then lowered my gaze to the black hole of the pool. If I were to throw myself into its *brea* sludge and never come up, I would make my escape from Rancho Cambridge West. Throw in a triceratops, too, and Charmian would have her plot.

VI

Those Who Are Left Behind

During the preceding month, I had become accustomed to awakening to the groaning of water through the pipes, the distant scrape of dresser drawers, and venetian blinds jangling against windows as they granted ingress to the day. Often cantankerous accusations over a missing hairbrush or a toothpaste tube were my reveille.

On this particular morning an astounding chatter awakened me. There were shrieks of laughter supplemented by snickering. I lay in bed listening and wishing for subtitles.

Even Lizzie, within moments of returning from the stable, noticed the peculiar atmosphere. "What the heck is going on?" she asked.

"Since you're so chirpy, why don't you flutter into the hall and peck for information," Twyla prompted her. A moment later we heard the scuff of Lizzie's boots across the rec room's tile floor. A door opened and closed.

"Stop treating Lizzie like a no-account minion," Melly told Twyla. Melly had moved into our room, maintaining a turbulent peace, soon after Twyla and I arrived.

"Don't think you can dictate my behavior," Twyla said, as though Melly were her minion, too.

My mind hadn't fully reckoned with the new day when Lizzie reappeared. Her cowboy hat hung down her back and her eyes bulged. "It can't be true," she exclaimed. "But they showed me proof. Reba left a note. They say it's really her handwriting. She's a goner."

"A suicide?" Twyla asked. She sounded almost tickled.

"Oh, no, please God," Melly gasped.

"And the Wozzums never to see the light of day?" Twyla turned the knife.

"Na-uh," Lizzie said, slumping down on the edge of her bed. "Worse. Reba's run off with the cook."

"Cook Ned? He's such a namby-pamby. But they do say love is blind," Melly mused.

"In this case, it's tasteless," Twyla said, making a bee-line for the bathroom before anyone else had the chance.

"I'll miss his pickle loaf," I defended him.

"Reba was my roommate until I moved in here, so I knew her pretty well. She wanted to leave this place in the worst way. It was just that she needed, um, subsidizing. So I guess she latched on to Cook Ned. Reba was a good kid," Melly said. "Gosh, I'm already talking about her in the past tense."

"Reba's gonna die of food poisoning any day now with

him cooking," Lizzie said. "So the past tense makes sense."

"Does this mean Cook Ned fathered the Wozzums?" I asked.

Melly and Lizzie shot amazed glances in my direction. "You mean you really thought she was pregnant?" Melly asked.

"Isn't she? I was thinking she must be sneaking off to have a litter. Like a dog or cat."

"When I met her a year ago, Reba's stomach was the exact same size," Melly said without noting my naïveté. "My assumption was an ovarian cyst. They've been known to reach watermelon size—I looked it up. But Reba consulted a doctor over the summer, and after X-rays and the rabbit test, he suggested she lose some weight."

"So Reba really snookered me."

"She did."

Curious to see what would happen without Cook Ned on the premises, the entire student body turned out for breakfast. We found cold cereal in unfamiliar boxes that had never merited an advertising campaign and several pitchers of powdered milk. Every student but me agreed that, straight from the box, the flakes or puffs or nuggets were far superior to the tepid, overcooked mush and watereddown syrup we customarily found on our plates.

Before we finished slurping down our breakfast, Dirk Swiggert stepped out of the kitchen, where he'd never been seen before, to make an announcement.

"They're going to let the handyman address Reba's breakout?" I asked, incensed.

"Dirk's not the handyman—he *owns* the school," Melly informed me.

"He couldn't."

"I know it's a little weird."

"It's preposterous."

"Y'all may have heard the news"—a hush enveloped the mess hall—"our cook's flown the coop."

The student body spontaneously applauded.

"Don't clap too hard. Till we find someone new, it's gonna be me an' Jo Ella feedin' you. But anyway, you got my word—we'll be hirin' a new cook soon's we're able."

"Jo Ella's finally getting her just deserts: working in the kitchen," Sparky said with glee. "That'll teach her to get engaged to someone who runs a dump like this."

"Why would a registered nurse want to marry a dud like Dirk?" I asked.

"Who says she's registered?" Sparky responded.

Assuming Dirk would now say some disparaging words about Reba, lest we followed her example, we shushed Sparky. But instead of continuing, Dirk ducked back into the kitchen.

"What's with him?" Brian complained. "What does he think? Out of sight, out of mind? If he doesn't mention Reba, we'll forget she ever existed?"

I admired Brian's reaction. Boys didn't often express such sentiments.

"Maybe Dirk doesn't know she's gone," Melly said.

"He knows," Sparky said. "He came into our room all puffed up and read her note. Then he confiscated Reba's old bra that was hanging over the tub."

"Why?" Melly and I asked in unison.

"To give to the bloodhounds, I guess," Sparky replied.

"Hey, let's hold a ceremony to keep Reba's memory everlasting. Something with candles and incense and dirges," Lionel brightly proposed.

As it happened, Reba had been Melly's only opponent for student-body president of Rancho Cambridge West. And Melly very much wanted to win, not because she could achieve anything in the strictly titular office but because college scholarship committees would be impressed. "The more you supposedly achieve in high school, the more money a college coughs up," Melly had explained. "Remember, I need high-octane financing for my higher education."

"You know, Melly, you mustn't run for office unopposed. It's unsporting and constitutionally unsound," Twyla later told Melly, when Lizzie had trotted off to the stable and the three of us had stretched out for a nap. "So I've decided to run against you myself. It'll be much more fun for everyone if we both campaign."

"But we're roommates," Melly argued.

"We won't let that stand in our way."

"Twyla, stop kidding around," I chided her.

"I'm not kidding."

"Of course you are. The presidency means so much to Melly's future, and it means zero to yours. You aren't even planning on staying to the end of the year," I said sternly.

"All the more reason! This is my only chance for . . . an experiment in American high school government," Twyla declared. Then her voice became eager and precious, too. "If my father is the all-American I suspect he is, think of how impressed he'll be with a daughter who is president of her high school. The only thing better would be home-coming queen."

"You're being ridiculous, Twyla. It won't make—" I began.

Twyla gave me a pleading look, discarding her usual bravado. "Did you ever think that my father might not want anything to do with me? Maybe he has a family. *If* he knows I exist. Maybe he's never mentioned me to his wife. The fancier the package I make my arrival in, the better chance I'll have of approbation."

Only desperation could have induced Twyla to divulge her plight within Melly's earshot, I realized.

"The kids will vote for Twyla because she's glamorous," Melly later complained. "Somehow I'll have to outfox her. Fleur, will you help me? Will you be my campaign manager? Please?"

"I have no experience as a campaign manager," I said, torn between my desire to help Melly and yet not hurt Twyla's feelings. "Well, I suppose I could make posters for you. Twyla knows I don't approve of her running for this office."

"There's more to campaigning than that."

"What?" I asked.

"We'll have to keep tabs on Twyla's tactics and then do some strategizing ourselves," Melly said.

"What tactics can there be in a high school election?"

We'll soon see."

At lunch on the day of Reba's disappearance, we were served baloney sandwiches on hot-dog buns. Cold cuts and white rice salad were set before us for dinner. Though I'd become an aficionado of adobe melt, tamale and shepherd's pie, and creamed-corn casserole, the other students agreed this was the best meal they'd ingested in the mess hall all semester.

"As soon as Dirk hires a new cook, you can be sure it's back to shit on a shingle," Sparky lamented.

"You know what?" Melly said, rising from her seat. "I've seen the light. I can be of assistance to the students *and* win the election."

"How?" Lionel asked eagerly. His fascination with Twyla had diminished since she refused to give him—or any of the boys—a moment's consideration. Again Lionel took Melly's every articulation to heart.

"Wait here. I'll let you know if things work out," Melly said mysteriously as she vacated our table.

Intent on her new enterprise, she didn't notice me following her. Like a gumshoe, I peeped into the kitchen while Melly penetrated its depths.

The kitchen at Rancho Cambridge West seemed a reasonable size to be feeding forty (now thirty-nine) students, but it looked antiquated, as though it had been built before the advent of modern appliances. Tatters of plastic packaging, as well as slices and tidbits of cold cuts and rice salad, had been strewn around the room. Perhaps Dirk and Jo Ella had engaged in an intense quarrel. But this would not explain why the stove, burners, and grill were encrusted with soot and grease. So were the counters, the table, the chopping block, the ceiling, and the floor. The sink might have belonged to a garage mechanic.

"I'M NOT MARRYING YOU TO BECOME A GALLEY SLAVE," Jo Ella ranted at Dirk.

I would have been frightened had not a tendril of her blue-black L'Oreal hair been caught in the corner of her mouth, giving her an inadvertent Salvador Dalí mustache.

"When people are married, the spouses pitch in an' help each other. You know, in a pinch. Like this 'un, they pitch," Dirk pleaded.

"WE AREN'T MARRIED YET," Jo Ella shouted so loudly that I thought her throat might tear. "Let me tell you here and now, if I haven't already: I hate cooking. And even if I liked it, I'd never cook in this death trap. And don't ask me to clean it. It's beyond redemption."

While they squabbled, Melly quietly gathered up the packages and scraps of food and put them in the trash.

"You got KP duty?" Dirk asked when he noticed her.

"No, I'd just like to help you in your . . . pinch," Melly said with her usual good-heartedness. Unfortunately the refrigerator's spasmodic rumbles kept me from hearing her scheme.

I didn't see Melly again until later that night, well after study hall, when she returned from town. Full of vivacity, she said, "Don't you think the way to the electorate's heart is through its stomach? Didn't Herbert Hoover promise 'a chicken in every pot'? That's my strategy, if you'll give me some help."

At six A.M. the following morning, my spirits somersaulting in anticipation, I joined Melly in the kitchen. "Who cleaned it up?" I asked as, unbidden, an image of Hercules cleaning King Augeias's stables came to mind. (Mr. St. Cyr's sporadic classes were having an effect.)

"I did," Melly confessed. "I got up at four. I made a stab at it, anyway."

"Isn't it bad for your disease if you don't get enough sleep?" I asked.

"I don't have time for a flare-up right now, and I don't have time to discuss it, either," Melly said, handing me two large skillets and a pad of steel wool that, I soon discovered, exuded magical properties in the guise of soap.

"How did you convince Dirk to buy the food you wanted?" I asked after I took a gander at what she'd stuffed into the rattletrap refrigerator.

"It wasn't so hard. He was grateful that someone was taking on the cooking chores for free. And saving his marriage, so to speak. I think he would have bought anything I asked. Well, maybe not caviar. Or lobster or oysters. Maybe not filet mignon."

I delighted in manhandling forty-eight grade-triple-A eggs, dispersing their contents into a bowl with only a scattering of eggshells. Then I observed Melly as she poured the eggs over sizzling crackers in the two large, clean frying pans.

While Melly dropped dough into boiling water and waited for it to puff, I asked, "Where did you learn to cook?"

"The food we're fixing is from recipes that were passed down through my family. My grandparents in the old country got them from their grandparents, and they got them from God."

No student at Rancho Cambridge West besides me had ever tasted or, for that matter, heard of matzo brai. But as soon as the breakfasters sampled Melly's treat, they waxed poetic: "Yummy." "Delish." "Fab." "Best breakfast ever." "Melly—a friend of the belly."

By the end of the day, I'd learned how to make borscht, bagels, cream cheese, latkes, holishkes, and kugel from scratch. And I had decided to apply to the Culinary Institute of America, a college for chefs.

During dinner there was a reprise of "Melly—a friend of the belly," and she left the kitchen to oblige her fans. "I'm glad you appreciate my efforts," she told them. "You must also thank Fleur Leigh, my partner and campaign manager. And on a more serious note, a part of why we did this is to prove our can-do attitude. If I'm elected president, I'll make sure you're always well fed."

The cheers and applause were so spirited, I assumed Melly had cinched the election.

"What kind of restaurants serve this food?" Babs asked when the mess hall had quieted. "Where can I get it?"

"Visit my family in Newark or find a good Jewish deli-catessen," Melly said with a laugh.

"This is Jewish food?"

I heard mutters from the diners, but, feeling gloriously accomplished, I assumed they were accolades.

Only Mr. Prail complained. In our presence he told Dirk that Melly and I had missed all our classes. "If their parents find out that you've put the girls to work, you're going to have a lawsuit on your hands. And rightly so, because they are paying for an education."

"The girls're gettin' a vo-ca-tional education," Dirk replied. "In the long run, it's for the best. Kids, 'specially girls, got to know how to do somethin' practical. They're readin' cookbooks, writin' recipes, and 'rithmatickin' the ounces and teaspoons, ain't they? So right there the girls got the three R's covered."

Unmoved, Mr. Prail forced Melly and me into retire-ment.

The following morning at breakfast, Melly and I sat down in our customary places and were surprised to find ourselves alone at the table. Brian and Lionel were absent, Twyla had remained in bed, and Sparky sat across the room.

"What's going on?" I asked Sparky as we left the mess hall, but she quickly turned away.

As we attended our classes, it became clear that none of the students were speaking to Melly and me. The silence had a familiar ring. My father was a master of the silent treatment, and I preferred it to his upbraiding, so I knew I could ride this out.

Melly brooded, "I thought we'd be receiving kisses and kudos for months to come. What is it we've done? What happened to 'Melly—a friend of the belly'?"

Not until late in the afternoon did Lionel slip Melly a note. Only Twyla could have written a better one. *If the new frosty climate in Tucson gives you the shivers, meet me at Ye Olde Car Wrecke at 3 for explanation. Don't breathe a word to anyone, and be sure you aren't followed. Your ardent admirer, You-know-who. (Please burn this immediately.)*

"I'm going with you," I told Melly. "There's something crazy going on."

"Only if you promise not to reveal your presence."

Arriving at Ye Olde Car Wrecke early, I knelt on the floor behind the backseat so that only Melly could observe Lionel as he tiptoed across the desert field.

"You don't know how courageous this is of me," Lionel whispered, climbing into the shattered Chevrolet. Once inside, he must have jiggled his foot continuously. The whole hulk kept vibrating.

"Spill it out. What's going on?" Melly demanded.

"Don't shout, someone might hear us," Lionel pleaded.

"All right, then. You do the talking."

Lionel swallowed so loudly I could picture the gymnastics of his Adam's apple. "I'll do it, I'll risk it, because of my love for you," he said.

"Do it because you're a good person, will you?"

"It's like this. It's Twyla who got the anti-you-Jew ball

rolling. She told us everything she learned about Jews at her Swiss boarding school."

There were no Jews at her boarding school, so how would anyone know anything? I wanted to say.

"'Ever hear of the domino theory?'" Lionel quoted Twyla in reasonable facsimile of her voice. "Twyla explained it. Then she said that Jews started communism because they wanted to dominate the world. 'They already rule Hollywood,' she told us, and she ought to know. They also govern the arts, the Nobel Prize, and the banks."

"Not the bank my parents owe money to, they don't," Melly angrily argued.

"Twyla said that Jews are planning to take over city governments, then states, and then the U.S. Congress until they can install a Jewish president in the White House. She said to watch out for Jews running for elective office."

"Lionel, even if Jews had a worldwide, world-conquering scheme, they would skip RCW."

"Listen, I've never told you this, but my father is a banker. He says just what Twyla does, that the Jews have cornered the worldwide market on money."

"Telling me that Jews have all the money when my parents work like dogs, when they had to borrow money just to send me *here*—this is too much," Melly railed.

"But there's this document called, uh, the Protocols of the Elders of Zion. It spells out just these plans. It's an authentic historical record of a meeting some bigwig Jews had about eighty years ago. But there's more. Twyla also told us—well, I know it doesn't pertain to you personally—that some Jews throughout history have murdered gentile babies because they needed the blood for rituals. You don't do any rituals in your temple, do you?" Lionel asked.

I knew theoretically and historically of the prejudice against Jews, but I had never experienced it firsthand. Was there a protocol? How should I respond? My hiding place became a chamber of torture.

Fortunately Melly knew what to do. "You're an ignorant, asinine fool, Lionel. Come on, Fleur, let's get out of here before I kick this simpleton in the you-know-whats."

In our haste, we unwittingly shifted the position of the derelict that had been resting precariously on rusty jacks and two tireless wheels. The creaky Chevy toppled onto its side, sliding Lionel abruptly into the gear shift and onto other unpadded mechanisms.

I turned to extricate him, but Melly yelled, "Leave him there. Leave him. He's a moron to repeat this prejudiced drivel. He deserves a great big . . . bruise."

VII

When the Mind Is Perturbed

Charmian had coached me at an early age to respond "nonsectarian" whenever filling out a form that asked for religious affiliation. I resented having to certify my religious vacuity. Hadn't I visited numerous, if not *all*, of the houses of Christendom in Beverly Hills? Since my parents required unimpeded calm to slumber till noon, our domestic help had spirited me to countless churches, chapels, and tabernacles.

The fact is, I became an avid churchgoer. I critiqued Sunday services as though they were productions. Some were achieved with shoestrings and some were full-feathered binges, but I revered clergymen who could ensnare an audience with no grander props than a rostrum, a floral bouquet, and a human voice. The organ music, even when badly played, infused a church with tenacious, omnipotent tones. Sometimes choirs invited parishioners to participate, as per television's *Sing Along with Mitch*, and though my parents cringed when I vocalized at home, I trilled along with congregations uninhibitedly. Churches lacked only the bouncing ball.

No matter which church I attended, if the contents of the sermons sometimes bewildered me, I extrapolated a common message: a grand, inscrutable parental Someone would take an interest in what I did, even love me, so long as I behaved in a principled manner and loved Him in return. This simple notion gave me solace for a time.

By my tenth year, I had been baptized by several denominations, but the pursuivants who'd wormed me into their faith never remained at our house for long. The replacement nanny, cook, or maid always had her own, more righteous basilica to attend. With the exception of our hirelings, almost everyone I knew was Jewish, so I remained a religious outsider. Only after I had entered seventh grade and spent a weekend at the house of my school chum Charlotte Douglas did I happen upon the truly pertinent Sunday-school class.

Charlotte's mother drove us past three historic Los Angeles locations that heretofore in my young life had been exotic destinations unto themselves: the aforementioned roiling, boiling La Brea Tar Pits, the tourist-engorged Farmers' Market, and the sleek and golden but squatty May Company department store.

Even farther away from my comfortable quarter of the world, we found the Wilshire Boulevard Temple, a building every inch as palatial as Grauman's Chinese Theatre. The auditorium seated fifteen hundred people and, I'd been told, had been decorated by the art department at Warner Brothers Studio. With no audience present, I found it darkly mysterious, as though a menacing, gloomy God might be crouched on the catwalk. I knew already, of course, that He had all the dignity the Phantom of the Opera lacked.

Upstairs in the temple's classrooms, I found a cozier stratosphere. Soon, scintillated and euphoric, I acquired knowledge of the dauntless Jews. My very own ancestors, I learned, had led more celebrated lives than anyone in Hollywood. The most continuously best-selling book in history had been written about them. (Even Jesus, as I came to understand, had been a Jewish black sheep.) For me Judaism offered the comfort of familiarity: Yahweh Himself was every bit as mercurial as my father. For eight divine weeks I had shed my nonsectarian condition.

On my ninth Sunday, after another engaging class, the teacher spoke to me privately. "Look," Mr. Blaustein said in a kindly manner, "you've been attending my lessons for two solid months. Unfortunately I must tell you that unless your parents become members of the temple, you really can't return."

At home I made an intensive effort to sway my parents. I approached my father just after he'd turned off his favorite television show, which happened to feature a preacher in sparkly formal wear who guaranteed his proselytes that they could have whatever they prayed for—be it drum sets, Cadillacs, skyscrapers, even stardom—if they followed his tenets. The listening was easy, because he had such a smooth and engaging oratorical style. The reverend distilled religion into what Maurice explained were the basics: *Have faith and send me money.* No one, not Sid Caesar, Ernie Kovacs, not Groucho, made Maurice laugh as heartily.

"Please, please, will you join the temple?" I begged my parents. "I'll never ask for another thing."

"Religion is the opiate of the dunderheads. What's the difference between giving your money to Rabbi Magnin, Reverend Ike, or Elmer Gantry? They're all con artists," my father said.

"But this is different. The Sunday-school teacher isn't promoting God or himself. He's teaching literature and history. He says that educated people still grapple with the metaphors of the Old Testament."

"Don't you realize that, outside Hollywood, being Jewish is a liability? Why do you think we changed our names?" Charmian sniveled.

"It's a liability inside Hollywood, too. Believe me, I'm doing you a favor, sparing you from . . . balderdash," Maurice said.

"All I'm asking is that you pay the dues."

"No can do. I'm not a hypocrite. Reverend Ike doesn't get my money, either. And *he* makes me laugh."

I stewed about this injustice for several days. The Thursday before the next Sunday-school class, I took what action I could. "I'd like to speak with Rabbi Magnin," I said when I phoned the Wilshire Boulevard Temple. I didn't know at the time that he was known as "the rabbi to the stars." Nevertheless, it surprised me that Rabbi Magnin, not some underling, took my call.

"I really love your Sunday school. It means the world to me, and I want to keep attending," I said, using a positive approach.

"Yes?" he asked, a little impatiently.

I didn't think it wise to mention my parents' atheism. Instead I said, "But my parents aren't what you'd call joiners. They don't belong to anything, not even the Automobile Club of Southern California."

"That's impractical," the rabbi said.

"So I'm wondering . . . I'd like to join the temple on my own. In my own name."

Rabbi Magnin didn't answer immediately. "Well, yes, why not?" he said finally, in a voice that implied a shrug. "We have no age restriction here."

"Oh, that's fantastic," I squealed.

"You understand that you'll have to pay membership dues, just like everybody else," the rabbi added quickly.

Thinking that I'd happily give him my entire allowance of three dollars a week, I cooed, "Oh, I'd be delighted."

"Well, then, we have a deal," he said.

"By the way, how much are they? The dues?"

"Eight hundred dollars a year," he said in a tone so staid that I gathered it wasn't a joke.

"Eight hundred?" I repeated, dumbfounded. "Gosh, don't you have a children's rate? They do at the movies. And when children fly on planes."

"No, 'fraid not," the rabbi told me casually, as though my situation made little difference to him.

"But . . . but . . . but," I spluttered. "I'm really interested in Judaism. I'd really like to learn the history of . . . my ancestors."

"Then talk to your parents again," he said.

"Please, please, Rabbi Magnin," I implored him.

"Jews are men of laws," he said.

I spoke quickly to forestall his cutting me off. "I don't understand. I would have thought you'd be glad to have a young person, the child of . . . atheists, wanting to get back into the fold. What about my children? What will I tell them? I think you're being so unfair. This is really so . . . so . . . un-Christian of you."

For Melly's sake rather than my own, I decided to breach my father's directive and call home.

"Leigh residence," someone (most likely a new maid) responded upon picking up the phone.

"Oh, hi, I'm calling for Mr. or Mrs. Leigh. This is their daughter, Fleur." I spoke softly, trying not to convey exasperation.

"Hang on a mini-min, will you, now? I'll see if they're in," the maid said.

I would have asked her name, but I knew full well that anyone caught saying *mini-min* by either Charmian or Maurice would not be in their employ for long. So I waited in the stuffy phone booth with nothing to do but peer into

the Cimmerian sludge of the swimming pool. Despite
the arid desert breeze, the surface of the water had nary a
ripple.

Chances were that turning to my parents in a time of
need would prove fruitless. Nine times out of ten, when a
cloudburst of trouble soaked my shoulders, they didn't
deign to hand me a towel. It was that tenth time, when
they supported me, that lured me back to them.

"Qu'est-ce que c'est?" Charmian asked when she came on
the line. "It better be something worthy of my time. We
have company—my new agent and his wife. She's dull as
an aluminum penny, but he's a wizard."

My downheartedness didn't staunch my cunning. "I
have a bang-up idea for you," I tempted her.

"That's different. Go right ahead." Given that Charmian's
efforts to bring herself and the triceratops to the big
screen had bogged down, her ears pricked up when a
potential plot drifted her way. She would find no role suitable to her talents in the Rancho Cambridge West caper.
But she wouldn't know that until she heard me out.

"Your friend should not have advertised her Judaism,"
Charmian commented when I'd completed my narrative.
"There's never any point in that. It's a fool's game. And
Daisy, anti-Semitic? I'm shocked. Who does she think gave
her parents their start? Or, for that matter, their middle
and end? But since Daisy is this far gone . . . well, I'll have
to think about it. Give me a minute."

"A mini-min?" I asked.

"Qu'est-ce-que vous dites?"

"You're supposed to be thinking," I said.

"Hmmm. All right. *One* thing is clear. You are going to have to fight. One always must—it's obligatory—when bigots rear their ugly heads."

"But the bigot is my dearest friend. What can I do? Charmian, can't I just come home?" I ventured, forgetting all about Melly or, for that matter, the Jewish race. "I didn't ask for this."

"I suppose you would have been a Nazi collaborator because it was easier," Charmian harrumphed. "Why aren't you taking umbrage? Why won't you defend the Jews?"

"I thought we were nonsectarians."

"We are. My ancestors were the first assimilated family in Germany," Charmian stated with pride, as she had many times before. "Nevertheless, I take a strong position when necessary. One must. Think of Hitler. Think of World War II. Think of all those horrid photos in *Life* magazine."

"Would you talk to Daisy, then?" I beseeched her.

"*Mon dieu*, you're in a school full of adolescents just like yourself. You should know how to approach them far better than I. Use the imagination I've endowed you with."

"Charmian, if only you'd come to Tucson. If you could see this dumping ground, you'd say to get the hell out. I know you would."

"Yes, yes, if I had the time. But at long last, your father is making a picture again. I will play the part—not the lead, to my regret—of a retired, very intelligent, and still beautiful ecdysiast. It's a shame she's retired, because I'd love to do a scene that shows her working. I'm perfectly capable of it. My body is as good as ever. Still, her wardrobe can reflect—"

"What *is* an ecdysiast?"

"*Chérie*, you head straight to the library and look it up. And while you're at it, study the definition of prejudice and, eh, genocide. The seeds of genocide are, well, germinating in that school of yours."

My mother rarely said good-bye before she hung up. I listened for a few seconds to the dial tone, the most desolate sound I know, before vacating the telephone booth. Fortunately I found Melly outside.

"Were you calling your parents for advice?" she asked.

"Uh-huh," I said.

"What was it?"

"The advice? Oh, I'm supposed to look up the definition of genocide," I said.

"Gee, do you think it's going to come to that?" Melly asked. "There're just the two of us here. It'll be such an itsy-bitsy *genocide*."

We both chuckled. Then I had an idea. "I bet your parents will know how to handle this. Will you call them?"

"No, I can't," Melly said quickly. "I wouldn't. They'd get worried and want to fly me home. Or, worse, they'd rush to Tucson. They can't afford to do either."

"So we're alone."

"We have each other," Melly said with false cheer.

If we had been students at almost any other school, the girls' dean or headmaster would have called a compulsory assembly and lectured us on the meaning of prejudice. At Beverly Hills High School, even more extreme measures would have been taken. Representatives of the Anti-Defamation League, the National Association for the Advancement of Colored People, and possibly the Bureau of Indian Affairs would have converged in our auditorium. If their rebukes didn't purge the bigotry, they would have postponed the election.

As we strolled away from the telephone booth, I noticed that Melly walked stiffly, as though her ankles had lost all motility. I also observed a rash on her cheeks and her eyes glistening like the glass buttons sewn on the faces of teddy bears. "Are you all right?" I asked.

Melly sighed. "I'm so tired."

As we passed the swimming pool, I noticed a crowd of students around its edges. Brian was standing barefoot on the diving board, staring at the stagnant depths. Though he wore a long-sleeve shirt and jeans to cover his psoriasis, he appeared to be contemplating a dive.

Brian bounced a little, just enough to flap the board's shredded lining. The very creak of the diving board solicited gasps from the sidelines. "I don't want to do this," Brian addressed the multitude. "I really don't, but I can't stand what's going on. Melly went to so much trouble. She cooked such terrific food. This is your thanks?"

"Don't jump," Sparky called to Brian. "Think of your skin. Your own health has to come before any so-called principle. Going into that pool is suicide."

"Okay. All right. If you really care about me, then proclaim your acceptance of, um, all creeds and colors. Think of me as representing them, the girls you're pushing over-board. I don't care who you vote for. I just care that you do it for, um, nonprejudiced reasons. So if all of you don't drop your bigotry right now, I'm dropping into the pool."

I peered around at Babs, Dena, Eddie, Cuyler, and all the others. No one moved or spoke.

Brian, at the very end of the diving board, now sprang more forcefully. With each bounce, a larger gap appeared between his feet and the precarious plank over the pool. As he landed, his weight threatened to break the diving board in half and spill him into the water. I fretted that Brian would lose his footing. I didn't believe—I couldn't believe—that he would do something so foolish as to allow any patch of his skin to come in contact with the contami-nated fluid.

"PLEASE DON'T JUMP," Melly implored. "You'll get sick." Then she whispered to me, "Nothing's going to stop him unless the kids do what he says. Brian's Catholic. And Catholics love their martyrs."

"This is the only way I can think of to get you to give up your ridiculous prejudice." Brian spoke powerfully even as he bounded several feet into the air. Then he unexpect-edly tucked his head down toward his chest, and his body seemed to crumple as he rolled forward and entered the water with a thunderous splash.

We all screamed and ducked the spray. When Brian didn't surface, we screamed the more. Perhaps his head had struck some forgotten fragment of Ye Olde Car Wrecke, sharp as Poseidon's trident, hidden in the black stew. But no one else dared to dive in. Even I, who could swim better than most native Californians, succumbed to cowardice. The newt-hatching, amoeba-germinating, slime-breeding broth bridled my better impulses. If Brian didn't surface by the time I counted to sixty, I promised myself, I'd take action. Sixty-five, sixty-six, sixty-seven. At last Brian's head, covered with blackened bracken, pierced the crust.

"It's the creature from the black lagoon," someone screamed, not meaning to be funny, just giving an apt description of what we all saw.

Cuyler and Eddie bent over and pulled Brian, panting and choking, onto the deck.

Even Jo Ella, when she finally arrived on the scene, recognized Brian's need for medical attention. "Get him out of here. Get him out of here," she yelled at the attendants when the ambulance arrived.

Despite the facts that Twyla was reclining on her bed industriously writing essays, and that our room reeked of cleaning solvent, Melly and I had no choice but to bivouac there. Conchita had lately attached herself to us, and today she had set about washing the unsightly light fixture. Straddling a stepladder, the maid glanced at Melly and me and, observing our glum faces, asked, "Sometheeng ees wrong?"

"I'm very sad," Melly told her.

"Ho no. *Por que?*" Conchita asked.

"Because this school is full of dunces. They're mistreat-

ing Fleur and me because we're Jewish. It's called prejudice, Conchita, and it's wicked, though I suppose you've
had your own experiences with bigotry," Melly said,
loudly enough to snatch Twyla's attention.

"Jou are Jouish?" Conchita asked, her tone conveying
both fear and astonishment. She climbed down from the
ladder as if to thwart any peril, and when both her feet
touched ground, she shook her head. "Jou are Jouish?" she
asked again, as though to be certain she had heard it cor-
rectly. "Oh well, I like jou anyway."

Despite her obvious pain, Melly laughed. "Well, thanks."

I peered over to see if Twyla had absorbed this
exchange, on the verge of saying, *There, you see, even this
maid has better sense than you.* But Twyla's mind seemed
concentrated solely on her dispatches.

Melly carried an economy-size bottle of aspirin into the
hushed mess hall. Students were speaking in low tones.
We were surprised to find Lionel seated at our table,
though it appeared he had joined us mainly to flaunt his
injuries. He had fixed a scarf around his neck and forearm
to indicate a broken radius or ulna.

Once Melly had observed the ersatz bandage, the
downturned corners of her mouth shifted to hint at a
smile. "It's nice of you to sit with us," she thanked him.

"Have you heard from Brian?" I asked.

"They're keeping him overnight for observation,"
Lionel answered. He ate exactly six beans from his six-

bean salad and the two ends of hot dog. He couldn't stop fidgeting and craning his neck to see if others were looking his way. Then, as though he were a ventriloquist sneaking words into a dummy's throat, he spoke through the side of his mouth. "What are you going to do about what I told you about?" he asked Melly.

"What *can* I do? I'm going to keep up with my studies and ignore the rest. I, for one, plan to go to college." Still, she sounded defeated. After she took a few bites of dinner, followed by a number of pills, she said, "I'm only eating this rubbish because I can't take aspirin on an empty stomach."

"I don't know why, but I like this dinner," I exclaimed, eliciting expressions of disgust.

After dinner Melly limped back to the dorm on ankles that appeared to have solidified into hardened cement. When she lowered herself into bed that night, I realized that her wrists and elbows had stiffened, too.

"If Mr. St. Cyr shows up for study hall, and if he misses me, which he probably won't, tell him I'm having an episode," Melly said. "He'll know what that means."

"You look like you're really in pain. Shouldn't I ask Jo Ella to do something for you?" I asked.

"Perish the thought."

"But maybe she has some medicine that will help you."

"I'm taking everything the law allows," Melly said.

Jo Ella's strident voice could be heard from outside the kitchen. Inside I found her haranguing Dirk as he attempted to mop the floor. Melly's efforts at cleaning it were no longer in evidence. "THE PLACE NEEDS SANDBLASTING, DIRK," Jo Ella roared.

"Excuse me," I said. "I don't mean to interrupt, but you have a patient. Melly's sick."

"Yeah? What's supposedly wrong this time?" Jo Ella asked.

"She's in terrible pain."

"Oh, all right. Anything to get away from this pigpen."

The nurse stopped by her office next to the classrooms to procure her medical kit, and I led the way to our dorm.

"Open your mouth, Melinda," Jo Ella demanded, looming over Melly with a wooden depressor. When Melly complied, Jo Ella jabbed the stick against her tongue. "Nothing wrong here," she quickly deduced. After taking Melly's pulse and blood pressure and listening to her heart with a stethoscope, she remained unimpressed. "I suppose you want to give me a rundown of symptoms."

"Look at Melly's cheeks. They're as red as stop signs," I pointed out. "Aren't you going to take her temperature?"

"I don't *take* temperatures. I've been burned too many times. Anyone can fake a high fever," Jo Ella elaborated.

"Melly can hardly walk or move her arms."

"And that can't be faked? Ha!" Jo Ella scoffed.

Melly hadn't the strength to argue, so it fell to me to caution the nurse. "You already have one student in the hospital. Melly could end up there, too."

"Dirk and I are going to catch a movie tonight, so I feel charitable. I'll let you stay in bed," Jo Ella told Melly.

* * *

Ever since our intervention, the Adjudicator seemed to have quashed his more outlandish impulses.

Still I approached him with trepidation. "Mr. St. Cyr? I need to talk to you."

"What is it?" he asked, as though I'd been pestering him all day.

"Melly is sick."

"Aren't we all?" He shrugged as if I were talking about pandemic neurosis.

"I mean really sick. *Elle est très malade.*" In an effort to seize his undivided attention, I gave my best rendition of Charmian's scattershot French.

"Did Jo Ella examine her?" he asked with more concern.

"Jo Ella berated her."

"I imagine she would," he mused.

"Melly is sick enough to go to a hospital, I'm pretty sure, and I don't want that to happen."

Mr. St. Cyr looked at me intently, and I fretted that he would solicit further explanation. But the Adjudicator asked nothing; he glanced at his watch instead. In a conspiratorial whisper, he said, "There's an hour and forty-seven minutes left of study hall. Do you concur?"

"I don't have a watch," I said.

"I think I can get . . . a friend over here to examine Melly with nobody the wiser."

Like Charmian doing undercover work, I lurked in the dark near the Rancho Cambridge sign. Soon enough, tires

crackled over the sand and gravel, and even with no headlights in evidence, I could see a sleek foreign car from a
flamboyant but bygone era rolling toward me.

When Mr. St. Cyr's friend, whom I assumed had medical credentials, began rolling up his window, I stepped
from behind a cactus and inadvertently startled him. He
didn't unlatch his door.

"Are you Dietrich?" I asked.

"Where's Cyril?" the man asked.

I hadn't known Mr. St. Cyr's first name; I hadn't considered that he had one. But the whole of it—Cyril St.
Cyr—made me giggle. "Mr. St. Cyr thought it would draw
less attention to your . . . house call if he stayed at his post
in the study hall. He entrusted me to take you to Melly."

Dietrich went through quite a rigamarole, which
required two keys and unscrewing the hood ornament,
before he retreated from his automobile.

"What kind of car is that?" I asked, more out of polite-
ness than interest.

"It's a 1938 Hispano-Suiza," the doctor said proudly,
just as a grandfather might enthuse about his grandchild.
"I bought it new." He spoke of the car's many mechanical
and handmade attributes as we wound our way to the
dorm.

By the light of our room's newly cleaned fixture, I
noticed that the doctor's well-pressed double-breasted suit
with wide lapels looked like suits my father wore in my
kindergarten days. His collar and cuffs were frayed, indicating hard times. Then, too, his facial features appeared
trampled by catastrophe. *An accident? A stock-market crash?*

Syphilis? "Pick one," Charmian would have said. Only his hair, thick and a vibrant white, had any real life.

I wished Mr. St. Cyr had mentioned Dietrich's last name. I felt certain that we'd met before.

The physician's hands shook as he took Melly's temperature and listened to her heart. He had a fastinating tic that momentarily lifted one cheek away from his mouth to give him, in profile, a fleeting smile. From the front, it appeared that the other half of his face had been left out of the joke.

"You're a sick girl," he murmured to Melly.

"She is," I rushed to tell him, thrilled to be talking directly to a doctor without my father running interference. "I think Melly tries to do too much."

"Rheumatoid arthritis is a disease that demands extra hours of sleep, up to ten hours a night. Will you keep that in mind, Melly?"

"Yeah, sure," Melly said weakly.

"She will from now on," I promised impatiently. "But is there a cure? Is there some medication—"

"I don't . . . write prescriptions anymore. I . . . I'm retired," Dietrich said regretfully, glancing nervously at the door as though someone might be listening. "But even if I could, there isn't anything much to prescribe. Melly could take some aspirin."

"She did already."

"As you may have noticed, her temperature will be fluctuating from very high to very low for the next few days. You can alleviate some of her discomfort by applying heat to her joints when she's cold, and cold when she's hot. If you could obtain some hot-water bottles and ice bags, your task would be simplified. And, need I tell you, she should have complete bed rest for the entire week."

"May I ask you something?"

Dietrich nodded.

"Could Melly's sickness be brought on by . . . gloom and doom? I mean, if she was badly upset, could her body break down?"

"When the mind is perturbed, so goes the body," the physician said. Then, utilizing Lizzie's escape hatch, he departed.

VIII

The Cure

Soon Melly slipped off to sleep, leaving me alone to cogitate on how, with no money or means of transportation, I could procure the proposed medical supplies. Taking up a collection for Melly came to mind, but since none of the students were speaking to her, I doubted they'd contribute.

I lay on my cot benumbed by the paucity of options until, over the hubbub of the girls returning to the dorm from study hall, I heard the thwack of Lizzie's cowboy heels on the rec-hall floor. The tinny percussion of spurs followed a half-beat behind like ideas hatched moments too late. "Lizzie," I whispered and pointed to the lump that was Melly asleep in her bed. "Please, could you walk in socks?"

"Yeah, sure," Lizzie said gruffly but softly. To her credit, she began struggling to dislodge her metatarsals from her skintight boots. "Is Mel okay?" she asked.

"She will be if she gets plenty of rest."

"I'll slug anyone who disturbs her. How's that?" Lizzie said with a smirk.

Either Lizzie hadn't been notified that Melly was a persona non grata or, more probably, she hadn't absorbed the data. Therefore, I supposed, I could use her ignorance to Melly's advantage. "I talked to a doctor while you were in study hall, and he suggested applying heat and ice to her joints. That would mean buying quite a few ice bags and hot-water bottles. Do you think we could shame Jo Ella into supplying them?"

"Jo Ella wouldn't lift a pinkie," Lizzie said.

"Well, I just remembered something. I have a checkbook. So do you think I could get a ride into town? Do you think the pharmacy will be open this late?"

"The pharmacy is closed, but the delivery boy is always open," Lizzie said, an expression of disgust spreading across her face.

"What do you mean?"

"See, durin' the day this guy delivers for the Medicine Man Pharmacy. His name is Denny, and by day he's the pharmacist's nephew or somethin'. At night he becomes Mr. Party Time! He'll scout around, pick up, and deliver anythin' you want, usin' the pharmacy van, naturally. Too bad he can't have his name painted on the side. So long as you give him his tip, he'll get you anythin'. Not that I'd ever tip him, no siree Bob, but do you want me to call?"

"Definitely," I said.

At that moment the bigot sauntered in, pretending not

to notice any of us. She pulled off her clothes, then stretched and yawned and yawned again, visiting octaves I'd never before heard.

"Quit your yapping," Lizzie warned her. "Melly's sick."

"What a shame," Twyla responded indifferently.

"The point is, she needs sleep," I beseeched Twyla.

"I won't make a peep," Twyla said, but at the word *peep* she hiccupped, whether by accident or design I couldn't determine.

"Shut up, shut up, shut up," Lizzie said. Then she slid across the room in her socks and left us.

I had expected Twyla to shimmy into her mother's mauve negligee, which she wore more frequently than her others, but she pulled on a striped Lanz nightgown, purchased in Salzburg, Germany, from Mr. Lanz himself. Twyla was the only person I've ever known, before or since, to look glamorous in flannel sleepwear. Throughout her disrobing and rerobing, Twyla continued to converse by means of yawns.

"It sounds as though you're trying to kill off your opponent. Please stop," I petitioned Twyla in a whisper.

"If only I could. Yawning is involuntary." She yawned again, as if to prove her point.

"All right. All right," I said angrily but softly. "Just step into the bathroom so we can talk."

"Not right now," Twyla replied, yawning again. "I've just heard from my detective, and I have to think."

I took a breath and enunciated as clearly as I could, "You do what's best for you, then, Daisy Belmont."

Sliding her feet into slippers, Twyla did as I'd asked. A moment later I found her sitting in the empty bathtub, so in an effort to tenderize our coming quarrel, I stepped back into our room and pulled the swan-down satin-covered comforter from her bed. (The swans themselves, minus last year's feathers, lived at Lake Como, Twyla had reputed.)

We sat facing each other in, on, and under the quilt in the otherwise empty tub. Once again Twyla had left me the faucet end, but this time I placed a pillow behind my back.

"Can't you show a little respect? You know I'm finished with that name," Twyla said. "You don't seem to under-stand—my mother has people searching for me. She and that cretinous little Jew want to abscond with my money. I can't believe that you, my oldest friend in the world, would break a confidence." (She pronounced the word *confidence* in the French manner, just as Charmian would have, though Twyla's pronunciation sounded authentic.)

"Tit for tat," I said angrily. "You can't turn the entire school against Melly and me and still expect me to respect you. Now, tell me, is it your squabble with the 'little Jew' that has turned you against the entire Jewish population? Is it your hoity-toity school? Or do you really believe that Jews—myself included—are inferior to you?"

"Oh, Fleur, not you," Twyla suddenly gushed in an apologetic tone. "I don't include you when it's as clear as distilled water that you're a *white* Jew."

"A white Jew?" I'd never heard the term and couldn't

help but connect it to the white-flocked Christmas tree my parents had purchased the year before. When I was able to discard the image, I replaced it with resentment. "I suppose in your parlance, that means Melly is a black Jew."

"There's no such designation," Twyla said. "But face it—Melly is crass, unrefined, loud, dresses shabbily, and has a Brooklyn accent!"

"Even if those things were true, and they aren't—except for the Brooklyn accent, though she is actually from Newark—they have nothing to do with her being Jewish," I argued. "Your big complaint, it sounds like, is that she's not as wealthy as you."

"Don't ever say *wealthy*," Twyla ordered. "Expunge that word from your vocabulary right now. Just say *rich*."

"What's the difference?"

"*Wealthy* is a non-U word. Non-U means lower-class. As opposed to upper-class, you see. And while I'm on the subject, stop saying *eether*, will you? People of breeding say *eyether*."

"What are you babbling about?" In my despair, I unconsciously tugged on the quilt and attempted to dislodge Twyla from the smooth, gently graded end of the tub.

"I'm telling you, and you should listen—Melly is a stereotypical Jew," Twyla said loudly, kicking at me a little to lend emphasis to her words.

All at once my thoughts centered on Rabbi Magnin. He'd pushed me into this tub of intolerance. If he'd allowed me to remain in Sunday school, I'd have an argument to set forth. Instead I had to defend a group, a race, a religion, or whatever it was, that hadn't accepted me. "Listen, Twyla, even though you're exempting me, I refuse to be your sidekick in this. I don't think you believe this bigoted hogwash. I think you're just using the other kids' stupidity to get them to vote for you."

"You're wrong. I'm repeating what cognizant people around the globe have told me."

"How can they be cognizant when they're prejudiced?" I asked. And then I was kicking Twyla with serious intent, though the quilt tended to cushion the blows. I'd never had such direct physical contact with anyone. But Twyla had raised my hackles. Ashamed of her, and of myself for giving in to corporal impulses, I climbed out of the bathtub. But an unconquerable urge seized hold of me. I reached down and yanked as hard as I could, trying but not suceeding to pull the satin quilt out from under my so-called friend.

After lights-out, while Melly slept and Twyla isolated herself in the bathroom to perform her cosmetic purgations, I crept across the windowsill with the stealth of a cat burglar while Lizzie kept vigil over Melly.

Unlike Dietrich, Mr. Party Time drove onto the campus with headlights aglow and music, or some excuse for it, thumping louder than the most obstreperous carburetor.

Denny was eighteen years old, Lizzie had said. Neither too fat nor too thin, awkwardly tall or too short, he would not have been tagged unattractive if a dark froth of acne hadn't coated his face and neck. I could spot his skin's volcanic topography even by moonlight. Perhaps Twyla could prescribe some unguents for him.

"So, I got the stuff for you," Mr. Party Time said in his nasal voice, a Peter Lorre up to no good. I had noticed the presaging Brody knob on the steering wheel before I saw the bags on the passenger seat.

"The pharmacy only had two hot-water bottles and five ice bags. I'll order the rest if you want."

"Yes, please. And how much do I owe you for these?"

"We'll call it fifteen even," Mr. Party Time said, sounding like my father when he wheeled and dealed.

Pulling my checkbook out of my jeans pocket, I asked, as I'd heard Charmian ask so many times, "To whom do I make it out? And how much is the tip?"

"A check? I don't take checks. I run a cash business," he said huffily.

"My check is perfectly good. My father—or his secretary—puts money in the bank whenever it's needed. The bank must call them when I run out."

Mr. Party Time pulled the checkbook out of my hands. "Beverly Hills! You're from Beverly Hills? I can't believe it. How many movie stars do you know?"

"My check is good," I answered.

"Yeah, okay, Beverly Hills. You can make it out to Denny Holtz," he said with a nervous titter. "Maybe I'm gonna pin it on my wall." He waited until I finished writing and then added with a contorted smile, "You asked about the tip."

"Is it included?" I asked hopefully.

"Nah, the tip isn't money. It's much better than that," he said, sneering lasciviously. "The tip is . . . for you to kiss me. One kiss per item. French with lots of tongue." He might have been ordering a sandwich. "Yeah, Beverly Hills, give me seven big smackeroos. Give me some of those big old movie smooches." Mr. Party Time leaned close and puckered his lips.

A mild paralysis overtook me, as if I had no fight-or-flight instinct whatsoever. Did I have to go through with this? I'd felt similarly discombobulated when confronted with my first kiss years before.

A typical celebration for new eleven-year-olds in my set at El Rodeo Elementary School entailed a Saturday jaunt to the Beverly Theatre in the heart of Beverly Hills to see a movie starring one of three actors—Tab Hunter, Russ Tamblyn, or Troy Donahue. We girls then lunched across the street at Blum's Restaurant. I remember nothing of what we ate beyond Blum's pastel-colored sugar-coated almonds and scrumptiously gooey birthday cake. When the time came for the birthday girl to open her presents, excruciating pains would fire up in the useless spaces below my eyebrows. As I watched the squealing celebrant unwrap pristine stuffed animals or feathery-soft cashmere sweater sets, I knew what shame awaited. My mother refused to buy "extravagant gifts for children," so she rustled up such items from the present closet as a patent-leather headband she'd originally bought for herself or an even more embarrassing bar of soap on a rope.

Accustomed to these "gifts," sometimes wrapped in

secondhand paper and ribbon, the reveler didn't waste time making snide comments. (The kinder girls didn't even unwrap them.) Nevertheless, I earned a reputation for asking the mothers of the hostesses to drive me home early.

For my eleventh birthday, Charmian, on hiatus from her radio show and "in between movies," as she called the time she had no work, decided to while away a day with a birthday "pairs affair."

"I'd like to go to the movies and then to Blum's with my girlfriends, just like they do," I said.

"And I suppose you also want one of those boring bake-a-cake mothers your friends have. Why don't you acknowledge your luck in being the daughter of an inordinately creative woman?"

"Couples" were delineated at school by their exchange of ID bracelets. My mother sent invitations to five of them and to one "unattached" boy for me. I liked Darcy Unger well enough, but we weren't linked by anything so tangible as jewelry.

Charmian had chosen a treasure-hunt theme. Indeed, she'd spent hours on the hillside behind our house and throughout the garden, hiding elaborate clues that she'd composed herself on squares of pastel paper folded into birds and airplanes and sailor hats.

All the guests but one were dropped off promptly at three P.M. We nibbled candied pecans and chocolate-dipped strawberries, served in my mother's delicate Haviland dishes, while shuffling around on the patio waiting for Darcy Unger.

It didn't take Charmian long to fume. "Who exempted this boy from his manners? The game is set up for partners. We can't begin until he arrives."

"It's all right," I told Charmian. "I can look for clues by myself. It's probably fairer that way, because my friends don't know our grounds the way I do."

"No." My mother stomped her sandaled foot. "I have to have an even number. Go call that slacker, for heaven's sake."

When I reported that no one had answered the phone at the Unger residence, Charmian enlisted our cook to walk down the street and lure a neighbor boy named Willy Gold with the promise of games, prizes, ice cream, and cake. But Willy was only nine years old, a baby next to my just-turned eleven-year-old self.

Charmian gave me no choice but to swallow my pride and lead the others toward the elaborate trails she had charted around our house and gardens. She'd created clues that were practical and witty, written in the curt but bewitching language of telegrams (though Charmian claimed they were influenced by Alexander Pope).

> Some will call me a tree, though verily I'm a bush.
> Toss my berries in your mouth and surely you will goof.
> Nestled in my branches, however, betwixt thorn and thistle
> Examine me cautiously to find the next epistle.

Victorious shouts rang out as the select few of my schoolmates unscrambled the messages and ferreted out the next clue. One team had to count off fourscore and seven paces. Another had to climb a tree. Another had to take off their shoes and step across the gap between the hillside and our tile roof. When we needed respite from our convoluted trails or became red-faced from the heat, crystal goblets of pink lemonade awaited us on a silver tray.

The inky-dinky spider will stay out of sight
If you round Fleur's domicile and look to the right.
Though there are no gargoyles standing guard
On gray days I divert rainwater from the yard.
When you peer into my piping
An arachnid might be sniping.

I have no recollection of the winning couple, but, proud that my mother would go to so much trouble for me, I felt victorious. While feasting on crustless egg-salad sandwiches with the bread dyed blue and green, I had to agree with Charmian that none of my friends' mothers could have devised so ingenious a party.

Our cook had made a delectable eleven-layer cake laminated with chocolate butter cream, but before I had a chance to lick the crumbs from the bottoms of my eleven candles plus one to grow on, Charmian said, "And now for the best part of the party—a game of chance." She bade us sit in a circle on a blanket she had spread over the grass. Then, like a magician, she pulled from a silken satchel an everyday object—an empty glass milk bottle. With a flourish, Charmian then demonstrated its whirling capacity. "Round and round it goes," she called out like a hawker at a county fair. "Who will be the lucky recipient of Fleur de Leigh's first kiss?"

When Willy understood the purpose of the milk bottle, he scrambled off the blanket and retreated from the party. I saw him scurrying down San Ysidro Drive and wished I could follow.

The bottle slowed its spin and finally stopped with its open mouth gaping at Emanuel Roth, a boy who was brilliant in math and science but undone by all other subjects. I felt terribly embarrassed for him, and for me. I wanted to say, *My mother's just joking.* But I couldn't disappoint Charmian; she'd worked so hard. She obviously placed importance on the kissing game and seemed almost giddy. "Go on, go on, go on," she urged us.

"We aren't really old enough for this," I whispered to her.

"Don't be a party pooper," Charmian admonished me.

In the foreground, Emanuel's lips loomed large. Once his flesh pressed against mine, I had no other feeling, no other desire, than to present him with a tube of Chap Stick. As quickly as I deemed appropriate, I withdrew my lips. Neither of us so much as glanced at each other until he put forth a few well-acted guffaws.

The following day I lay in bed, sick with a belated birthday-party headache. At three P.M. the discordant buzz of our doorbell heightened the pain. Creeping across my bedroom lest my movements be heard outside, I arrived at the window overlooking our front door. And there, under the portico, dressed in a suit and tie and holding a box wrapped in floral paper with a matching bow, stood Darcy Unger, punctual as a school bell, if twenty-four hours too late.

Now fury jostled my insides. "Let me ask you something," I confronted Mr. Party Time. "Why do you want to be kissed by a girl who doesn't want to kiss you?"

The boy laughed a mean whine of a laugh and, grabbing hold of my shoulders, pulled me toward him. I quickly considered the acting technique my mother claimed she utilized for loathsome love scenes: she visualized my father. Not an experienced actress, I feared I would sully Brian's image if I attempted to substitute his face for the delivery boy's.

What transpired could not fall under the definition of a kiss or even one long, unendurable osculation—our lips coincided. But, like one of those bantamweight prizefighters on television, Mr. Party Time, using his tongue instead of his fist, jabbed his weapon of torture into my mouth. Like his external skin, his tongue was covered with bumps. If I hadn't kept an image of the ailing Melly foremost in my mind, I would have pushed, kicked, screamed, and made an unforgettable ruckus. Instead I counted to seven, turned away from him, grabbed the bags, and started running.

"Don't forget," Mr. Party Time called out, "I'll expect another tip when I bring the rest of the stuff."

"The order is canceled," I shouted without turning around.

Before I attended to Melly, I turned the shower on full force and stood, mouth gaping, under the spray. In the shower tray were a choice of cleansers: Twyla's speckled lavender-scented soap, Melly's Ivory, my Dial, and Lizzie's no-nonsense bath bar. Picking up a sliver of Lizzie's Lava, I swished it around my mouth and all over my body, counting on the abrasive texture to scrape away Denny's copious germs. Before even toweling off, I brushed my teeth, my gums, my tongue, and the roof of my mouth, first with Ipana toothpaste and then with Listerine antiseptic liquid.

After pulling on fresh clothes over a not entirely dry body, I pawed through Melly's belongings until I found the key to the kitchen. Once there I spent half an hour trying to wrench open the metal dividers and dislodge cubes from freezer trays that were furred with age-old ice crystals.

Melly dozed and awakened many times during the night. When shivers wracked her body, I laid the hot-water bottles and heated towels on her moving parts. When she radiated heat, I applied the ice bags. I'd never realized how many joints exist in the human body.

The following day at lunch hour, Twyla made a campaign speech in the mess hall. "I've lived on two different continents under three different governmental systems," she said. "That surely qualifies me for the office of Rancho

Cambridge West student-body president more than my . . .
callow opponent."

She received no applause, I noticed with delight.

"And if I am elected, the first plank in my platform will
be this: 'mess hall' is such a, well, messy, unappetizing designation for our . . . dining room that I propose—in keeping with the unavoidable western theme—from now on
we call it the canteen." Twyla spoke in the manner of an
actress trying on a role at an early rehearsal, as though she
didn't wholeheartedly trust the dialogue or hadn't yet cal-
culated her emotional motivation.

Twyla left the subjects of Melly and Jews alone, perhaps because the headmaster and Mr. St. Cyr were lunch-
ing on baloney sandwiches along with the rest of us. Or
perhaps Melly's character had already been assassinated.

As soon as Mr. St. Cyr exited the canteen, I accosted
him with the injustice of Melly's situation. "You've got to
help Melly. She certainly helped you."

"You better learn to choose your battles, Miss Leigh.
Winning the presidency of this Hooverville has no meaning whatsoever."

"But Mr. St. Cyr, that's not the point." I tried to engage
his empathy as I followed behind him down the path.
"Don't forget, Brian practically gave his life on Melly's
behalf."

Brian *had* made a substantial sacrifice: the polluted pool
had aggravated his condition. Only time, the doctors said,
would lessen the effects. So after spending one night in the
hospital, Brian returned to school but refused to leave his

room until his skin returned to its normal texture and color.

"I have no further comment," the Adjudicator declared.

When I later approached Mrs. Prail in her dollhouse living room, she became teary-eyed. "If only you and Melly were . . . Christians," she replied, "I'd know how to help you."

"How?" I asked.

"We'd go to church," she said, applying a hanky to her nose. "We'd . . . pray."

When I later consulted Mr. Prail, he paused so long before responding that I wondered if he'd entered a trance. But finally, after I'd forgotten my exact question, he said, "Yes, Twyla is using prejudice to sway the election. I would give a lecture on discrimination to the entire student body. But sometimes"—and here he sighed—"I think my talks have the opposite effect of what I intend. Better for you to resolve this for yourself. Tonight look up into the heavens and notice all the planets, stars, and other unearthly delights. Then you'll realize that what happens in our tiny, obscure corner of this universe is insignificant."

Although I appreciated Mr. Prail's cosmological response—it possessed some of Charmian's flair for the grand scheme of things—I didn't think that the headmaster of the school should express such a philosophy. It seemed to me that he should assume responsibility. Fairly certain I would not receive the solace I sought, I took a chance and telephoned Charmian again. There were times when she relished giving advice.

"Is there any way I can swing the election in Melly's favor? Think of it as a plot on *The Mystery Half Hour* and then tell me how to resolve it," I appealed.

"You know I never would have presented a mystery on my show that I couldn't unravel and then sew up again before the tag line," she said. "There actually are a few topics that are simply too ponderous for a half-hour show. Anyway, I'm just dashing out the door."

Though Melly read medical books and listened to Sparky's collection of 45-rpm records for hours on end, she was unable to move far from her bed for three days. She therefore missed meals, classes, and, finally, the election. The votes were counted on Wednesday afternoon, and Twyla won by two votes. Only thirteen students had cast ballots.

"It's akin to landing a role in a really bad film," Twyla said, shrugging it off. "You want to list it among your credits, but you don't want anyone to see it." On Melly's first day out of bed, Twyla took Melly into her confidence. "You can understand, can't you, Melly? I'm just lining up as many merits as possible to impress an unknown and unsuspecting father."

"No, I can't understand," Melly said with solemn composure. "Nobody worth his salt *should* understand. You basically trampled on me and mine for your own selfish reasons. I'm going to stay vigilant, and I won't forget what you've done. I never, never will."

IX

How I Spent
Thanksgiving Vacation

"Fleur, dear, dear *chérie*." Charmian's facsimile of sweetness and light traversed the telephone lines a few days before Thanksgiving vacation. "Whichever it is, left or right, put your more rational ear to the receiver, will you, please?"

"Okay," I said, preparing to be chagrined.

"Listen to this. The nerve," Charmian said huffily. "I've received a letter from your school saying they charge extra if you stay there for Thanksgiving. *Quel Gaul!*"

"But it's a *moot* point." I tried to soothe and amuse her by using one her favorite words. (Indeed, bevies of moot points had regularly been made on *The Mystery Half Hour*; they helped to fill airtime.) "Because, after all, I am coming home."

"Don't be so quick to count your hatchlings," Charmian replied.

"Meaning what?" I asked.

"There's no earthly reason for you to come home. To fly all this way for only four days—two of them spent in transit—when the airfare is exorbitant."

"Paying the airfare will counterbalance the cost of keeping me at school," I quibbled.

"And the cook we have now . . . *En réalité*, roasting a large bird is beyond her capacity. The closest she could get to a Thanksgiving dinner would be to scramble some turkey eggs," Charmian lamented.

"I'm not coming home for the turkey. I just want to be home. Be by myself in my own room."

"There'll be time for that at Xmas. Two paltry days just don't warrant my moving out of your room," Charmian said.

"You've moved into my room?"

"Just to sleep, Fleur. Your father's snoring has become *tympanic*. He's a kettle drum."

"But you have a bed in your bathroom," I said.

"Don't worry. As tormenting as it will be for me, the nuisance of it, I'll move out of your room in time for your Xmas visit. You just be sure to have an outstanding day on Thanksgiving with your Tucson friends."

Even Lizzie's parents had paid her passage home, though the fare did not include Gwendolyn. I therefore generously agreed to slip Gwendolyn's bridle over her head and take her for an outing once a day from Wednesday through Sunday. This peripatetic journey would not be too onerous if we both remained on foot.

But on the second day, Thanksgiving, as Gwendolyn ambled out of her stall, she happened to step on me. She didn't just tread on my toes and move on; she pressed down her hoof and refused to advance. Then, making a U-turn of her neck, she gazed at me and—I felt certain—smiled.

Pinned there, I mentally stumbled upon the memory of a slapstick comedian named Parkyakarkus. That was what the horse had done—parked her carcass on mine!

"Don't you realize, I'm trying to do something nice for you?" I attempted to reason with Gwendolyn. Then I tried pushing the bulk of the hot chestnut nag with my shoulders and hands. I tried wriggling my toes. I tried digging them into the dirt and tunneling out from under her hoof. I called for help. I mimicked Charmian's most thrummy actor's voice on such phrases as "Giddy up" and "Let's go, big fellow" and "Hi-ho Silver." The horse whinnied but wouldn't budge. Gwendolyn kept me trapped for a good fifteen minutes.

"We're all trapped," Twyla later remarked, plainly uninterested in my calamity. "The Thanksgiving revelers went home. You, Melly, Sparky, and I are underfoot or, more appropriately in your case, under *hoof* of ominous forces."

It did seem that way. The day before Thanksgiving, the Prails, Dirk and Jo Ella, Mr. St. Cyr, and even the new cook abandoned us; they had families who welcomed them home. *We* four had been invited to watch over one another as well as warm up our own lackluster meals. Therefore we ate, or attempted to eat, white-bread stuffing and canned cranberry gel that garnished—or camouflaged—a tough, dry presliced fowl. Twyla appraised the turkey, accusing him of being "in the winter of his discontent." Lest the meal seem bleak, a large can of Hi-C grape drink had been chilled on our behalf.

Dessert, as desserts have a way of doing, saved us from utter desolation. Someone had left behind a passable pumpkin pie. This we divided evenly and consumed with gusto. Only when we found ourselves scraping the pie plate for crust crumbs did Melly begin to cry.

"Hey, Melly," Sparky said in an uncharacteristically maternal manner. "You know why you're crying and we're not?"

"Because I'm a ninny," Melly whimpered.

"Because you've got a real nice family. You know they love you and wish you were with them now. You know you'd be with them if they had the cash. Plus, you'll be seeing the whole bunch at Christmastime. Of the four of us, you're the lucky one by a long shot," Sparky said.

Melly closed her eyes tightly, as if shutting a door on her tears. "It's true," she bravely admitted. "I have no right to feel so sorry for myself. I *am* lucky. If my family were here, I'd portion them out to you just like the pie. But since I can't, isn't there something we could do to have a little Thanksgiving fun?"

After a while Twyla said, "Here's a thought. The night is young. We'll do something out of the ordinary to be thankful for. We'll throw ourselves a Thanksgiving extravaganza. By that I mean a formal party, with champagne and caviar, or the closest to it that Tucson can provide. So I suppose we'll have to hitchhike into town to buy our party supplies."

"Hitchhiking could take a lot of time," Sparky said. "Especially on a holiday evening. But if you're interested, I've got some pot in my room that I'll donate to the cause."

"Not for me," Melly said. "It might aggravate my condition."

"I'm not really wild about smoking anything," I put in my two cents.

"I don't smoke it, either. Because of my allergies," Sparky admitted.

"A night like tonight calls for champagne," Twyla said. "Not something so crass as grass."

"Okay. I get the picture. How 'bout I phone our favorite delivery boy?" Sparky suggested.

"You don't mean . . . ?" I asked suspiciously.

"You met Mr. Party Time? He'll deliver anything, anywhere, anytime. For a price, naturally. He's such a moron," Sparky added with a chuckle.

"Oh, no," I protested vehemently. "I've already paid his price. Once is more than enough."

"Why is that?" Twyla asked, and I filled her in.

"Mr. Party Time and his pustules is the most revolting male I can think of," Sparky corroborated my story.

"Leave him to me," Twyla said, then called in her order.

Mr. Party Time brought the provisions, two cartons of clinking bottles, directly to the girls' dorm. Twyla greeted him in her white satin evening gown, clear Cinderella slippers, and white opera gloves that climbed her arms, with her hair twisted into a chignon. She easily could have held her own with Grace Kelly, Audrey Hepburn, or Jackie Kennedy.

Denny's eyes bulged. He'd gone gaga; he'd gone googly-eyed.

"So good of you, so gallant, to bring our party equipage," Twyla said in a cream of society hauteur meant to awe Denny further. She glided toward him, removed the cartons from his arms, and set them on the table. Reaching slowly into the bosom of her dress, she retrieved the check I'd written for the whopping sum of $78.57. "Well now, Mr. Party Time," Twyla said as she handed it to him. "My friend told me that you require *further* payment." She cocked her head in a way that anyone would have interpreted as a solicitation.

"Um, yeah, um, that's right, the tip," Mr. Party Time said, but he seemed apprehensive. Gulping air, he stepped close to Twyla and placed his hands on her shoulders. His spine seemed to cave in as his lips jutted forward.

"What an asshole," Sparky whispered to me from our hiding place under the rec-room couch.

For a second Twyla made it appear that she would comply with the boy's desires, but a split second before their lips actually made contact, she reached for Mr. Party Time's wrist and grasped it firmly. Then, staring into his eyes, she slapped the back of his hand several times. "You naughty, naughty boy," she said coquettishly. "What makes you think I would kiss a boy who hasn't bothered to ask my name?"

Her words seemed to pulverize Denny; his vertabrae looked so perilously off kilter that I thought he might fall on his face. "Wull, it's strictly business," he said. "I didn't think your name mattered. Wull, if you care that much . . . I mean, *I* do—tell me what it is."

"Someday when we are properly introduced, you will find out. But now you really must depart. Our . . . teachers are arriving momentarily, and we must prepare our fête," Twyla said.

"Your teachers are going to drink with you?" the befuddled delivery boy asked with amazement.

"Would you care to join our . . . Roman banquet? We'll be speaking only Latin tonight. Do you . . . *deus ex machina*? Do you *amo amas amat*?" Twyla coyly asked.

"I don't know," Denny said.

"I didn't think so," she replied smugly. She then clamped his previously slapped hand between her thumb and forefinger, as if picking up uncooked organ meat to feed a cat. "Bye-bye, Denny-poo," she called as she shoved him out the door.

"He didn't know what hit him," Sparky said.

Twyla convinced us that in order "to derive the maximal enjoyment from our festivities," we needed to dress appropriately. We therefore dragged her three trunks from the storage room and inspected her plentiful formal wear. Twyla quoted the maxim Mrs. Belmont had recited when bequeathing a dress to her daughter.

> *The first time is stellar.*
> *The second is not.*
> *Always remember:*
> *Thrice is a lot.*

The actress never wore clothes more than three times.

Since Twyla had already dressed, she thought it only fair that the wine tasting begin. She removed from a drawer in one of her trunks a lacquered marquetry box. Inside, fitted into a silk-covered receptacle, were four elaborately etched crystal champagne flutes. "My grandmother's," she explained, setting them on the dresser. Next she twisted a champagne cork with aplomb, and we applauded the detonation.

First sniffing and then sipping and swishing the liquid in her mouth, Twyla disparaged the champagne. "I should have known it would be Californian, not French. Well, it's not *too* bad a vintage." She poured the fizzing elixir for each of us and then held up her glass and said, "Skoal."

"Skoal," we repeated. We sipped champagne leisurely as we pawed through Twyla's trunks and tried on French-bikini panties, garter belts, merry widows, and strapless bras. We covered our bosoms with costume jewelry. We took turns modeling, a pitiable sight, since we were not physically equipped enough to do the lingerie justice.

"It really does tickle the nose," Melly said of the champagne as she poured us each another glass.

"I dreamed I waltzed through Thanksgiving in my Maidenform bra," Sparky said and executed some Arthur Murray–style rotations in Twyla's mother's merry-widow corset and earrings that resembled rhinestone candelabras.

"I dreamed I flew home in my Maidenform bra," I said as I, too, twirled, sending garter-belt snaps flying out into space.

"I dreamed my family came to see me in my Maidenform bra," Melly said dreamily.

"Well, *I* dreamed I found the father from whose seed I sprang in my Maidenform bra," Twyla said. Inspired by the champagne, she proceeded to give Sparky a detailed account of her lineage.

"So you've never met your real father? That's sick," Sparky said. "Shows what kind of bitch your mother is."

"What I don't get is why she never told you," Melly said with compassion. "That's unforgivable."

"I don't plan to forgive her," Twyla said. "And I'm not going to let her take away my money, either. I—"

Quite certain that Twyla would regret getting into the economics of her life, I hindered her storytelling by creating a dance à la Imogene Coca wherein I did grande jetés and triple off-center pirouettes around our room. This time the snaps on the garter belt slapped against my thighs, making me into a human tambourine.

"Silly Fleur, what's a garter belt without the stockings? Go on, try them," Twyla goaded me.

"No thanks," I objected and halted my *pas d'une.*

"Why ever not?" Twyla asked. "Nothing makes me feel more like a woman than gossamer nothings squeezing my legs. Besides, a woman looks nuder in stockings than in the raw.

"My tongue already unfettered by the champagne, I recounted a personal story. "My misadventures with stockings happened when I was almost thirteen years old and invited to a bar mitzvah party for a boy named Gary Heidnisch."

Twyla's eyes narrowed at the words *bar mitzvah,* but I continued. "The party took place at the Coconut Grove, a swanky grown-up nightclub at the Ambassador Hotel."

My nanny had curled my hair, I recalled, and Charmian had bestowed on me an ice-rink-pink low-cut doozy of a cocktail dress. It had been worn more than thrice, or my mother wouldn't have given it up. I adored the dress, and if I positioned myself before the mirror in three-quarter profile, I looked a little like Charmian. Minus the bust.

"With a cocktail-length frock, you must wear hose. And to hold them up, a garter belt," my mother had informed me.

The archaic aspect of garter belts intrigued me. I imagined them being forged along with chastity belts by medieval blacksmiths. So I'd said, "Fab," and began to roll on the stockings just as Charmian did every day.

"Wait a minute! *Mon dieu.* What are you doing?" My mother's voice sounded an alarm. "Ye gods, you can't wear stockings over those hairy appendages. Get into the bathroom. We'll have to shave them right now."

I'd always liked the hair on my limbs. My legs were muscular, and the hair softened their effect while giving them a golden hue. Whenever I noticed it glistening in the sunlight, I regarded myself as touched, just once and very gently, by Midas. I voiced my objection decisively. "I don't want to shave my legs. I like them the way they are."

"I won't have you seen in *my* dress with scruffy extremities. Dora, Dora," my mother called my nanny, who was really the maid. "Come here and help me, will you, please?"

After my mother screwed a new blade into her indestructible double-edged razor and filled the bathroom sink with warm water, Dora, a Herculean woman, lifted me onto the countertop and continued to hold me there. When I saw the short swaths Charmian made through my hairs, I screamed angrily, "Stop, stop it. You're hurting me. They're *my* legs, and you're spoiling them." Two things kept me in Dora's grasp: the fact that this was the most intimate thing Charmian had ever done for me and the fear of becoming an amputee.

"But you let your hair grow back, didn't you?" Melly asked tentatively, taking another swig of the bubbly.

"It came in stiff and not so golden. I'll never get back what I lost." I sighed dramatically. "And I don't plan to forgive my mother. I've made a vow about that."

"What a pisser," Sparky said.

"Shit," Melly agreed.

"It's a kind of rape. With a rapier, yet," Twyla said sympathetically. "Here, forget your woes with another glass of *vino.*" She had such a generous and friendly mien that I worried there'd be hell to pay.

But I didn't mind when Twyla opened her cosmetic kit and smoothed pancake makeup on us. She said her makeup contained light diffusers and reflectors, in case we were photographed. Twyla's colors didn't necessarily match my particular flesh tones, but I had always wished for an olive complexion, and it went with the Cleopatra look I was trying to achieve. The movie wouldn't be out for a year or more, but sketches of Elizabeth Taylor's maquillage had already been circulated. We curled our eyelashes and applied mascara and eyeliner. Then, since none of us had black ancient-Egyptian type hair, we nested bobby pins in an attempt to fasten what we had into French rolls. "Shit," we cursed whenever a bobby pin pinged on the tile floor. "Shit, shit, shit," Sparky said when her hair refused to do anything but cling to her neck.

At last I was atop three-inch heels in a fire-truck red sequined sheath slit to the thigh. It flattened my stomach and made my waist look tiny. "Do you think I'm a knockout?" I asked my friends, angling for compliments.

"Beautiful. Fab. Wow. A glamourpuss," Melly and Sparky exclaimed.

"If you wanted to rival Tokyo Rose, you've done it," Twyla said.

Melly thought she looked like Natalie Wood in *Marjorie Morningstar.*

"A pygmy Marjorie Morningstar," Twyla told her.

"The fuck she does," Sparky defended Melly. She had

dragged her record player into our room, and because she didn't want to go back for more records, we had been listening to *Deuces Wild* by Frankie Laine over and over. We tried couples dancing but kept stepping on the hems of one another's dresses as we debated who should lead.

Frustrated, we sat on our beds and crossed our legs. I touched one heel to the floor, on a crusade to look ladylike while we washed down potato chips, Fritos, and Oreos with the third bottle of bubbly.

When I glanced up, I noticed Sparky rummaging through the shopping bags. "That cocksucker," she said, referring to Denny. "There's no more champagne. The rest is beer."

"He's an asshole," Twyla responded. "What did you expect? But give me one. As long as it's here."

Evidently I didn't mind the taste of the beer that night. I quaffed the contents of an entire six-pack.

"Fleur, you're not only mixing your liquors, but you're chugalugging, too," Sparky apprised me.

"Well, fuck. I want to get drunk," I exclaimed, teetering across the room even without the heels.

"Listen," Twyla said, raising herself to a standing position on Lizzie's bed. She spoke so sharply that the rest of us ceased talking. "*Listen* to yourselves. Listen to your *slanguage*. Sadly, I'm guilty, too. Our English has gone to hell."

"In a handbag," Sparky said.

"No, this is a serious problem. Remember, we're all going home at Christmastime. Our parents will disapprove of our speech," Twyla insisted.

"Since your parents are essentially dead, what do you care?" Sparky asked.

"I shall have a new father by Christmas. I'm certain of it," Twyla said emphatically. "So you could say I'm doing this for him." Then she became dramatic. "Now, this instant, you must join me in excising—no, *exorcising* all the putrid words that have been oozing from our mouths. If we don't, we'll be home for five minutes before accidentally unleashing these words like—"

"Pandora's box?" I interrupted.

"Like unbidden belches and farts," Twyla completed her thought.

"What can we do?" Melly asked.

"Think about it! If you ate seven boxes of candy in one sitting, you'd never eat candy again. That's why candy makers are always slim," Twyla said.

"Are they?" Melly asked. "Not in my experience."

"Just follow my lead," Twyla continued, genteelly pouring beer into her champagne flute. She swallowed a goodly amount, then grabbed the box of chalk that Melly had purchased for the campaign posters I never made. Positioning a cylinder of chalk between her thumb and fingers, Twyla began to scrawl on the wall above Lizzie's bed. *Fuck, shit, cocksucker,* she printed while the rest of us laughed, cheered, and jeered.

Because I acutely valued the tangible items in life, I had never been a destructive child. The notion that I should leave the room flickered on my mind's movie screen, but in a moment I joined the others in laughing heartily and taking swigs of beer straight from the bottle. Caught up in Twyla's impetuous logic and under the influence, I viewed her actions as restorative.

"That's nothing," Sparky said, and with another piece of chalk, she scratched *piss, prick*, and *suckass*. They were ugly words befitting our brown walls.

Energized, Melly then scratched out *clit, cunt*, and *twat*, words her older sisters had whispered in the dark.

"Is that how to spell *twat*? Are you sure it isn't *t-w-a-u-g-h-t*?" I asked. "Or *t-w-o-t*?"

"Fleur has always been the worst speller, the first eliminated in any spelling bee," Twyla tattled on me.

To change the subject, so to speak, I pulled out a word Charmian particularly liked so long as my father wasn't at home. *Balls*, I wrote in large, loopy cursive.

Each time the chalk—pastel orange, dainty pink, or cradle blue—made a streak on the walls, we squealed with satisfaction. And when Sparky began to bounce on my bed in an effort to scrawl on the ceiling, we roared with laughter at the way her violet chiffon overskirt flew over her head and her heels punctured the blanket. We each mounted a bed. What with the laughing, jumping, exhibition of obscenities, and all-around alcoholic carousing, I fancied us participants in a Dionysian rite.

Unfortunately one, or possibly more, of the bars that held my mattress in place followed a course contrary to Sparky's. Without warning, it cracked—I could have sworn I heard splintering—and the mattress slumped onto the floor. Our bouncing ceased, and we rushed to help

Sparky. "Oops, oh fuck, I broke your bed," Sparky apologized, barely stifling her giggles.

"How are you going to fix it?" I growled.

"Don't stop now," Twyla shouted. "Keep going. We're in a word purge. This is serious business. We have to write them so many times we can't stand to even *think* them ever again. Or, oh well, maybe it is only *I* who must. Once I find my father and take my rightful place in society, I'll definitely have to sound upper-class. As it is, I'm losing my accent."

We came up with other words, all the obvious ones, until Melly began spelling out proper nouns that she found obscene: *Jo Ella, Dirk,* and *Mrs. Prail.* We each emblazoned the name of a personal nemesis on the walls. *Mr. Prail* and *Mr. St. Cyr* appeared. I took profound pleasure in writing *Gwendolyn.* For some reason I wrote my own name, too. *Fleur de Leigh. Fleur de Leigh. Fleur de Leigh.*

Those names taking their place among the smut turned us into laughing hyenas, as Ivy, one of my nannies, would have said. We chuckled and snorted and cackled until, all of a sudden, we were crying.

I had little time to absorb our collective state, because in very short order I began vomiting. I say *began* because my nausea and its related manifestations continued for four more days.

X

What Can't Be Cleansed

Suppose someone sees this? were the words that penetrated my stupor the following morning. When not fending off the pinpricks of light that sneaked around the venetian blinds and stabbed my eye-shadowed eyelids, I rued my position on the bathroom floor where I'd remained for hours, trapped in Mrs. Belmont's glowing red gown and garter belt, poised as close to the toilet as possible. The night before, I had been unable to remove the dress, a ruination after my first trip to the john. Melly had unzipped it, but not before I'd begun retching. Consequently the stays at the side of the gown, which reached from hip to just below the armpit, jabbed me intermittently. I preferred that outward pain to the nauseating vertigo that any motion brought on.

"Drink some water," Melly coaxed as she held a glass to my lips. "Fluids are a necessity."

"Take it away," I pleaded.

How could this be? My mother downed her martinis and pills with abandon and never experienced repercussions. I'd always suspected her of being made of kryptonite.

"Twyla, Sparky, wake up," Melly sounded an alarm to our roommates. "We've got work to do, and we better do it quick as a wink."

"Please don't talk so loud," I beseeched her. I couldn't lift my head without gagging. Having nothing left in my stomach, I expelled a fetid bright yellow liquid. ("It's bile. Rhymes with vile," Melly had said.) The very stink of my breath redoubled my nausea. But the sound of Melly's plaint filled me with such guilt that I crawled—not on hands and knees but rather on thighs and forearms—into our bedroom, where I remained on the floor, hoping my physical presence would convey my moral support.

"We have to clean this up," Melly said earnestly. "It's so . . . incriminating."

From my lowly vantage point, I observed a puddle of beer on the tile floor. One whiff of hops sent me back to the bathroom. I emerged to the sight of empty bottles, upturned trunks, limp clothes, and crumpled bags of snack food. Makeup and beer had spilled over hairbrushes, lipsticks, powder puffs. Worse, far worse, we had practically flocked our walls with smut.

"All right. All right. It's just chalk." Twyla rose from her bed. A reincarnation of Miss Havisham, the jilted bride in *Great Expectations*, Twyla still wore her now almost corrugated white satin gown. "This mess will take twenty minutes max to clean up," she announced, brushing casually with her hand at the nearest four-letter word.

Sparky tried using the sheet from her bed. Then she tried spit and elbow grease, with the same disappointing result. In a fury, she ran out of the room but soon returned with the three erasers she'd found on a blackboard ledge in one of the classrooms.

"Now, there's an obvious thought," Twyla congratulated her. But the erasers, whether applied lightly or with full force, had no effect on the scribbling.

Melly brought in Conchita's cleaning caddy. Stepping over me to get into the bathroom, she mixed water and soap flakes in the sink and, using her hands as beaters, created suds to rival the finest meringue. Into this amalgam Twyla and Sparky dipped their own bath towels.

"How could soap and water not wash away chalk?" Sparky asked as they scrubbed without success.

"Chemically speaking, it doesn't make sense. There must be something in the paint that binds the chalk to the walls." This was Twyla's way of conceding the point. They next made a paste of water and Bon Ami cleanser; alas, with no better results.

"It's the words that won't quit," Melly decried them.

"So, Miss Smarty Pants, what do you suggest?" Sparky addressed Twyla.

"This is all a part of our four-letter-word-ectomy," Twyla replied calmly and knowingly. "To expel them from our systems takes effort. It's figuring out how to eradicate them from the walls that will release them from our vocabularies." With that she lay down on her bed, rested her head in her hands, and closed her eyes. "I have the most dreadful headache," she admitted.

"Me, too," said Sparky. Her face looked as wrinkled as the chiffon dress she had slept in. I watched listlessly as she dropped down on Lizzie's bed and pulled a pillow over her head.

"I'm hungover, too," Melly named our mutual malady. "But we simply can't quit. Well, maybe if we just lie down a little while . . ."

"I'm lying here thinking of what we did to Mr. St. Cyr," I told Melly. "Putting him in a tub of ice water when he was as sick as I am now. How cruel we were."

"He wasn't as sick as you are now. He's accustomed to all that alcohol. Oh, he throws up once in a while, but mostly he drinks until he passes out. When he wakes up, he has an ordinary hangover. Of course, in the long run, he's annihilating his brain as well as his liver and kidneys."

"Don't I have an ordinary hangover?" I asked feebly.

"It's totally different with you—I think you have alcohol poisoning. I read about it when I was trying to find out what to do about Mr. St. Cyr. Alcohol poisoning is what fraternity boys sometimes get during initiations. That's why I'm keeping vigil over you and plan to force fluids," Melly warned. "Alcohol poisoning can be fatal."

All afternoon my three friends tried, in turn, Breck shampoo, Luster Crème shampoo, Wild Root Cream Oil,

Sea Breeze astringent, witch hazel, Twyla's turtle-oil soap, Lizzie's Lava, three brands of toothpaste, and lanolin. They succeeded only in peeling a bit of paint: the profanity was *that* defiant.

Sparky had one last idea. She skulked out of the dorm and returned with a bottle of white vinegar that she'd managed to snag from the kitchen. "My mother uses vinegar on every spot you can think of: coffee, tea, pee, poop, blood, wine, barf. It never fails," she assured us.

With my head inside a marching band's drum and my stomach a Mixmaster, it took all my strength to suggest, "Why don't we just cover the entire surface of the walls with chalk? I hate the color in here, anyway."

"The chalk dust would kill us," Melly contended.

A desperate call to Mr. Party Time and the promise of one of my checks produced a remedy. Denny guaranteed that a cleaning crew would arrive no later than Sunday evening at six P.M. "Maybe I can get them sooner, but maybe not cuz, heck, it's a holiday," he had whined. "They go out and get drunk."

By Sunday morning Twyla, Melly, and Sparky had fully recovered from their debauchery, but all of my symptoms remained in full effect. My nausea kept me slumped in my drooping bed, wondering if anything short of decapitation could cure my headache.

Not until late Sunday afternoon did my roommates interrupt their vigil over me. "We won't be gone for more than half an hour," Melly softly explained as she placed a bucket on the floor next to me. "Before the cleaning crew shows up, we're going to the stable to exercise Gwendolyn. The three of us can manage the one of her, we figure."

I'd forgotten the horse entirely. And because it hurt so much to speak, I didn't mention my gratitude for the solitude.

Not twenty minutes later, into my dark, fouled lair stepped Mr. Prail. "Hello," he said, sounding almost cheery. "I'm making the rounds. Mrs. Prail and I have just returned from far-flung Maine. I inhaled pine trees, mountains, and ocean, and I am refreshed." His next thought, born of innocence, was for me. "What's wrong? You're ill, are you?"

My veins pulsed with fear. "A migraine. Any light hurts my eyes. Any sound—" I moaned. "But I'll be all right, really, if you'll just please leave me alone."

"Maybe we better get Jo Ella in here to examine you," he said in a worried tone.

"NO, I beg of you!" I cried out even though it hurt to do so.

"Well, then, I'll ask her to bring you some broth."

"No, *please*, I'll be fine if you'll just let me sleep."

Mr. Prail had nearly taken his leave when he turned back to check on me one last time. Like Orpheus's affectionate backward glance at Eurydice, it proved cataclysmic. "What *is* this? What's happened here?" he asked. "Surely my eyes deceive me." He switched on the light.

* * *

Into my runnel of self-pity swept Dirk and Jo Ella. One would have thought they were clearing brush by the side of a highway, the way they whooped and shoved the furniture around. "You're going for a ride, sister," Jo Ella shouted, using the lingo of criminals on *The Charmian Leigh Radio Mystery Half Hour* as she pulled my bunk away from the wall. "This room has to return to normal before the other students arrive," she announced so loudly that the hammer in my inner ear pounded what I thought must be a sickle. "While we paint, you are going to scour the bathroom. Whoever throws up, cleans up, that's the law."

"I promise to clean the bathroom just as soon as I can," I told her. "Right now I'm still queasy. I get . . . seasick if I change positions. If I just move my head . . . maybe you have some medication . . ."

"You brought this on yourself." Jo Ella's voice rocked my cranium. "So you just get yourself out of that bed and start making amends. THIS MINUTE."

While they painted, I laggardly attempted to scrub the bathroom, but the chemical odor of Bon Ami, my own dried vomit, the turpentine and paint fumes, Dirk and Jo Ella's constant bickering as they slapped a dismal color over our bad-girls' argot provoked my stomach again and again. Hercules must have felt just as repulsed when he endeavored to clean King Augeias's stables. And yet *he* triumphed, I tried to remind myself.

By Monday afternoon I had recovered sufficiently to make a command appearance, along with Melly, Sparky,

and Twyla, in Mr. Prail's empty classroom. "Bring notebooks and ballpoints," we'd been told.

The four of us hesitantly took the last row of seats, but
Mr. Prail ordered us to the front, where, when he began to
sermonize, I had the unavoidable misfortune of staring up
his woolly nostrils.

Hands shaking with anger, he turned to the blackboard
and wrote:

> intercourse
> fornication
> coitus
> copulation
> excrement
> urination
> urethra
> urine
> lavatory
> rectum
> anus
> penis
> testicles
> genitals
> vagina
> vulva
> reproductive organs

Mr. Prail dropped the chalk in the tray and turned to
face us. "Do you know the meaning of these words?"

Twyla tittered softly, possibly out of contempt, and
Melly's cheek, which I could see in profile, puffed maroon.
Sparky clamped both her lips between her teeth, her usual
half-baked technique to keep from giggling.

I kept my eyes averted. Why did these words embarrass me, shame me, when the more-than-four-letter words we'd chalked on the walls had not?

"It is an understatement to say that you've made a spectacle of your obloquy, your most pitiful and deficient vocabularies," Mr. Prail said stonily. "I'm therefore assigning you to copy these nouns, which are acceptable to society, into your notebooks. You are to treat them as you do any other vocabulary lesson: look up their meanings in *The American Heritage Dictionary of the English Language* or *Webster's Collegiate*. Then write the words using complete sentences and proper English—*not slang*. Never again slang. Then commit them to memory. I will check your papers and test you a week from today."

I dutifully copied Mr. Prail's anatomical wordage on a sheet of lined notebook paper, but I used a left-hander's prerogative, the only one there is, and transposed the letters so that they could be read only when held before a mirror. (I thought I alone invented this secret, sinister code until a few years later when, at a museum, I saw a page of Leonardo da Vinci's journals.) As an extra precaution, I planned to tear the page into fragments no bigger than confetti immediately after the test.

"As for your punishment . . ." Mr. Prail started up again.

"Have you noticed the color Dirk and Jo Ella painted our room?" Twyla interrupted him. "It's punishment enough, let me tell you. Taupe happens to be the exact color of moles and eels and uncooked cows' livers. If you don't believe me, look it up in your prodigious *American Heritage*. How do you expect us to think we aren't already imprisoned when we're surrounded by such a virulent shade of dung?"

Mr. Prail blinked with incredulity at her insouciance.

Sparky tried something else. "Isn't the test supposed to be the punishment? Isn't it enough?"

"The *test* is a means of improving your vocabulary and educating you. The *punishment* must stave off your destructive impulses. It must be an exact correlative of the crime." At this Mr. Prail allowed a rare though parsimonious smile to skim his lips.

"It seems to me that your long-winded tongue lashing is enough," Sparky said so impudently I was afraid she would garner further penalties.

Mr. Prail seemed to be attempting to ignore her remark, but his hands and head trembled like martini shakers, and his Abraham Lincoln countenance looked waxed in the way that famous figures in inferior museums so often did. "I haven't fully formulated my thoughts on your penalization," he said in a quiet rage. "But as headmaster, I must teach you that every action generates a consequence. What I've come up with so far simply won't do. Won't do at all. Perhaps not until next week or possibly after your Christmas break will I arrive at the apt discipline. I am going to give myself plenty of time, as much as it takes, to be thorough, practical, and judicious with you four. You incorrigible four."

"Do we really want to be known as the incorrigible four?" Twyla asked, trying to make light of our predicament after Mr. Prail left the room.

"It's so blah," Sparky said.

"How about Sacco and Vanzetti and Sacco and Vanzetti?" Melly suggested.

"Who?" Sparky asked.

"We could be the *Chalk*-o-block Four," I said.

"The Something Four," Twyla said, warming to the task.

"The Four-Letter Four?" Melly said.

Everyone laughed. "Yeah." "Yes." "Perfect."

"That's it. That's who we are. Don't mess with the Four-Letter Four," Sparky shouted it out.

On the way back to our dorm, Twyla appeared more downhearted than the rest of us. "I heard from Al Mandell today. He said my father's trail has gone cold. I guess I wasn't being realistic. I thought for sure I'd be spending Christmas vacation with my father."

Once we reached our dorm room, Melly admitted, "It's not the punishment, it's the test I'm worried about. I can't do anything to jeopardize my grade-point average."

"Damn it to hell. I mean, darn it to heck," Sparky said. "Can't he just tell us what the punishment is now? It's the waiting that's going to kill me."

"Yeah," Melly said. "I've already pictured myself pilloried about a dozen times."

"It's my fault," I told Sparky and my roommates. "If I hadn't had so much to drink, I wouldn't have gotten sick. If I hadn't gotten sick, we would have repainted the room on Saturday and never been found out. So when we find out what the punishment is, if there's any way I can take it on by myself, I will."

"Ofter accepted," Twyla said.

"We are all at fault," Melly said. "We all have to shoulder the punishment."

Later that night Twyla sat herself on my repaired bed. "Do you understand what I was trying to tell you this afternoon? That I expected to be spending Christmas with my new father? And now it seems highly unlikely."

"Yes, I'm sorry that it isn't going to work out," I said, and meant it.

"But do you understand the impact of it?"

"Not exactly, I guess."

"I simply have no place to go," Twyla said, looking weepy. "And after our Thanksgiving fiasco, you can imagine why I wouldn't want to hang around Rancho Cambridge West alone for two whole weeks, can't you?"

"It would be awful," I agreed.

"It would be . . . excremental," Twyla said.

XI

On Furlough

A new cook, Fern, and a new maid, Paladrina, greeted Twyla and me on our arrival. Our house seemed to have shrunk since I'd seen it in October. Its majesty had been replaced with vacuity.

"Not one molecule of this house has changed since I saw it five years ago," Twyla said as she glanced around our cathedral-like living room. "It reminds me of the catacombs."

"The carpeting is new," I quickly defended my home.

Just then something as ignoble as a creaking floorboard or ceiling beam drew our attention to the balcony that traversed the hillside end of the room. Backlit by a golden glow, Charmian, hands resting on the banister, posed in a spun-sugar chiffon negligee. Studio technicians might have worked all afternoon to show her off to such advantage.

We watched as my mother promenaded the full length of the balcony and floated cloudlike down the staircase, her gown flowing behind and outlining her exceptional figure. "*Bienvenue à vous*," Charmian hailed us as her slippered toe made contact with the living room carpet. On the ground at last she did not hug or kiss us; as ever, she detested displays of affection. She simply spread her arms wide at shoulder height, fluttering her fingers with balletic grandeur, to offer a more extensive panorama of her costume.

"*Bienvenue à vous*, too," Twyla responded.

"*Enfin*, my little girl has returned," Charmian said, implying that I had been the one to leave her.

"And you got me in the bargain," Twyla said brightly.

"Yes, haven't I? Well, dear Daisy, I'm sure you have exciting stories to tell," Charmian said warmly, gliding to one of the long blue divans and seating herself with monarchical grace. She gestured for us to sit facing her. "How is your mother? Where is she? And with whom? All I know is what I read in the trades."

"Charmian," I said, "don't you want to hear about school? Twyla and I are really anxious to bare our souls. Also, the headmaster is planning to punish us after Christmas vacation because we were involved in a . . . fracas. You better hear our side of it now."

"First things first. Daisy, I asked you a question, so I cede the floor to you," Charmian said. Looking at me, she added, "After all, Daisy is our guest."

"I'll be glad to give you the lowdown on Maman and Papa," Twyla told Charmian slyly, "over a drink."

"Oh, *mais oui*. What would you like?" Charmian asked.

A soigné Twyla ordered Scotch on the rocks, and my mother never flinched. But when I asked for a Coke, Charmian disdainfully said, "I must remind you that your father disapproves of such opiates."

Coke consumption at our house had been a persistent tribulation for Maurice, who believed all soda pop to be lethal for the liver, kidneys, and teeth. Yet, ever since Charmian had plugged their beverage on *The Radio Mystery Half Hour*, the Coca-Cola Company had rewarded us with two cases a month. Ultimately Maurice's parsimony won out over his quest for good health.

"How will Maurice find out I drank one?" I argued.

"You know he counts them," Charmian said.

"How could he trace the missing bottle to me? Paladrina—is that her name?—might have drunk one. Fern could have used one to flavor a stew. Or you might have had guests."

"You're absolutely right," Charmian said. "I'll have a Coke, too. We'll let Fern and Paladrina take the dive."

Once we were served and my mother's cigarette had been kindled, Charmian persevered, "Well, dear Daisy, tell me all."

"There's something I must apprise you of first, Mrs. Leigh," Twyla began.

"Please, call me Charmian. You're almost my age now."

"All right, Charmian, this is to inform you—I've changed my name. It's Twyla Flint. I explained that to you when I phoned from Europe, remember? You gave my new name to the RCW administrator, whoever that could have been."

"*Qu'est ce que c'est?*" Charmian inquired with dismay. "If you don't mind my saying so, you're making a foolish choice. Daisy Belmont had dulcet tones, while Twyla Flint is so . . . truncated."

"You changed your name, didn't you?" Twyla asked.

"And I would recommend the same to you if your birth name had been Gretel."

"Gretel's kind of cute," Twyla remarked.

"Not if your brother's name is Hansel."

I had never heard this particular account—it sounded like improvisation—but I knew better than to advertise surprise.

"How awful," Twyla said sincerely. She tossed back her Scotch and then chiseled an ice cube with her teeth. Setting the glass on the coffee table, she covered her mouth with her hand, making sure we noticed her yawn. "*Pardonnez-moi,*" she said in an accent that undermined the authenticity of Charmian's French. "I plan to be a thoroughly unobtrusive houseguest. I'll just go upstairs and rest while Fleur reports the school news."

Charmian arose from her divan at the same moment. "*Mais oui, bonne idée.* I was thinking of a nap myself. Maurice and I are attending *une grande fête ce soir.* The Christmas season is upon us."

"But what about our hassle at school?" I babbled.

"You really should give Fleur a hearing," Twyla advised my mother.

"*Chérie*," Charmian said curtly to me, "you'll be home for two whole weeks. I'll have untold time to hear you out."

Both Twyla and I noticed the alterations in my room. Numerous hot-off-the-press paperback novels had crept onto my bookshelves. A television—an appliance that had heretofore been considered too *moderne* for my Victorian decor—now roosted on my desk. One of Charmian's peignoirs, of black and gold tulle, was hanging on a satin-upholstered hanger in my closet. Later that night I would find king-size Hershey bars in my nightstand drawers, along with packages of Lucky Strikes and matches. If Charmian had moved out of my room, it had been a half-hearted effort.

"Face it," Twyla said. "You're just as homeless as I am."

While nibbling "dinner sandwiches" (thus termed because they were open-faced and slathered in gravy) in the breakfast room, Twyla and I waved Charmian and Maurice off to their gala.

"Your parents take the cake. They don't even pretend to be happy to see you," Twyla said. "Even my two deranged progenitors would have made it a celebratory homecoming. They would have thrown a champagne party, mixing my friends with theirs. A good time would have been had by all."

As we talked, the maid departed for a roller-skate date,

and the cook retired to her bedroom. Soon we could hear the robust voices of the *Bonanza* brothers.

"What shall we do with ourselves?" Twyla asked.

"Would you like to play cards, chess, or Parcheesi?" I suggested, assuming these board games remained in the rear of my closet.

Twyla cast me a look that transmitted both pity and condescension. "Are you crazy? I want to go out."

"Where?"

"I'll decide in the car."

"Okay, but Fern will ask where we want her to drive."

"Fern? The cook? Forget her. I'll drive."

"You can't without a California license. We'd get in trouble."

Twyla glared at me. "I have an *international* driver's license. I can drive legally anywhere in the world."

For years my mother had been restricted to automobiles provided by the Oldsmobile Company, one of her corporate sponsors. Once her show had left the airwaves permanently, she had indulged her aspirations for more à la mode vehicles. Notwithstanding, I was entirely unprepared for the new Jaguar in the garage. The flashy black four-door coup had the lines and panache of a London taxi.

"With what Charmian saved on your private schooling, she could afford the next best thing to a Rolls," Twyla said, praising the auto. "The English love motoring. Their auto designers are second only to the Italians. Oooh, I've never driven one of these. Too bad they didn't leave the steering wheel on the right side."

With the windows rolled down and the radio tuned to the Southern California Gas Company Evening Concert, I happily occupied the passenger seat. The heads of pedestrians would have whirled in our direction, I felt certain, had there been any. Only the shadowy figures of pepper trees, scrub oaks, and palms greeted us as we sped up the canyon. After Mary Pickford's mile of curling white wall, Twyla removed her foot from the accelerator so that the Jag's momentum could carry us past Charles Boyer's vine-heavy fences and Fred Astaire's modest, unfenced facade. Rolling on, we came upon the Chaplin estate. Epitomizing dignity, it made Twyla homesick for Europe.

Abruptly, near the junction of Summit and Cove drives, Twyla pummeled the brakes. The tires squealed as the Jaguar fishtailed to a stop, and our bodies slid perilously forward. A full minute must have passed before I could focus on what had seized Twyla's attention.

We were parked, if *park* is the correct word for the angling of the tires, at Twyla's former street address. She had spent her early years in an authentic half-timbered Tudor mansion surrounded by banana trees of the *giganticus* species. Her home contained so many rooms I sometimes got lost on the way from the Ping-Pong pergola to the projection room. One wrong flight of stairs beyond the library on the mezzanine and I would find myself in the large bedroom that had become Mrs. Belmont's dressing chamber, or a room under the eaves devoted solely to Daisy's puppet theater, or another that housed Mr. Belmont's collection of chinoiserie. Where all those resplendent rooms had heretofore existed, we now gazed at a massive muddy hole.

Twyla pounded the steering wheel and shouted at the empty lot, "Look at that. LOOK AT THAT GORGE! Someone's bulldozed a chasm right out of my heart."

"It makes me ill," I said in commiseration.

"Don't say *ill*, it's very low-class," she snapped. "Just use the word *sick*, will you, please?"

"What I mean is, how could anyone tear down so nice a house? What do they think could replace it?" I asked.

"I should have guessed this would happen. Everything about my childhood has disintegrated. What made me think that any single part of it would remain standing?" Twyla said bitterly.

But while I attempted to formulate words of consolation, Twyla's thoughts proceeded in another direction. "On the other hand, Fleur, why should I care? I don't live here anymore. My parents were never going to return. And soon, very soon, I'll be living with my father." Her cheeks remained dry, but I heard the tears in her throat.

"We had so much fun here," I told Twyla. "Well, we can have fun again."

"Oh?" she said, challenging my optimism. "Do tell me. Where and how?"

I rummaged through my mental White and Yellow Pages, seeking a safe haven for her, but my desire to compensate for the entire oppressive void of Twyla's circumstances benumbed my thought processes. "If only Charmian were here," I mused aloud. "She'd have dozens of suggestions."

"Charmian. Charmian. I'm so sick of hearing about your damn mother and what you think she thinks! Don't you ever do any thinking of your own?" she almost spat at me.

It was clear that Twyla needed to discharge some of her animosity, so I said nothing while she raced the Jaguar at Indy 500 speeds for miles up Benedict Canyon. We zoomed by the historic Harold Lloyd estate, then the newer, less impressive models, including Chuck Connors's plebian ranch house. Twyla drove erratically and with no courtesy for others. I thanked Artemis, the lady god of wild things, that no cats, dogs, deer, or raccoons had chosen to cross the road. Only when the engine shifted into low gear to compensate for the steep grade did I stop clutching the door handle with both hands.

We eventually arrived in what I considered "country," where very few houses interfered with the natural landscape of scrub brush and scree. Twyla didn't step on the brakes until we reached a long dirt driveway that led to a shuttered cottage surrounded entirely by eucalyptus and pines. We couldn't see the city or neighboring homes. The moment she yanked on the emergency brake, I sprang from the Jaguar, a cat myself, and gulped the clear December air.

Twyla jabbed the bell at the cottage's entrance until a face appeared behind the beveled glass set into the door. Despite her beleaguered countenance, unrelieved by makeup, and her ungoverned hair, prevaricating ashen brown and leaden gray, I recognized the actress immediately.

Odiline Marchet opened the door tentatively, then

placed her body, lithe even in a stained and wilted house-coat, in the crevice between door and jamb. I could see that she'd been crying, and she spoke in an octave of torment. "You've come at a most inconvenient time."

Rarely, and then only as a favor, did Odiline Marchet take a small role in movies. Whenever she did, every actor in town, including Charmian, made a pilgrimage to observe the master's technique. Her skills were so revered that studios beckoned her to the set whenever they had trouble with their stars.

Possibly because Odiline had become the highest-paid coach in Hollywood, Charmian had never consulted her. "Acting and writing can't be taught. One has to rely on one's own natural abilities and perspicacity," my mother had often said, but she had made a study of the actress. "Odiline has never succumbed to the chisel," she once told me, using her own euphemism for plastic surgery. "She's loath to tinker with her natural tools. That's the one piece of advice none of her students follow. But they don't have Odiline's marvelous cheekbones, her unfurrowed brow or regally long neck."

"Odiline, don't you remember me?" Twyla asked now, as though she hadn't noticed the woman's sorrow.

Odiline blinked over her glasses and relaxed her stance slightly. "Yes, Daisy Belmont, how could I not? You are the duplicate of your mother twenty years ago. And I do appreciate LaGiana sending you all this way to make a condolence call, but I am talked out, wept out, worn out. I'm not receiving visitors."

I glanced at Twyla, whose lips were pressed together in

resentment, not sorrow. She swallowed. "Condolences for what?" she asked almost peevishly.

A seepage of tears moistened Odiline's cheeks. "You didn't know that Viktor died? Dropped dead is more like it. Six days ago he was in the garden, innocently snipping mint leaves for our tea, and he . . . he keeled over. I don't know how long he lay there. It was only when I missed my tea . . ." A sob prevented her from continuing. "Well, you didn't know of the death in my family, and now I've started up again," she said, wiping her cheeks roughly on the lapels of her housecoat. "You might as well come in."

We entered a room that, under ordinary circumstances, would have been cozy, full of books, scripts, framed photographs and elaborate paintings of Odiline, as well as many of her celebrated students. An indifferent orange cat lay on a cushion in front of a brightly tiled fireplace. Tonight, however, the room had the aspect of a forsaken hothouse: innumerable bouquets, some small and precious wreaths with fairy roses and baby's breath, some garish arrangements of tropical flowers, others large enough to accommodate Kentucky Derby winners. These bouquets, in various stages of bloom and decay, covered every horizontal surface.

The actress cleared an armchair and wearily sank into it. "I have played the role of a grieving widow many times, and taught others how to do so, but it didn't prepare me," Odiline lamented. "Not for a minute did I ever imagine the pain." Again she wiped her cheeks and her nose with her sleeve. Then, noticing that we were still standing, she said, "Slide anything you want out of your way and sit."

"I'm sorry about Viktor," Twyla said once she'd burrowed into the couch.

"I am, too," I said. I had found a place to rest my bottom on the upholstered arm of a chair.

"I had no way of knowing about your travails—not where I've been," Twyla said.

"Ah, I understand now. You have something to tell me that has nothing to do with Viktor. Well," Odiline said solemnly. "What is it?"

Though occasionally Twyla repeated verbatim the phrases and inflections that she'd used with me, for the most part she employed an altered vocabulary and manner more suited to Odiline's age and antecedents. She tucked in new particulars, elaborations, comments, and opinions. I didn't mind in the least hearing her narrative again.

While Twyla spoke, Odiline never once permitted her concentration to stray. She appeared to mobilize all her energy into the act of listening, registering Twyla's every thought with the subtlest movement of her unchiseled facial muscles. Charmian would have said Odiline was playing for the camera, not for life's stage, but I took her reactions as genuine.

When Twyla finished, Odiline asked, "Do you want commiseration, or do you want dispassionate advice, as you would expect from your Mr. Quincy at the bank?"

"Well, I want your . . . sympathy, I suppose. I would like to feel at least one person I value truly cares about me right now."

"But you must value your little companion here. You brought her along," Odiline replied.

"Oh, right. This is Fleur Leigh, but she's only fifteen," Twyla explained.

"I'll be sixteen in three and a half months," I said and immediately regretted sounding so childish.

As if to explain her association with me, Twyla added, "Fleur lives just down the canyon."

"Fleur Leigh? You're not *Charmian* Leigh's daughter?"

I nodded. "Do you know my mother?"

"I know her . . . work," the coach said. "Let's hope you haven't inherited her pretensions. No, I take that back. I can see that you haven't."

Odiline had meant this as a compliment, but I couldn't summon a thank-you. I couldn't help myself; I accepted criticism leveled at my parents as my own. Accordingly, I lowered my head to avoid the issue.

The actress returned her attention to Twyla. "In response to your calamity, I have only my own to offer. That is, if you want to hear it." She didn't wait for Twyla to answer. "How well do you remember Viktor?"

"He was funny," Twyla said, "but I never knew if it was the way he looked or what he said that made me laugh. I hope you don't mind my saying so, but he seemed as round as he was tall: an overgrown dwarf. My mother said that despite his . . . disfigurement, he was one of the most fascinating men she'd ever met. Viktor knew everything and read everything—he was a great raconteur, she said. She'd been begging him to direct her in a picture for years."

"I met Viktor when I was Fleur's age," Odiline began. "In 1933 he was thirty-six years old, and his parents had just bought the summer estate where my parents had lived and worked all my life. On farms the weather is the major topic of conversation, but Viktor never noticed the heat or clouds. Already renowned as the greatest living Hungarian playwright and also a director of pictures in Germany, he had a thousand other interests.

"That bittersweet summer I met Viktor, the political climate was on everyone's mind. It made Viktor impatient to immigrate to America. It made his parents fearful they would never see him again. Well, they were right.

"Naturally, looking the way he did, Viktor had never married, but he now wished to acquire a wife from his own country. I was a very pretty girl, studious and malleable. Without consulting me, Viktor asked my parents for my hand. You might not understand that they saw our marriage as a grand opportunity for me. And they weren't adverse to accepting the large tract of land Viktor's parents offered them. I agreed to the marriage because, frankly, I didn't like farm life. Viktor, after all, lived in a world of theater and books and films.

"True to his word, Viktor filled my life with the riches of the mind. He always made me laugh and gave me an education no university could have equaled. When I was studying the novels of Thomas Mann, Viktor made sure we spent time with the great author—he lived not far from here, you know. When I was trying to grasp the theory of relativity, Viktor invited Albert Einstein to dinner. And as you know, Viktor's directorial skills were in demand in America. He made me his ingenue. Thus, I learned the theory and practice of acting from the master. What more could a farm girl have asked for?

"You can understand why Viktor and I decided not to have children. We were both terrified that any baby of ours would suffer from Viktor's . . . deformities. So sex had no objective for me, and unfortunately neither of us knew anything about its pleasures. There were no books; the subject was not discussed publicly." Odiline began crying softly again. "So . . . Viktor made love, if you want to call it that, out of need. And I out of obligation. But I never made it a loving act. I didn't whisper sweet nothings, as they say. Instead I told Viktor, 'Hurry up, hurry up. Get it over with.'

"Only on the afternoon, six days ago now, when I found his poor, sad body did I comprehend how much I'd truly loved him, even his physical being. Honestly, I've cherished Viktor since the day we first talked. But—here is the rub—I never once told him. *Never.* I never said, 'Viktor, I love you.' Not once. Not one time. Now, *that*, dear Twyla, is tragedy."

When Charmian and Maurice came home that night, I waylaid them by sitting at the top of the stairs so they couldn't ignore me. "Everything has gone wrong. We went to Twyla's old house. It's been torn down, and she's very, very, very sad."

"I'll take care of it, don't worry," my mother responded. She pushed past me and hurried to her bedroom.

In a few minutes she marched into my room with two bottles of prescription pills. "Twyla, look here. These pills are for sleep. And these are for pain," my mother said. "If the sleep pill doesn't work in half an hour, take two of the pain pills. You won't feel anything for at least twelve hours, I guarantee."

I snatched up the bottles and carefully read their labels. Once, when I'd had the flu, Charmian had dispensed pills to me, and I had lain awake until daylight, painfully alert. Only twelve hours later did Charmian realize she'd given me the wrong medicine.

"You want to share your pills with me?" Twyla laughed. "How sweet of you, Charmian, I guess. But I'm a fine sleeper. Even in times of crisis."

"Twyla has the same talent for sleep as the heroine in *Saratoga Trunk*," I offered.

Charmian's shoulders sagged under her peignoir. She abhorred discomfort of any kind, for herself or for others. But pills were the only remedy she knew. At that moment I felt even more pity for my hapless mother than I did for Twyla or Odiline.

The next afternoon, over cocktails—martinis for my parents, a highball for Twyla, and tea with sugar for me—my father said, "Well, Fleur, I noticed you took Charmian's car out last night without asking permission."

"You weren't here to ask," I responded snippily. "Besides, Twyla drove, not I. Twyla has an international driver's license. She can drive anywhere in the world. She's almost eighteen."

"Even so," Maurice said, his tone immersed in hurt feelings, "I notice the Jag is dusty. It needs a wash. And why didn't you refill the gas tank?"

Charmian, never hospitable to negativity, broke in. "Fleur and Twyla, we have some news for you." She nodded at Maurice to fill us in.

"That's right. We're taking off. This is business, you understand. We have to go down to the Caribbean for a couple of weeks to sail on some screwball's yacht."

"You're taking a vacation? Now?" I asked.

"I *said* it was business," Maurice grumbled at me. "Business is never convenient or timed to fit the ideal schedule."

"*C'est un grand dommage*—we have to cancel our Xmas party this year," Charmian said with a little girl's pout.

"There you have it. We have to go," Maurice summed up.

"Why?"

I could see Maurice debating with himself about whether to grant me an explanation. "Well, if you must know, the owner of this yacht is a retired florist. Who'd ever dream that anyone could make the millions he did in flowers? Now that he has all this dough in a savings and loan, he wants to invest it. In something artistic," Maurice said with a laugh. "The flower peddler wants to produce motion pictures! Art! High-class stuff, wouldn't you know? Consequently, your mother and I have agreed to help him any way we can."

Twyla and I devoted ourselves to Odiline's cause. We threw out the rotten flowers and installed the potted plants in the garden. We ordered printed cards from a stationer and helped Odiline write her myriad thank-you notes. We phoned the fawners and sycophants to whom she didn't wish to speak. We cooked the hams that had been sent to the widow and learned to make Eggs Benedict Canyon, one of Viktor's many creations and Odiline's favorite meal.

Despite the actress's grief, and Twyla's, we began enjoying ourselves. One night we visited a local theater to critique an acting student; another night we went to the movies and discussed for hours the patent mistakes actors make. The following evening we attended Odiline's advanced acting class.

On our return flight to Tucson, over the racket of the engines and the shuffling of cards, Twyla sang Odiline's praises: "If there were any justice in this world, she's the kind of mother we both would have had."

"You really like her?" I asked. I'd been waiting for this moment.

"I love her," Twyla responded.

"Then there's something I'd like to point out to you. Odiline Marchet is Jewish."

"What makes you think so?" Twyla asked coldly.

"Well, I told you, Charmian has made a study of Odiline through the years. And once Odiline's name came up in a funny way. Charmian had made a list of historical personages whom she believed should have received Nobel Prizes for their contributions to humankind. Some of the nominees were: Moses, Jesus, Einstein, Freud, Karl Marx or

Groucho, and Odiline. 'I don't have any bias about this in the least,' my mother said, 'but do you notice every one of them is Jewish?'"

"Who would trust your mother on any sort of facts?" Twyla scoffed.

"I would on this one. Charmian knew that Odiline was Klára Kértesz when her feet first touched the shores of New York. And if Odiline hadn't been Jewish, her parents wouldn't have needed to send her away. But not only that, just to be sure, I asked Odiline. She said of course she's Jewish. She's so obviously one of the Chosen People."

XII

PUNISHMENT

"See the U.S.A. in your Chevrolet, America is asking you to call," Sparky crooned. A brave show, I thought, since we had no concrete idea where we were headed or how long our journey would be.

Per Mr. Prail's requirement, the Four-Letter Four had returned to Rancho Cambridge West before noon on the last Sunday of vacation. He had devised a new approach to our "discipline." We would be spending three months of Sundays—thirteen of them—doing penance. No sooner had we changed our clothes than the headmaster ordered us into the station wagon. Declining to explain or accompany us, he'd said only, "Dirk will drive you to your destination. Then you must do the rest."

A drizzle disparaged the usual Tucson sun as the rachitic vehicle ferried us on dirt roads through desolate terrain.

Demeter, the enraged goddess of the vegetable kingdom, must have hexed this soil.

"See the U.S.A. in your Chevrolet, America . . ."

A lurch of the rattletrap signaled that we'd arrived at the periphery of a vast bemired field. I would have thought we were the first humans to stumble into this region had I not seen a distant hill clustered with rough-hewn huts not unlike those where garden tools and soil amendments were stored on the Chaplin estate.

The station wagon bucked and then plowed into the nucleus of the lowland. The motor coughed, gagged, and convulsed until it died. I felt the car settling into an unfamiliar viscous substance.

"Okay, end of the line," Dirk said. "Go on, git."

Was this it? Our punishment? Were we to be slurped into a plat of quicksand like bad hombres in a western?

"I think we've rolled into a semidry lake bed," Melly speculated.

"Pish," Twyla said, not stirring from her seat. "I have no intention of getting out just to ruin my shoes."

"What we need are life rings," Sparky declared. "Dirk wants to abandon ship."

"Excuse me for asking, Dirk." Melly spoke politely but without budging. "What exactly are we supposed to do here?"

"Any point in my askin' you to dig this automobile out of this here hole?" Dirk prompted.

"None whatsoever," Twyla responded.

"That's what I thought," Dirk grunted. "Well, then, the

rest is between you and Mr. Prail. He shoulda brought you out here, but I got the license to drive kids. So, till I call fer you, go on, do yer Peace Corps stuff. Skedaddle. Go build the natives a volleyball court, and maybe they'll push this car onto solid land."

"Natives?" Sparky repeated with alarm, as though envisioning naked warriors with spears.

"Is he speaking about . . . aborigines with fuzzy heads?" Twyla asked. I couldn't be sure whether she meant to amuse us.

Only when I peered very carefully through the smudges on the windows did I perceive movement. In the distance between the gray lake bed, if that was what it was, and the toolsheds, if that was what they were, there appeared to be an irregular line of people climbing the hill toward the shacks.

"What *are* those?" Sparky asked.

"The natives?" Melly said with a nervous chuckle.

"Them's migrant workers," Dirk informed us, sounding pleased to know something we didn't. "They pick the crops. Cotton and citrus is big around Tucson."

"Crops? Where? I haven't seen anything green for miles," Sparky challenged him.

"Now, you don't think they're gonna let them folks live on land that's irrigated and all set to grow, do you? They truck migrants off to where they need 'em in the mornin'," Dirk explained. "Then it's back here at night."

"What are they doing right now?" I asked.

"Let's go find out," Melly suggested. Following her own counsel, she opened the car door.

I couldn't allow Melly to face the natives alone, so I followed her lead. Together we traipsed slowly, our shoes sucking up muck, toward the mass of humanity about a hundred yards away. Long before we reached the odd queue, Sparky and Twyla joined us. We each wore a scarf—as was in vogue—to protect us from the drizzle, though Twyla had tied hers across her face bandit-style.

"Why the outlaw getup?" I asked.

"People like these are crawling with lice, fleas, and hives," Twyla said sotto voce from behind her bandana.

"How would you know?" Melly asked.

As we approached, we could see adults and children carrying sheets of cardboard covered with the same sludge that had sunk our car. They were headed up the hill to the toolsheds.

Melly *would* be the first in any group to do something. "Hello there," she said as we neared the line. "Hi, how are you? Do you need some help? What exactly are you doing with that . . . clay?"

But they didn't respond, whether out of timidity or lack of comprehension, I couldn't tell.

"You're talking to them?" Sparky remarked with wonder. "They won't understand. They're either niggers, cholos, or igorotees."

"Please say Negroes, not the other word," I urged.

"They could be Gypsies," Twyla advised us. "If so, look out. Gypsies would just as soon slit your throat as look at you."

"Nah, igorotees," Sparky said.

"What is that?" I had to ask.

"Igorotees are coons who also have tails. They hide their tails in their pants unless they're on the warpath. If you're captured, they use them to whip you or tie you up," Sparky explained.

"That's ridiculous," I told her.

"Stop it, you guys. They're obviously busy, and we've interrupted their work," Melly said.

"On Sunday?" Twyla asked.

We were on dry ground now, and Melly tried, with halting pronunciation, a few words of Spanish. *"Bu-en-os dios. ¿Como está us-teds?"*

"Jeeze, you're speaking Mexican to them?" Sparky muttered. "You really think they're beaners?"

Beaners were Mexicans, I happened to know. A few of my nannies had used this word to describe people who lived at the dilapidated, faraway end of Los Angeles. With the exception of Conchita, the only authentic Mexican I'd ever met was the actress Delores del Rio. She had hair as sleek and inky as a raven's wing, and embroidered her English with long, operatic R's.

"Don't say *beaners* in front of them," Twyla chastised Sparky. "It's possible, though unlikely, they're mongrels who speak some English."

"Try *hola* on them," Sparky, a dubious student of Spanish, told Melly. "If they don't know that, they don't know a thing."

"Hola," we all said in unison.

"Hola," a little chorus of children responded softly. A tingle of satisfaction prompted me to smile. It must have

struck Sparky, too, because she excitedly said to us, "Did you hear that?" She asked the children directly, "*¿Habla español? ¿Habla inglés?* Or what?"

"Tell them not to be afraid, that we come as friends," Melly told Sparky.

"*¿Habla español?*" Sparky asked the children again.

Some of the children left their parents and came forward. "*Sí. Hablamos español. Somos de Mexico,*" a very small but determined girl responded.

"Did you hear that? That kid answered me," Sparky said, her eyes asparkle and voice full of amazement. "This makes studying Spanish almost worth it. So they *are* greasers! Guess they're wetbacks, too!"

"I didn't hear the little girl say any of that," I said. Then I tried one of the phrases I'd recently learned. "*¿Como se llama?*"

"Becillia."

"Becillia? Becillia is her name," Sparky informed us, triumphant.

"Do any of you speak English?" Melly asked, speaking as distinctly as a girl from New Jersey possibly could. "Please answer. We want to be friends."

"Speak little," one boy said.

"We speak little," another carefully followed suit.

"Oh, that's wonderful," Melly told them.

I noticed that even the youngest children were grubby and ragged. Several of them had knots of snot parked under their noses, prompting Twyla to ask, "Hasn't anyone heard of Kleenex around here?"

"So, *muchachos*," Sparky said. "What's with the muck? Where are you carrying it to? And what for?"

"You really want to find out?" Melly asked Sparky.

"Yeah, sure," Sparky said.

Melly very gallantly took a piece of cardboard with a large lump of sludge from the smallest girl. "Please, let me help you," she said, her sunny voice conveying what her English could not.

The other three of the Four-Letter Four followed suit, and as if we'd said *abracadabra*, the line began to move. With our shoes full of what I believed to be clay in the mooshy stage, and clumps of it now in our arms, we trudged uphill to the structures I had mistaken for toolsheds. They were simple squares of plywood loosely tacked together, with cutouts for windows and doors.

"You don't think they live in there?" Sparky asked. "There aren't any floors."

"Some of them have put down pieces of cardboard instead of linoleum," Twyla said with a disapproving arch of an eyebrow. "Not too shrewd when the weather gets wet. Like today."

"You know what I think?" Melly said. "I think they're using this clay as insulation. It gets so cold in Tucson at night, I think they're padding their . . . bungalows."

We helped the adults do just that for an hour or two, until we had covered three whole shacks with the gray gunk and become completely encrusted with it ourselves.

"Jou nice," a woman said by way of thanking us.

"Jou nice," a few other women chimed in.

Then Twyla said, "You like us so much? Then show me to the ladies' room, please."

"Twyla," Melly said, "can't you wait? I don't think their bathroom is going to meet your standards."

"No, I can't. I need to wash up as well. This stuff is drying on me. It's going to ruin my skin." (I couldn't help but recall that some of the emollients Twyla swathed on nightly looked very much like this clay.)

"Gosh, heck, I can't remember learning the word for *bathroom*," Sparky said. But using the words *donde está* with *toilet* and pointing to her crotch, Sparky made the predicament clear. Nodding and beckoning, Becillia indicated she would lead Twyla to the lavatory.

"Come with me," Twyla beseeched the rest of us. "I don't think I should travel in these parts alone."

Becillia led us some distance from the shacks and farther from the lake bed. With no other structures and no trees, Twyla became suspicious. "Where are we going? There's only dirt out here."

The ladies' room consisted of a long open trench. The stench and the visible excrement indicated it was an open latrine.

"Disgusto," Sparky said, taking a stab at Spanish.

Even Melly said, "Gross."

"No doubt this is the men's room, too," Twyla said.

I had staunch reservations about pulling down my pants in public, but once Becillia squatted nonchalantly over the trench, the rest of us did the same, albeit holding our noses. A few moments passed before Twyla imperiously said, "And where is the toilet paper, I'd like to know."

I hadn't even faced the fact that my underpants would be sodden the rest of the day when Sparky, hurriedly pulling up her jeans, appeared to have an epiphany. "Oh! Wow! Don't you get the message? These beaners can't afford toilet paper! We've got to do something about it."

"What do you think they do about their periods?" I asked.

"I for one am going to tell Mr. Prail I simply can't come here again," Twyla told us, removing a Kleenex from a jeans pocket and blotting herself. Then, holding just its edge with her forefinger and thumb, she dropped it into the trench. "I'm not paying my own good money to Rancho Cambridge West to be doomed as a do-gooder."

"What I'm talking about is how do we get some moolah to these people?" Sparky said as we headed back toward the cluster of huts. Since the evening when she had burst into laughter in the sickroom, I hadn't heard such zest in Sparky's voice.

"I don't know about money, but we can at least give their lives some joy," Melly said. "And maybe we can bring some food."

An obstacle prevented our leave-taking. Both Dirk and the station wagon were exactly where we had left them. Dirk grimly handed Sparky a shovel, a four-by-four plank to Tywla, and told Melly and me to push when he gave the signal. We dug and scraped and pitted our weight against the vehicle, but it wouldn't come unglued. Finally the children and their parents—who'd been watching us with, I thought, bemused expressions—ventured close enough to help. They swarmed around the station wagon as if it were a soapbox-derby entry, and after a chorus of grunts and groans, I felt something give. The car shifted and lifted. Everyone kept pushing until it rolled out of the quagmire.

"Adios, adios," the children cried. *"Adios pelirroja,"* they shouted in reference to Sparky's red hair.

When we returned to our dorm room that Sunday evening, January 6, 1963, after our first full-dress brush with injustice, the cheeriness of our quarters surprised me. The floors may have lacked the touch of a rug, but the tiles were glossily clean. The jade-hued serapes hung square and flat on the beds, giving the room a tidy air. And thanks to Conchita, even Twyla's perfume bottles gleamed. Most important, all four of us had the certainty that we could now indulge ourselves in long, hot showers or baths.

Twyla implored and petitioned Mr. Prail relentlessly all week, but he compelled her to remain allied with the Four-Letter Four on the second excursion to what we alternately called the Prison Camp or the Leper Colony. This time we came prepared.

With newspapers wrapped around rocks, Melly and I laid out a rough-cut diamond of a baseball field. Then, lining up the children into two groups, Melly commenced her tutorial. Though I'd occasionally seen the Hollywood Stars at Gilmore Field with my sports-minded nannies, I'd never heeded the rules of the game.

"Okay, we need teams. What's the word for *team?*" Melly asked Sparky, who just shrugged. "Well, okay, I'll *show* them what I mean," she said and briskly began rustling newspapers. As we all watched in fascination, Melly crimped and folded seven double sheets into seven tri-tipped hats.

Melly made a ritual of bestowing the head coverings, conveying the idea to each child that he must first say his name, then bow his head as if to be knighted, before receiving his "sombrero." The boys and girls took the ceremony seriously and, in turn, murmured their names. José, Pablo, Becillia, Sonia, Maria, Eduardo, and Jaime beamed with pride under their newspaper crowns. Sonia and Maria, who had sleeping papooses on their backs, wanted baby-size hats for the infants Imelda and Rigaberto. Melly crimped them quickly with expert fingers.

The Helmet Team, as Melly dubbed them, struck poses in their finery, but the unadorned team sat on the ground and folded their arms and legs in protest. Their position gave Melly an idea, and in moments we four girls set about making newspaper bandoleers.

Sparky and I didn't have much trouble hitting the soft-ball when it was pitched within a yard of our bodies, so Melly placed us on opposite teams. Twyla, on the Ban-doleer Team, still wearing her bandana, had the aura of a TV outlaw who'd sneaked across the border to rob and pillage.

Unfortunately neither Twyla nor Melly, nor any of the children for whose benefit the game was being played, could make a connection between the ball and bat. The children and even parents, passively standing by their huts, lost interest quickly.

"Baseball's too hard for them," Melly said. "They're weak and don't have much coordination. You know what? I think they're malnourished."

"So what'll we do?" Sparky asked.

"Think. We're the Four-Letter Four, aren't we? We should be able to come up with something," Melly urged. "But right now I don't know."

Idly picking up the beach ball we'd brought, I tried whacking it with the bat and was surprised to see it fly easily past the pitcher's mound. Several of the children laughed and scrambled to catch it. After a noisy skirmish, Eduardo victoriously squeezed the ball to his chest. After looking around to assess his options, he threw it toward me. Delighted, I happily batted it back.

"Aha! You're a sports genius," Melly hailed me.

When José took his turn at bat, he held it in one hand. As the beach ball bounced to knee height, he struck it so that the airy globe headed heavenward, its red, blue, and yellow panels spinning cheerily through the drizzle. When a current of air picked up the ball and transported it fifty or so feet away, we all watched in awe. Both the Helmets and the Bandoleers swarmed to it like ants to a cheddar cube. Certainly no stickler to the rules of Hoyle would have approved of our game, but the children kicked and ran and chased the ball, laughing all the way, for what seemed like hours until they fell to the ground in a happy tangle.

"I can't believe a beach ball held its air after treatment like that," I said.

"*Something* had to go right for them," Melly answered.

"They look hot and thirsty," Sparky said. "Aren't you glad we brought lemonade?"

We spilled out a box of old toys collected from the neighbors of Rancho Cambridge West: miniature cars and trucks with missing wheels, dolls minus arms or their clothes, hundreds of denuded wooden spools. The children seized upon the items as though they'd been handed the keys to FAO Schwarz. The boys immediately assembled the spools into towers and flew cars over them with Evel Knievel devil-may-care. The girls used their spools as chairs and couches and pedestals for the dolls.

"*Muchas gracias,*" one of the parents humbly thanked us.

"Jou nice," another woman said to me. "Jou nice." She stroked my arm and my hair.

"I haven't really done anything," I tried to explain. I felt exhausted with embarrassment.

She kept speaking words I couldn't understand until almost pleadingly she said, "Jou help?"

"What does she want? Can you translate?" I asked Sparky, vowing to skip ahead in my Spanish workbook.

Sparky shrugged, but Becillia reluctantly left the group of children. "*Mi madre,*" she introduced the woman solemnly. "He want jou come with heem."

Melly, Sparky, Twyla, and I reluctantly followed the mother and daughter into their shadowy shack, where a couple of wooden crates served as furniture. A lumpy mattress made of hay, perhaps, lay on the dirt floor. "This is where they live!" I said. I had to say it because it seemed so utterly absurd.

A cough, ever so infinitesimal, pulled my gaze toward the mattress, where a baby lay very still on a tattered blanket.

"Jou help?" Becillia's mother asked.

"Baby ees sick," Becillia explained.

Melly immediately bent down and felt the baby's forehead. "He's burning up," she murmured.

"Melly, you shouldn't," I warned her. "He might have something you could catch." I knew I should snatch the baby away from Melly but I momentarily felt fearful for myself. Wouldn't germs congregated on this fragile, diminutive representative of the human species prefer a pampered girl like me?s

Once, when I lay abed in my room, where Maurice had confined me until I recovered (from what I couldn't have said), a telling incident occurred. The heavyweight nanny Glendora, whom I'd venerated for the few months she stayed with us during my eleventh year, was bringing me a dinner tray. First I heard her footsteps across the hardwood floors in the dining room. Then, when her feet were silenced by the living room carpeting, I heard the tinkle of spoons and forks shivering on the moving tray, the clink of a teacup rocking on its saucer, and a glass of milk thudding against the china. The aroma of a T-bone steak preceded her, and in anticipation of a hearty dinner, I propped up my pillows.

A few moments later Glendora's feet made contact with the hardwood of the stairs, and I could hear her lumbered but measured gait as she climbed with, I supposed, one hand on the banister. Taking me completely by surprise, Glendora made a misstep. A second later she, the china, the silverware, the milk glass, the teacup, the saucer, and the tray struck the steps with the various thuds and thwacks and clunks and clicks and clatters that were their own particular franchise.

"GODDAMMIT TO HELL," Glendora shouted. The glass, emptied of its contents, rolled freely to the bottom of the stairs along with pieces of porcelain.

I couldn't stop myself: I laughed. I laughed at the auditory slip on a banana peel, the pratfall, the unexpected belly flop of a blimp. Then I laughed at Glendora's misfortune and at my own for going along with my father's orders when we both knew I had no need for a dinner tray. I laughed at Maurice making suckers of Glendora and me. I laughed at the inequity of our respective situations. I laughed and laughed.

Glendora, her white uniform stained with what had been my dinner, eventually limped into my room and, as she later described it, let me have it. But truly I didn't mind. She had a right. Besides, I'd enjoyed my moments of laughter without restraint. I'd laughed instead of cried because I knew with certainty that I wasn't sick.

Exhibiting none of my or my parents' antipathy toward bacteria, my stalwart friend Melly swooped up the baby, held him tightly, and carried him outside to the light.

Though his body was quite plump, his face appeared thin and colorless. When he opened his eyes and squinted into the dull sun, he seemed lethargic and indifferent to his surroundings.

"Could you go get one of those orange crates from inside?" Melly asked me.

"Sure. Why?"

"I need to look at this little guy so I can describe whatever's wrong with him to a doctor."

"What doctor?" Sparky asked.

Kneeling in the dirt next to the box, Melly unwound the material that had been wrapped mummy-style around the baby. His plumpness decreased with each revolution. As she neared the end of the fabric, we could see that he was pitifully scrawny. Yet, when at last she came to the end of the swaddling, Melly laughed. "Look," she exclaimed. "It's a girl!"

I didn't know why the baby's gender made me suddenly care for her. But unexpectedly, she mattered to me. And this caused me anguish, because I saw in the infant something I'd never known before—what sickness really looked like. She was sicker than even Melly had been. She was too sick to squirm or moan.

Despite Sparky's and Twyla's admonitions, Melly rested her ear against the infant's chest and listened intently to the insides of the little human. I watched as Melly stuck her finger in the baby's mouth to try to look down her throat. When Melly raised her head, she herself appeared stricken. "If ever someone needed a doctor, it is this little bitty thing. What's her name?" she asked the mother, and Sparky translated.

"Tesora," the mother responded.

"Tesora," Melly repeated, as if talking to the baby. "Tesora, we're going to get a doctor. We're going to get you well."

"Yeah? How?" Sparky asked.

Handing Tesora back to her mother, Melly bowed her head as if making a solemn promise. "We come back," she said. "We bring medicine."

XIII

ANAMNESIS

With me a half-step behind her, Melly scurried to the Adjudicator's room. We found him soberly absorbed in his journal. He made the act of setting down his fountain pen one of sacrifice.

"We wouldn't interrupt you unless it was very important," Melly apologized. "We need a doctor."

"You may be covered in sludge from head to foot, but underneath it, you look quite fit," the Adjudicator said, cynical as ever.

"Don't worry, we won't sit on your furniture," Melly promised.

Once she explained our predicament, Mr. St. Cyr began to snicker. "So that's what old Prail contrived for you. That'll teach you to destroy Cambridge property, huh? But what do you know? The punishment seems to have had the desired effect."

"In what way?" Melly asked.

"Prail sent you out to better the lives of the migrant workers. And now look at you. You're chomping at the bit to do them a good turn."

"What is actually meant by the migration of workers?" I asked. "Does it have something to do with birds?"

"There is a connection," Mr. St. Cyr said with amusement. "Like certain birds, migrant workers flock to wherever crops are ready for harvest. They live on the farm until all the beans, cotton, cherries, popcorn—whatever produce—are picked, pulled, or plucked."

Never once had I considered how asparagus, the one vegetable Charmian sanctioned at meals, advanced from the field to our dinner plates. "Do the workers always have to build their own . . . nests?" I asked.

"No, the farmers provide housing."

Melly stamped her foot. "In the case of *our* migrant workers, the farmers forgot the bathrooms and floors."

"And windows and doors," I chimed in.

Mr. St. Cyr shrugged.

"What's supposed to happen when the migrants get sick?" Melly asked. "Do the farmers take care of them?"

"If they're extremely ill, I suppose they go home to Mexico." Mr. St. Cyr raised an eyebrow. "Why do you ask?"

"We met a baby, a very sick baby," Melly said.

"Influenza?"

"It could be. Or whooping cough or rheumatoid arthritis, like me, or anything. I just know it's serious," Melly said. "I know she needs medicine right away."

"Might it be contagious?" Mr. St. Cyr asked, recoiling just a little. "If it is, public agencies should be contacted, the Department of Health, Immigration—"

"The baby's mother barely speaks English. And there's no time. We have to get that baby to a doctor right now. That's why we've come to you, so you could call your friend Dietrich. We need his help," Melly said.

Mr. St. Cyr rested his jaw in his hand. He creased his brow. "I regret to inform you that I shall never ask Dietrich to resume the practice of medicine," he said.

"We'll pay him. Whatever he wants. You can tell him. Fleur and I, Twyla and Sparky, too, the whole student body if need be, will raise the money to foot the bill."

"It's not that," Mr. St. Cyr said, his voice for once remorseful. "Dietrich would never take your cash. Though unquestionably he could use it. There's something else."

"What? What?"

"I'm not at liberty to tell. I don't betray confidences," the Ajudicator said. I could have sworn the Jesus on the crucifix over his bed winked at me.

"Then don't," Melly said. "I wanted your support, but I can ask him. I have Dietrich's phone number. He'll do this for me, I just know it."

Mr. St. Cyr spoke sternly. "You mustn't disturb him with this. It would mortify him. You must accept the fact that he can't help." Then he hesitantly added, "Dietrich isn't permitted to practice medicine anymore. He's been . . . disbarred."

"Dietrich took care of me, didn't he? He's helped you a few dozen times. This baby—her name's Tesora—won't be asking to see his credentials. A doctor, licensed or not, could get her breathing properly. Honestly, Mr. St. Cyr, without a doctor, I think she'll die." Melly braved his misanthropic stare with a scowl of her own. "Is Dietrich's embarrassment more important than a baby's life?"

The Adjudicator glanced at the winking Jesus, then said in a defeated tone, "All right, I can't guarantee his compliance, but I'll put in a request."

Melly and I raced to our room to shower. On our return, we sat ourselves on the poufy rugs that covered the tile floor so that the doctor could avail himself of Mr. St. Cyr's plush chaise longue. But before Dietrich seated himself, he lifted his trouser legs, just so at the thighs, to prevent them from creasing. He might have been a celebrity engaged in badinage with Jack Parr, if the thinning threads in said trousers hadn't been so conspicuous.

"I'll take a look at your baby, but please take note: I'm no pediatrician," Dietrich told us. "Mumps, measles, chicken pox—they're Greek to me. Furthermore, just so you know, I'm not up-to-date on new techniques or drugs. I no longer write prescriptions. I'm . . . retired."

"If you could just examine her and advise us what to do," Melly said.

"All right, then, where is she?" Dietrich rose and headed toward the door as though he expected to find Tesora in the next room.

"She's at the migrant camp. I'll show you," Melly explained as she unfolded the map Dirk had left in the station wagon. She traced her finger along the route we had taken while Dietrich thumped his pockets to locate his glasses.

"That's a long way out. Dirt roads. Sand," the physician grumbled, glancing down at the trousers. Then he remembered something else: "My car! It's a priceless antique. It isn't meant for trips into the hinterlands. You weren't counting on me for transportation, were you?"

"A baby's life is at stake," Melly reminded him. As she spoke, we heard hoofbeats outside the dorm. I was wondering if Lizzie had decamped with Gwendolyn when someone tapped on Mr. St. Cyr's window. With the blinds drawn, we couldn't see the noisemaker.

"Hey, Saint," a manly, laughing voice burst through the window. "Get ye ready for the big guy. I'll be right back."

Mr. St. Cyr pushed past Melly and me as he hastened to the window. "Royzy, Royzy, listen to me," he implored through the blinds. "The time isn't opportune."

"It's the only time I've got, fella," the cordial voice volleyed back.

"I've got people here," Mr. St. Cyr whined.

"People?" The man laughed. "Some of those pesky kids, you mean? Throw them in their sacks. I'm leaving town in the morning, so tonight's got to be ours. I'll take Trevor to the stables and come right back." The clamor of hooves chased the voice out of earshot.

"Girls, you're going to have to withdraw. I have a"— Mr. St. Cyr giggled—"gentleman caller."

I had risen from the floor, ready to leave, in fact wishing to do so, when Melly said in the most casual way, "I know exactly who that is. I've met Royzy before, remember? And I never told anyone he comes here. So why would I tell anyone now? Anyway, I'm not leaving this room unless Dietrich leaves with me."

Dietrich shrugged to convey his helplessness in the matter when, with explosive force, the two metal-framed vertical windows burst inward. The next thing I saw were the soles of cowboy boots. Then a large, virile body swung into the room with a swashbuckler's flair and landed lightly on foot-long feet. Smiling with self-satisfaction, the proprietor of the aforementioned body peeled the strips of venetian blinds from his clothes while giving Melly and me a jolly wink. He giggled. "And they say I need a stuntman."

I recognized the gentleman caller immediately. Though to Mr. St. Cyr he was known as Royzy, to the world he had a distinguished movie star's name.

Charmian claimed that certain actors—some politcians, too—positively radiated good looks and confidence and joie de vivre. "It spurts right out of their pores," she'd said. "It's some chemical mélange that draws people to them like parrots to crackers."

Royzy offered proof of Charmian's point: he glowed not only on the screen but right here in Mr. St. Cyr's room. (I planned to ask Odiline how he did it.) Royzy had played every type of melodramatic leading man, from sheriff to doctor to war hero, but it was in romantic comedies that he'd won my moviegoer's affection. So affable, so comfortable in his skin, so sophisticated yet waggishly naive with tantalizing blondes, brunettes, or redheads, the actor appealed to men as well as women. Then, too, his slow burns, his double and even triple takes—all the more difficult to achieve by someone so handsome—were legendary.

Notwithstanding his talent, good looks, and virility, I had no wish to become acquainted with him. I had learned long before that familiarity with one's favorite actor bred, if not contempt, disappointment or even despair.

"Hi, Royzy," Melly said demurely before anyone else could utter a hello. "You're just in time to solve a complicated problem."

"Talk away," he encouraged while giving Dietrich a pat on the back. Then he boldly swatted the Adjudicator on the backside. Mr. St. Cyr, however, didn't seem to notice. He lay down on his bed and placed his hand over his eyes like the saturnine Camille my mother had once played at the Coronet Theatre. That show had died a sour death, worse than the heroine's, according to Charmian.

Melly ignored the Adjudicator and explained our dilemma. She ended with "This is a true emergency. Royzy, I know you came on horseback, but do you by chance have a car that could get us where we need to go?"

Royzy studied her map. "Yes, ma'am, I know where this is. We shot a stampede out that way a couple months back." He spoke the words as a cowpoke might, purposely, comically, drawling. Dirk should have sounded as good.

"We're in a terrific hurry to get there," Melly said.

"May I suggest," Royzy suggested, breaking his cowboy character, "that a horse will get you there quicker than the gutsiest automobile."

"A horse?"

"The roads take you miles out of your way. A horse, a good horse, my horse Trevor, for example, can gallop a straight line across the desert. He'll save you about forty-five minutes. And the ride will be a kick and a half."

"That's all very well and good, but you're the only one here who knows how to ride," Melly said. "We have to get Dietrich out there."

His lips pursed, his feelings bruised, Dietrich displayed his pique. "I wouldn't expect you to know that *I'm* the expert rider here. Royzy took how many—two? three? riding lessons so he could play a rancher in an epic, but I've ridden all my life. I had a ranch out in Malibu, California, with a dozen quarter horses at my disposal. A day didn't go by that I wasn't in the saddle."

I believed Dietrich. Charmian had told me that many stars who acted in the occasional western never bothered to learn to ride: "The grips or gaffers or best boys, I forget which, install the actor on a machine that simulates a horse's gallop or trot or prance, whatever they want. Then they run the scenery on a screen behind it. That's why the cowboy's hat never blows off, his hair never gets mussed, and he can carry on intelligible conversation or sing ballads in the saddle."

"The problem is," Melly told Royzy, "there's only one horse. And Fleur and I have to get out there, too."

"That's all right," I said quickly. "I'll be glad to stay here and . . . hold down the fort."

"Mr. St. Cyr, I bet you'd like to accompany us, too," Melly said, but it seemed that the Adjudicator had buried his head under his pillow.

* * *

The most difficult part of our eventual excursion became convincing Lizzie to lend us Gwendolyn.

"She'll get to spend time with her boyfriend. His name is Trevor," Melly whispered persuasively. "Trevor is a movie-star horse. He's been in hundreds of films."

"But if something happened to Gwendolyn . . ." Lizzie said.

"Royzy and Dietrich have spent most of their waking hours in the saddle," Melly lied. "Haven't you seen any of Royzy's westerns? Isn't he a great horseback rider, Fleur?"

"A great horseback rider," I said, making no commitment to a verb.

"Don't say *horseback rider*. Just say *rider*," Twyla interjected. "*Horseback* rider is low-class."

"Anyway, Fleur and I will be there to make sure they treat the horses right," Melly told Lizzie.

"It still won't work," I reminded Melly. "There are four of us and only two horses."

Royzy, whom we'd brought along to persuade Lizzie with his famous face, spoke to me in a jaunty, easygoing manner, "We'll just double up, sweetheart."

Gleaning his intention, I said, "I think Lizzie should go in my place."

"No, Fleur, you and I have to go," Melly said firmly.

"I don't see why."

"Because Lizzie's not one of the Four-Letter Four."

Only when Royzy agreed to ride Gwendolyn himself did Lizzie, unaware of his measly three riding lessons, finally consent to the equine arrangements. "You won't wear Gwendolyn out? You'll stop when she needs water? But not from some hole in the ground. You'll take water with you."

"Rest assured, I love Trevor as much as you love Gwendolyn," Royzy declared and chucked Lizzie under the chin.

And so it transpired that Royzy and Dietrich took the respective reins of Gwendolyn and Trevor. Dietrich, in an obvious attempt to save his good clothes, had metamorphosed into a singular jockey. He now wore Mr. St. Cyr's white tennis shoes, paisley pajamas, and would-be Sigmund Freud cloak. He looked like Zorro Senior.

Due to Melly's weakness, Dietrich placed her behind him on Trevor's rump. I was in Royzy's charge. "Okay, put your arms around me and hold real tight," Royzy said. "If you only knew how many women would give their right arm to take your place."

"Then how would they hang on?" I asked, having locked my hands into a death knot on the other side of Royzy's muscular girth.

"Fleur, legions of women will pester you for details the rest of your life," Dietrich promised.

The doctor's statement didn't mollify my discomfort. While observing Melly bobbing up and down behind him, I silently bewailed my own benumbed backside.

"Isn't this magnificent? Smell the air. Feel the night," Dietrich told us.

"*Vámanos* to the campesinos," Royzy shouted excitedly, as though playing the lead in the definitive motion picture of *Viva Zapata!*

Never a horse girl, I was not a nature girl, either. As we rode through the empty, caliginous dessert, Royzy sang and Dietrich whistled, but I felt apprehensive. The vast firmament of frozen stars, some in sudden-death leaps into antagonistic atmospheres, made me feel as insignificant as the pebbles under Gwendolyn's hooves. Speaking of which, I had no doubt that snakes and iguanas and scorpions were creeping out of their crawl spaces while sidewinders sidled toward Gwendolyn's naked ankles.

It seemed an eternity before we arrived at the giant field of quicksand. "You know, the horses might frighten the people in this camp. I think Fleur and I should go alone on foot to Tesora's hut," Melly told Dietrich and Royzy.

"Me, too," I quickly agreed, so anxious was I to dismount.

Following the phosphorescent bobbing line of our flashlights, Melly and I trekked toward the huddle of huts. "What if the migrants think we're here to rob them? What if they jump us? What if they shoot first and ask questions later?" I whispered.

"You've seen too many westerns," she answered.

"That's true," I agreed.

"But okay, we'll turn off our flashlights." As soon as we did, Melly whispered excitedly, "Hey, listen. Listen to the night."

It was a mistake—I heard our footsteps shatter the desert floor. Wings flapped ominously. Animals howled. Fear must have deadened my vocal cords, or I would have been screaming. As we rounded the corner of the first shack, though I had never heard such weapons in person, I thought I heard the salvo of tommy guns. I froze, a one-girl glacier, in my own footprints.

Melly grabbed hold of my sweater and pulled me along, unconcerned. "I guess if we did stoop labor like these people, we wouldn't have trouble sleeping, either," she said and laughed. "That's snoring you're hearing, dummy."

As we tiptoed past the vibrating hovels, we couldn't distinguish the one where a baby lay close to death. Even in daylight they had all looked alike. In the dim gleam of a quarter moon, our quest seemed hopeless until, circling the encampment for the second time, we smacked into a man returning from the latrine.

He screamed and we screamed, and in a second the steady cadence of snoring halted. Moments later our flashlight beams were dimmed by the luminescence of a kerosene lantern.

Melly recovered her sense of urgency. "The *bambina* Tesora?" she asked the eyes. "*¿Donde está?*"

One of the children, José or Eduardo, took Melly's hand and mine and led us to the right hut. I was shocked to discover that the two parents, Tesora, and three other siblings slept on the one tattered mattress.

Melly beckoned to Becillia. "Tell your mother we brought a doctor," she said, having exhausted her Spanish. "He's just outside the camp. I'll go get him now."

"No, let me," I said and ran off before she could argue. I had no trouble leading Dietrich and Royzy to the right shack, due to the glow in the open windows and the door; more kerosene lamps had been lit. In their tempered radiance, Royzy and Dietrich, still wearing his cloak, loomed large. Their shadows bunched together and hulked on the ceiling and walls.

It surprised me how easily Royzy slipped behind the others and made himself, if not invisible, inconspicuous. I hadn't known that actors were capable of giving up even the dimmest rays of limelight.

"I need some room," Dietrich snapped. I thought his costume would give the migrant workers pause, for surely they had a conception—no different from my own—that doctors on the job wore white coats and ties. But Becillia took his orders seriously and, as instructed by Melly, gently shooed as many people as possible out of the room. Even Tesora's parents stepped outside and stood looking at us with equanimity through the window cutout.

Melly aimed a flashlight directly at the baby while Dietrich hunched over her. He had brought along a small doctor's kit with a stethoscope, tongue depressor, and otoscope and knew how to use them. Melly had already unwound Tesora's swaddling so Dietrich could go straight to work. He sniffed Tesora, examined her eyes, checked her throat and ears, and listened with care to her chest and back. After several minutes he shook his head. "This is something I hate to see," he said. "My guess is she has TB. Of course, we need chest X rays to confirm it. The whole camp is probably infected, but you were right, she's in very bad shape."

"What can we do?" Melly asked.

"Well, if her parents had any sense, or clout, or I guess it comes down to money, they'd get her out of here," he said. "There may be medicine for TB now. When I was in med school, which is the only time I ever saw it, the only hope was trying to build up the patient's strength and immunity. Funny, they sent patients who could afford it out to Tucson."

"Okay, okay, I know what to do," Melly said, as if it were a simple assignment.

"You can't do anything," Dietrich told Melly.

"Yes, I can," Melly said with a finality that left no room for argument. Then she turned to Becillia and tried to convey her thoughts. Becillia quickly grasped the English words and clarified them to her mother and father. The couple nodded in agreement.

It took Dietrich longer to understand Melly's intentions, since he'd been concentrating on the baby. "Just a minute." He spoke harshly. "Where are you planning to take her, Melly? Any hospital you care to name will isolate her in a tuberculosis ward. Don't kid yourself, they won't allow you to visit."

"So I understand," Melly said. "That's why I'm taking her back to school."

"You're off your rocker," Dietrich grumbled.

I personally agreed with the doctor, but Royzy stepped in. "What's the harm?" he asked. "Is there any question that the little babe will die out here? Melly plans to be a doctor one day—so here's her first case."

"Melly could contract TB. It's highly contagious," Dietrich said indignantly.

"But she's already had contact," Royzy said with such authority that even Dietrich didn't argue. "Let Melly do what she can."

"Wait a minute," I interjected. "What about the other kids at RCW? What if they get infected?"

"They won't. Tesora won't leave our room," Melly said.

I had never held a baby before. I'd never even cuddled baby dolls, because Charmian wouldn't do me the injustice of treating me like a child. If, by chance, anyone presented me with a replica of a human infant, Charmian briskly removed it from the premises. "I'll just pass this piece of frippery along to a foundling home and take the deduction," she'd say. "All one can expect from charity children is procreation, so we might as well give them something to practice on."

Therefore, I felt an abysmal aversion on being handed the small, clumsily breathing creature. I saw at once that her tender skin could easily be lacerated with a frayed fingernail, of which I had several. And in the first moment of my taking possession, Tesora's head fell to her chest so vehemently that I thought it had severed from her neck. But since Royzy and Dietrich were busy controlling the horses, and Melly didn't have the strength to hang on to the doctor and the baby, it fell to me to cradle Tesora in one arm while clutching Royzy's belt with the other.

When Tesora began to cry, softly though it was, I didn't know whether to jiggle her, say something soothing, or change her position to my other arm. I tried all three but couldn't prevent her whimpering. Tesora, a sick and motherless child, and I, a hapless substitute, balanced on a horse's behind—what chance did she have to survive?

Fearfully bobbing along, I recalled the one time in my life when I had been legitimately ill, at the age of ten. That is, if being attached to an IV to remedy "dehydration and complications" at Children's Hospital counted.

Both my parents were working fifteen-hour days at the studio, or so my nanny Eileen told me, otherwise they would have merrily spent all the visiting hours in my room. But possibly out of guilt—because she planned to quit before the end of my hospital stay—Eileen hinted that each night at the end of their exhaustive workdays and well after I'd fallen asleep, Charmian and Maurice tiptoed down the silent corridors of the hospital to steal a glimpse of my weak slumbering self.

Because the rudiments of life, like falling asleep, eluded me even then, I ceased trying altogether. I lay all night in my mechanical bed, listening for the clapping of high heels and the drumming of wingtips, audible signs of my parents' entrée. Hearing only intonations of emergencies and distress, and the occasional slam of a distant fire door, I attempted to calm myself by synchronizing my breathing with the oscillations and vibrations of the machines that operated the oxygen tent across the hall. Because patients' doors remained open, I knew the blurred shape of the three-year-old who resided there. Her name was Ginger Mahn, a nurse had told me.

Ginger's parents spent every day at her bedside; each night one of them slept upright on an upholstered chair while the other sat on the bed holding Ginger's hand. They left their daughter only for trips to the bathroom, the cafeteria, or to huddle with a doctor in the hallway. The discussions were of a grave nature. Mrs. Mahn often sobbed, and Mr. Mahn always fixed one arm securely around his wife, even when blowing his nose.

By refusing to eat the institutional bill of fare, or bare my behind for an injection, or hold still for the blood-pressure cuff until my questions were answered, I garnered the information that Ginger had kidney disease, loved the color pink—"Not a good color for redheads, but her mother lets her wear it, anyway," the nurse said—and insisted on being told the story of Snow White several times a day.

With the deluxe Crayola set and sketch pad I'd been sent by the cast of *The Radio Mystery Half Hour*, I drew countless pictures for Ginger of a character named Snowy Pink. Wearing a pink tutu and a pair of pink wings, Snowy Pink could flutter out of reach of doctors' syringes or flap all the way to Will Wright's for an ice-cream cone. In my most elaborate drawing, Snowy Pink, with a parent in each of her arms, soared all the way to her home. Via a nurse or candy striper, I sent each of my illustrations to Ginger. Mrs. Mahn, her soft, dark hair touched lightly with an angel's perfume, frequently stepped into my room to relay Ginger's delight.

Very late one night or very early in the morning, I heard garbled sounds emanating from Ginger's room. Only when a nurse and a doctor came running did I realize that adults were crying. Sitting up and leaning forward in my bed, I could see the two uniformed figures and Mr. and Mrs. Mahn hovering over Ginger. The abrupt silencing of the machines conveyed more than I wanted to know.

Eventually Ginger's parents stumbled into the hall. Mrs. Mahn's wailing and the low register of Mr. Mahn's sobs coalesced into an inharmonious, angry requiem. I heard a doctor gently saying, "It's time to go home. You did everything you could. We all did. Ginger knew how loved she was." Without the hum and pulse of the machines, the Mahns' footsteps were all the more plangent. I listened as they traversed the long corridor for the last time. The sound of their steps, even the echoes, and the scent of Mrs. Mahn's perfume weakened as they traveled farther and farther from Ginger. The slam of the fire door squelched the last of my hope.

Though tampering with the IV could lead to instant death, a nurse had told me, I jerked the adhesive tape away from my skin and, with trembling fingers, extracted the needle from my inner arm. Only a little light-headed, I slid out of my elevated bed to the floor.

Without knowing that *I* would derive pleasure from her deed, Mrs. Mahn had taped the Snowy Pink drawings on the walls and ceiling where Ginger could easily see them. But the little girl's eyes were closed to them now. With the plastic tent removed, I saw her clearly for the first time. No wonder her parents had cried; Ginger's features appeared so precious and perfect. I touched the child's cheeks with my fingers. "Good-bye, Ginger," I said. "Never forget that your parents loved you more than anything else."

Still awake and waiting for my own parents to make their suppositional dawn visit, I heard something rattling and rolling down the long hall. Sitting up again, I witnessed a large wooden box on wheels being pushed into Ginger's room. Its paint—the drab, deadly color of battleships—matched the hospital worker's suit. He stepped over to Ginger's bed and, with one practiced motion, swooped her from the bed and placed her in the hideous gray box. Casually, as though nothing out of the ordinary had occurred, he wheeled the box out of the room.

Being in charge of the dead, he might have been able to tell me why Mr. and Mrs. Mahn had been deprived of a lifetime with Ginger while my parents, who had other consuming interests, were not going to lose me.

With Tesora in my weakening arm, I angled her so she could see the desert sky's arcade of stars and planets. They were named for Roman gods, who I hoped would lend me their puissance to restore the baby's health.

XIV

PANGS

The next morning as Lizzie climbed through the window, a little yelp and then another and another coaxed the three of us awake.

"What is that?" Lizzie asked, excitedly looking around. "Did you get a puppy? Oh goody, where is it?"

Before we could answer, Twyla had spotted Tesora in Melly's bed and verbally stamped her foot. "What have you done? What ever possessed you to bring that little octoroon back here to school?"

"If, by that derogatory word, you mean Tesora, I'm trying to nurse her back to health," Melly said.

"Not here. She's not staying in my room," Twyla said, cringing at each of Tesora's cries. "You're not turning this school into *Magic Mountain*. As it is, ever since we saw that disgusting latrine, I've been horribly constipated."

"This baby is sick and needs our help," Melly said. "And that's that."

"A puppy would be more fun," Lizzie said, slumping onto her bed. "If babies had fur and a tail, I might like them."

"The first order of the day is to give Tesora a bath," Melly announced. "And burn her infected clothes."

"I'll do that," Lizzie volunteered. "The clothes, not the bath. Love fire, hate water, you know?"

"Doesn't she need to be fed?" I asked sleepily. "I thought babies had a schedule. My mother had a baby in a movie called *He Who Takes the First Step*, and he needed a bottle every two hours."

"If you don't shut up about your mother," Twyla warned.

"Oh, no! Oh, no!" Melly struck her forehead with the palm of her hand, mortified. She bounded from her bed. "You're so right. It only dawns on me now—we don't have anything for Tesora to eat."

"There're Fritos and Chips Ahoys in my drawer," Lizzie offered.

"And Gwendolyn would share some of her hay," Twyla mimicked Lizzie.

"Yeah, thanks," Melly said as she pulled off her pajamas and wrestled into clothes. "But I don't really know what Tesora eats, solid food or pabulum or what. I forgot to ask her age."

"With a horse, you look in his mouth. The grinding of his teeth tells you how old he is," Lizzie explained over Tesora's cries.

"Unfortunately she doesn't *have* teeth," Melly said. "I'm just thinking—Tesora needs a lot of things." The baby cried a little harder, as if for emphasis.

"Melly, can't we just get some milk from the kitchen?" I asked.

"And feed it to her how? We have no bottle or nipple. Plus, babies drink formula, not cow's milk."

When Twyla steadfastly refused to appeal to Mr. Party Time for delivery assistance, Melly phoned for a taxi.

"I'll go. I'll be glad to," I implored Melly. I dreaded the thought of being left alone with the baby.

"Well, I'm going to breakfast," Twyla said as she left our room.

"It would take longer for me to describe what to get than to pick it out myself," Melly insisted. So, armed with a lengthy shopping list and one of my freshly signed checks, Melly spirited herself off to the Medicine Man Pharmacy.

Consequently, with the skipping of breakfast as well as my first class, I made my debut as a baby-sitter. Within seconds Tesora sensed my discomfort. Her face reddened. Her chin wobbled. Her arms and legs shuddered and flailed. She obviously felt the pangs of hunger and fell into a rhythm of crying that involved every aspect of her body and soul. I didn't know what to do. I lifted her so she could see over my shoulder. I walked her. I made my arms into a cradle and rocked her. Nothing would calm the little crying machine.

"Shushushu," I said, hoping I sounded like the calming

sprinklers on the hillside at home. "Please don't cry. We're going to feed you right away. Well, in another half hour or so. Please be patient. Please have faith in us."

My pleas had little effect, and I considered the possibility of filling Tesora's stomach with water. But how? From a glass? From my hand? From a thimble, if I had one? Suppose she vomited? Or choked? Or swallowed her tongue? Without warning, I was crying, too. My cries drowned out those of the baby.

Maybe my tears fell onto her face and surprised and delighted her, or perhaps the convulsing of her body wore her out, but one second she was crying like a champion and the next her eyes closed and her entire body relaxed.

Had Tesora stopped breathing? With fear nipping at me, I placed two fingers on her tiny wrist in an attempt to take her pulse. To my horror, I felt no throbbing under her skin. *Please don't die*, I prayed. "Please don't die," I beseeched her. I propped my ear against the baby's heart and heard the cadence of life.

The crying resumed abruptly and quickly escalated along with my own. I needed to calm myself, or I'd never be able to comfort the baby in my arms. And so, as I'd done to soothe myself for as long as I could remember, I recited the names of my nannies out loud:

"Mrs. Young, Carina, Jenna, Cheryl, Princess Bernadette, Mrs. MacKenzie, Miss Nora, Corinth, Tamar, Patricia, Madame Claudette, Violette, Phoebe, Meg, Mrs. Graham, Idalia, Lise, Janyce, Ivy, Cathy, Paige, Susan, Suzanne, Susannah, Marcella, Dora, Mignon, Cordelia, Amanda,

Christine, Laurie, Denise, Cosima, Nancy, Kristen, Penny, Eileen, Linda, Miss Elizabeth, Zelda, Sharon, Yola, Mrs.. H., Genie, Aurora, Emily, Joan, Glendora, Bettina, Helga, Clover, Miss Hoate, Victoria, Julie, Lauren, Odette, Colleen, Tara . . .”

The abundance of bulky packages Melly lugged into the dorm implied a shopping spree of major proportions. Enough diapers for tens of thousands of bottoms, twin magnums of diaper powder and baby oil, countless cans of pabulum, rubber panties that looked like shower caps, baby nightgowns, bottles, nipples, distilled water, a pan for heating the bottles, nipples, distilled water, a thermometer, rubbing alcohol, cotton balls, a baby spoon and dish, masks to protect Tesora from our germs, and multiple jars of variously colored baby food emerged from the bundles.

“Has Tesora been crying for long?” Melly asked through the gauzy mask she’d put on. She handed one to me. It looked a little like a pig’s snout.

“Just get the food ready. Do whatever you need to do as fast as you can,” I begged her.

The lid of the vacuum-packed jar of baby carrots made a thawp on opening and raised my hopes. But when confronted with a little mound of the orange root on a tiny spoon, the baby turned her head away. Melly kept following her mouth with the spoon, but Tesora’s lips were pressure-sealed.

“Try spinach,” I said. And then, “Try apple sauce.

Everyone likes apple sauce." Everyone except Tesora, evidently.

"Maybe she doesn't know about food yet. Maybe she only knows about sucking," Melly said. While I held what I took to be a hysterical baby, Melly filled a bottle with formula, heated it under hot running water, and tickled Tesora's lips with the nipple.

In seconds an expression of contentment smoothed Tesora's face. She sucked voraciously *and* gratefully. Only I cried now—with relief as the baby sucked her bottle in rhythmic rapture. Melly was holding her, and I noticed that Tesora's eyes were following me, that for the first time she appeared interested and expressive. How odd, I thought, that being watched by the baby makes *me* feel significant.

"You should probably go to your classes now," Melly told me. "We don't want to raise any suspicions."

"You're right," I said, but I hated parting from the baby. How could I concentrate on math or English or even mythology when I understood perfectly that mastery of these subjects couldn't possibly make a sick baby well. Just as a gesture, I prayed to Hestia, goddess of hearth and home, to give Tesora a chance.

By the end of the school day, our room had become a nursery. Despite Twyla's protests, Melly had already begun washing diapers in the tub and hanging them from the shower-curtain rod to dry. Though we were very careful about who entered our room—we propped a chair under the doorknob as an ersatz lock—the girls in our dorm learned of Tesora's presence faster than Zeus could have thrown a lightning bolt. We were bathing Tesora when the onslaught came. "Oh please, let me hold her? Look at this little *ookie-pookie. Ookie-ookie. Pookie-pookie.* What a *loveums,*" Babs baby-talked. She gave Tesora a little splash as though raining affection on her. "Come to me, come on, little loveums."

"Look out, Babs, your curlers are going to fall on her. She's sick, remember," Sparky said.

"And slippery," Melly added.

"Look at her cute little baby body. What a *cutey-ootey,* what a *cookie-wookie,*" Tammy goo-gooed.

The only naked babies I had ever been in proximity with were depicted in paintings and embodied by statues, and although Tesora didn't make eye contact or bill and coo as she soaked in the tepid water, I found myself charmed by her corporeal presence. Once it was washed (with Twyla's turtle-oil shampoo), Tesora's one-inch output of tar-baby hair stood straight out from her scalp. Her pitch-colored eyes appeared to be faraway planets orbiting in illuminated skies, carrying with them the mysteries of the universe. Her body and limbs, though exceedingly thin and frail, were perfectly formed and offered promising intimations of the girl she would become. Even her private parts, the section of the female body I deemed grotesque, became precious in miniature.

I felt a warming sensation throughout my own body

that I had never felt before. I wanted to kiss and caress Tesora's clean, delicate skin, to feel it on my cheeks, to stroke and hug the little human surprise package. Instead my teeth came together in a painful clench.

Had anyone ever felt such emotion about me? Had anyone admired my infant body, the depth of my eyes, the curve of my cheeks both in front and in back? Had one of my sixty-one nannies ever wanted to hold me and never let go?

"Oooo, I love her little nightgown. Look at those ducks. Can I hold her now? Really, I know all about babies, and she's so cute. So *itty-bitty-cutey-wootey*," Dena declared, sweeping her hands under Tesora.

"No, I don't have a mask for you. You wouldn't want to give her any germs or catch any of hers, would you? Tesora really isn't supposed to have visitors. But when she's feeling better, I bet she'd love to play," Melly said diplomatically.

Dena wouldn't take the hint. "Boobie-baby. Wou want to be my wozzums? I wust wuv babies."

"GET OUT," Twyla shouted harshly enough to make everyone who didn't actually belong with us leave the room. "Listen," she told us. "It's enough that I have this baby bunking here. Not that anyone asked if I minded. And since her presence breaks every health rule known to modern medicine, I could easily turn her in and, as a result, turn her out. And worse than that mess of a baby is the constant traffic of asinine girls who would rather be nursemaids than exercise their brains. The next one who comes near us is getting hell from me."

As if on cue, there was a knock at our door.

"WHO THE HELL IS IT?" Twyla shouted.

The voice of a bird, but definitely not a songbird, responded. "It's . . . it's Mrs. Prail."

"Oh, no," Melly murmured.

"Do you think she knows?" Lizzie asked in a whisper.

"Who would have told her?" I mouthed.

"Please, I need to speak with Twyla. There's someone on the phone who wants to speak with her. He says it's urgent," Mrs. Prail's voice filtered through the door.

"Oh!" Twyla leaped from her bed and slid into her slippers, her disposition now sweetly girlish. "I'm coming. I'm coming. Oh, oh, oh, pray for me, knock on wood, anything, that it's Al Mandell. Pray that he's found my father!"

How close to the surface Twyla's longings were. "Don't get your hopes too high," I counseled her. "I don't want you to be disappointed."

"That's the trouble with you, Fleur," Twyla upbraided me as she grabbed her sweater and pulled the chair out from under the doorknob. "You always think disappointment is in store."

"Wait, wait," Melly said, halting Twyla's momentum. "Your mask. Take it off. We don't want anyone getting ideas."

Twyla flung her mask at Melly and left, brusquely closing the door.

"What do you think this is all about?" Melly inquired.

"You mean Twyla's phone call?"

"I mean Mrs. Prail trekking all the way down to our dorm herself," Melly said.

"Incoming calls go to the headmaster's apartment, and Mrs. Prail no doubt answered the phone. There's no inter-com. How else could she summon Twyla to the phone? *I* just think it's horrid that Twyla has to talk with her in the room," I said.

"But normally Mrs. Prail would ask one of the kids to fetch Twyla."

"Maybe there was no one around."

"I think Mrs. Prail is spying on us," Melly said, her brow creased with suspicion.

"Well, Melly, I know a thing or two about sleuthing—or a writer's version of it, at any rate—and if Mrs. Prail's making an investigation, she's pretty inept. She didn't even try to come in our room," I said.

As we argued, the doorknob began to rattle, and the chair, which I had just reinstalled, rocked slightly. The person on the other side was intent on entering.

"There. You see?" Melly nodded. "She knows some-thing. She's back."

"Who is it?" I called out in a deceitfully friendly voice.

"Why jou are lockeen me out?" came the muffled voice of Conchita.

"There, you have it," Melly said smugly. "Mrs. Prail sent her."

The doorknob shook more vehemently.

"I have to let her in," I said.

"No, you don't," Melly almost growled at me.

Now Conchita was pounding.

"Melly, I don't know how to say this, but motherhood seems to be making you awfully mistrustful."

When I opened the door, Conchita looked neither left nor right. She simply headed to the bathroom with a bucket and toilet brush.

"I'll take care of the toilet," Melly said. "It's time for you to go home. *Now*, Conchita."

But the maid continued into the bathroom, where she couldn't avoid noticing the infant paraphernalia. "Jou girls are learneen, how you call it, home eeconomeecs?" she asked. "That ees sometheen I am teach."

Melly began to laugh. "Conchita, can you keep a secret? If you can, look over here."

"Oooh, oooh, ooh, a *bambino!*" she said.

While Conchita enlightened us on the ABC's of diapering technique, Twyla returned. She wore a surly expression, and none of us dared ask about the telephone call. But when she caught all three of us staring, she said, "No, it wasn't Al. Or my father. It was—who else—Mr. Party Time. The cretin wants to play Rumpelstiltskin with me. I'm only sorry that with Mrs. Prail standing over me, I couldn't tell him what an asshole he is."

"You couldn't tell him because it would prove that our word purge served no purpose," Melly said.

That second night of our collective motherhood, long after the master switch had been thrown and we'd convinced Lizzie to retire to the stables—lately she didn't want to go—we heard a tapping on our window.

"What now?" Twyla complained.

"Who is it?" I whispered through the glass.

Moments later Brian and Lionel crawled through the window. Brian had brought a little pink package tied with even pinker grosgrain ribbon. He was holding it awkwardly, unsure whether to place it near the baby or toss it on a bed. "Go on, open it," he said, handing it to me.

"Don't you want to see Tesora first?" I teased but accepted the gift.

"Eeew," Lionel squealed as he and Brian caught their first glimpse of Tesora. "She's so scrawny and gray. She looks like a possum. You're absolutely sure she's human?"

"She's beautiful," Melly and I said in unison.

"She looks all right. For a baby," Brian said with an embarrassed smile.

Opening the package, I found a pale pink rattle with cat faces at either end. "It's darling," I said and held it close to Tesora's face.

Melly and I, and even Twyla, were flabbergasted when a little hand reached up and clasped the narrow grip as though this were the most natural act imaginable. Tesora held the rattle all by herself, and after Melly gently demonstrated how to make it jangle, our baby eagerly brandished it on her own. Brian and Lionel therefore witnessed Tesora's first smile and my second bout with tears of the day.

"It's okay," Brian said to me, sweetly concerned. "No need to cry. You should be happy. She must be feeling pretty good."

Despite my tears, I noticed Brian doing the oddest

thing. He had crossed his forearms to better scratch his upper arms through his shirt. He scratched as though he meant to tear through the fabric.

"What's wrong?" I asked.

"I can't stop myself," Brian said. "I'm really itchy." I could hear the shame in his voice, but this didn't prevent him from trying to lacerate his arms.

"He sometimes keeps me awake all night with his scratching," Lionel complained. "Brian's never figured out that the more he scratches, the more it itches."

"Shut up," Brian told Lionel. "Just shut up."

Brian's malady and my desire to find a remedy halted my tears. "Isn't there something you can rub on your skin? Calamine lotion, maybe?" I asked.

"Nah," he said and continued to scratch. "Nothing works."

"Ice water?"

"No good."

"Soaking in warm water and baking soda?"

"Good for nothing."

"Well, okay . . . I have an idea. Would you let me see your arms?" I asked. I wanted to be sure his scratches warranted my antidote. And, I admitted only to myself, my curiosity was on the prowl.

"Do I have to?" he asked plaintively.

"No," I said. "But I think I can help."

Brian followed me into our bathroom, and there, amid the diapers and cosmetics, he rolled up his sleeves. "My skin is pretty disgusting," he said. "I'm just giving you fair warning."

The rough red crust that covered his arms didn't look any worse than a virulent case of poison ivy, but the long gouges embroidered with blood, both moist and dried, assaulted my eyes. "Okay, I hope you don't get mad at me. Don't watch what I'm about to do," I demanded.

"Of course I'm going to watch," Brian said.

His scrutiny made my job harder, but I audaciously prepared to relieve him of his armament. Appropriating a pair of cuticle scissors from one of Twyla's cosmetic bags, I attentively trimmed each of Brian's nails down to the nub. True to my upbringing, I allowed the detritus to remain where it fell.

Brian waited until I had completed the operation before commenting, "My fingers look like stumps now. But thanks, I guess."

The following morning, when Babs summoned Twyla to the telephone, my old friend cast a glance in my direction that defied me to say a disparaging word. "There, you see? it was Al Mandell!" she exclaimed on her return. "His detective work is finally paying off. He's narrowed the field. He says it won't be long before he positively pinpoints my father!"

"That's great news," I told her.

Twyla became friendly and confessional. "Fleur, I can feel him. I can feel my father's presence. It's difficult to explain, but there's a spot, a kind of orb, on the other side of those mountains," she said, pointing toward the Santa

Catalinas, "that is exuding warmth and love. I can feel it moving toward me. I really can. I know it will be here before my birthday. I know in my bones that I'll be spending my eighteenth birthday with my one and only true father."

I didn't ask Twyla any penetrating questions. Neither did I try to shield her from a possible fiasco. Instead I used the blandest words, the least offensive, the least likely to draw criticism: "I was hoping we'd be together to celebrate your birthday with the Four-Letter Four. But I'll keep my fingers crossed for whatever you want most."

XV

Bon Voyage

Wearing a Mexican poncho but no sombrero under the cloying Tucson sun ordinarily would have placed Melly in the category of mad dog or Englishman, but she had reason: the concealment of Tesora. Without Twyla, who refused to relinquish her proximity to the telephone, the Four-Letter Four minus one walked to the Landmark Laundry for a rendezvous with Dietrich. Tesora had been in our care for almost a week and had undergone a patch test, administered by Dietrich, that confirmed she had TB. He had therefore made the first available appointment with a specialist. I carried a bag with diapers and bottles and formula, wrapped in a sheet to look like laundry, and Sparky lugged the real laundry in an effort to make our outing appear to be an ordinary Saturday errand.

In the parking lot behind the Landmark, I received my

first daylight glimpse of Dietrich's transportation. A foreign car, it had the luster and authority of a concert piano, though the doctor himself called it an automotive Stradivarius. Not a car enthusiast per se, I coveted only the ornaments, an opulent silver swan at the forward end of the engine hatch and its elegantly etched twin swirling its tail around the trunk lock.

Dietich treated his vehicle as he might an elderly and revered patient, but I, a collector of sorts myself, felt compelled to say, "This car belongs in a museum. It could get damaged on the road."

"I quite agree," Dietrich said, his eyes downcast. "But she's all I've got."

"If you sold it, you'd have enough money to . . ." I didn't finish, because the doctor muffled his ears with his hands.

The Adjudicator had evidently decided to join our excursion. When he stepped out of Dietrich's car, his cloak furled and unfurled around his arms as though keeping time with a nervous throb. And when Melly pulled Tesora out from under her poncho, he glanced about apprehensively as though anticipating arrest for baby snatching.

On the open road, Dietrich's hangdog expression vanished. Honking his classic horn as he shifted in and out of the fast lane, he bantered jovially. "And what do you girls do with the baby when you're supposed to be in classes?"

"There's a maid at RCW by the name of Conchita. Mr. St. Cyr knows her, don't you?" Melly asked.

"She's a pip," the Adjudicator said.

"Conchita carries Tesora around like a papoose while

she works. She loves the baby. And now that Dirk and the Prails have seen her with Tesora, they think the baby is hers. They are incensed that the school maid has *disregarded the institution of holy matrimony*," Melly said, imitating Mrs. Prail.

"She's a pip," the Adjudicator repeated, making it his only utterance during our entire trip to and across the border.

Dietrich refused to utilize an ordinary parking place. He scouted the Mexican streets until he located a private garage, dusty and decrepit though it was, where a burly young gaucho, for a ten-dollar fee, agreed to situate the antique where no commonplace cars could scrape or dent it.

"Speaking of parking, I'll just park myself in the bar across the street until you return," Mr. St. Cyr informed Dietrich. "Then I can keep my eyes on the watchman as well as your only asset."

"Suit yourself, Saint," Dietrich said. I couldn't tell if he meant to convey disapproval or relief.

"Shouldn't you come with us?" Melly asked the Adjudicator. "Bars are so full of temptations."

"I won't jeopardize the safety of the Hispano-Suiza, I promise you that," Mr. St. Cyr said. Then he sallied forth to the other side of the street.

Though the denizens of Nogales were obviously poorer than the citizens of Tucson, the town itself had a far more vibrant air. Mariachis strolled everywhere, gaily playing the same four or five songs, in and out of taquerias, around vegetable stands, and in front of the hawkers of lottery tickets. The economy may have been based on the sale of trinkets. Key rings with tiny sombreros or ten-gallon hats were on sale in every tienda, along with serapes, stuffed rattlesnakes, sandals with tire treads for soles, and piggy banks that looked like cacti. I looked for one that matched the Rancho Cambridge West logo, but only fleetingly, because on several street corners, mustachioed men with no apparent vocation whispered menacingly at us.

Dietrich was in no mood to let us dawdle. He led us with rapid strides through the streets until we arrived at an undistinguished two-story building that had no ornamentation other than a sign that read CLÍNICA.

Trailing Dietrich like a brood of pullets, we entered the clinic, where, for the first time, I heard him give his full name. It sounded familiar, and when, as a lark, I tried the title of *Dr.* in front of Dietrich Stanhope, I recognized it as one attached to a Hollywood scandal. I'd heard Charmian speak disparagingly of him, but I couldn't remember why.

In the waiting room, children with runny noses played with others who had rashes and sores. Toddlers rolled on the floor. To tempt the children, tortillas spread with beans were lying on top of paper bags. Though many of the youngsters could stand and talk, some of them leaned against their mothers' bleached-out dresses and nursed.

The hubbub in the *clínica* canceled out everything I'd learned on Bedford Drive about preventive medicine. I missed watching Gene Kelly—a billed cap pulled low over his forehead—shamble, not dance, into our mutual sinus doctor's office. Ingrid Bergman, in an old raincoat, sometimes made an appearance in my general intern's well-appointed antechamber. Among Dr. Krusoe's celebrity patients, I'd been told, only Elizabeth Taylor had license to enter the offices through a private door.

When at last we heard the call for Señor Dietrich Stanhope, Melly, holding Tesora, Sparky, and I arose to accompany him into a room badly in need of paint. A cumbersome X-ray machine usurped most of the space. Though Melly stroked Tesora's arms and hair in an effort to soothe her, the baby cried softly on a table while her interior organs were exposed on film. (On Camden Drive in Beverly Hills, the X-ray technician would have asked us to leave for our own protection.) A few minutes later we were conducted to a small examination room.

Each of us, nervous for our own reasons, hardly spoke for the forty or so minutes we waited for Dr. Martinez. At last a round-faced, gray-haired grandfather of a man entered the room carrying Tesora's X rays. "Ah, Dr. Stanhope, I presume," he said and held out his hand.

I smiled because I had often seen that particular greeting—though it referenced a Dr. Livingston—as a caption in *New Yorker* cartoons. It required a jungle setting, two befuddled Englishmen, and several bristly-haired, bones-through-their-noses natives with cooking pots. Just who were the Englishmen here, I wondered.

"As I told you on the telephone, I'm a doctor no longer,"

Dietrich responded, his tic more active than usual as he shook the doctor's hand. "That's why I've come to you."

⁓ "We have different laws governing medicine south of the border, but they have been beneficial to many North Americans. So I can extend professional courtesy while you are here. I am very glad to be at your service." Dr. Martinez spoke distinctly and politely as he lifted Tesora from Melly's arms. He said, *"Muchas gracias, Señorita."*

"Please be careful with her," Melly said.

"But of course I'll be careful," the doctor promised, tenderness infusing his soft Fernando Lamas English. I approved of the way he held Tesora, letting her get familiar with his voice, touch, and smell before he set her down for the examination.

No doctor in my vast experience had ever given *me* such a thorough examination, but we all knew Tesora had an authentic disease.

"There is no question," Dr. Martinez said while cradling the baby in his arms, "that Tesora has TB." After handing her back to Melly, he showed us eerie shadows on her X rays.

"She won't have to stay in a hospital," I blurted out plaintively, "will she?"

"A superb hospital would be ideal for her," Dr. Martinez said. "But there is no such place here. Fortunately babies aren't very good at spreading the tuberculosis bacilli. It's an airborne disease, and babies can't cough hard enough to disperse their germs."

"But shouldn't we wear masks just in case?" I asked.

"Especially Melly? Melly sleeps with Tesora." I wanted to explain to him that Melly was sick, too, but if he was privy to that information, he might remove Tesora from our care.

"Yes, absolutely, the wearing of protective masks is a reasonable precaution," the doctor said.

"Okay, now *we're* safe," Melly said, a little impatiently. "But what's going to happen to Tesora?"

"On that score I have good news. There is a medicine recently developed that I am able to prescribe for Tesora. I will give you a prescription for Isoniazid, and you can buy it here in Nogales. It costs very much less in Mexico than in the States," Dr. Martinez said. "Tesora should begin medication today. If you take very good care of your baby, if you bring her back to me monthly, I think we can, eh, relieve her of the symptoms for a long time to come."

Melly smiled so broadly that her eyes closed. "I'll do whatever it takes," she vowed. "By the way, do you have any idea how old she is?"

"She might have as many as six months or as little as three," Dr. Martinez said. "The disease has probably decelerated her growth."

"Will she be able to catch up?" Melly asked with urgency, perhaps because her own growth had been abbreviated by disease.

"I am optimistic," Dr. Martinez said.

As we were leaving, I heard Dietrich say to the doctor, "I'm surprised you didn't ask who this baby belongs to. In the States—"

"I can see she is getting excellent care. What more could such a baby ask for? Mexico is a poor country. We have learned to be flexible," the doctor said. "All I ask is to examine her each month to determine the correct dosage."

On the way back to the car, we stopped at a *farmacia* and purchased a month's supply of Isoniazid, along with needles and a syringe. (I added one garish, oversize Mickey Mouse piñata to the tab.) The pharmacist himself administered the first dose, demonstrating to Melly and me just how to do it. During the process Melly asked countless questions.

Since Sparky had no idea that pesos were the currency of the Mexican realm, she couldn't help me with the mathematics of paying the bill in dollars. I'd discovered that I enjoyed writing checks for whopping amounts. One of these days Maurice would notice that I'd bought *drugs* in Mexico for hundreds of pesos.

Nudging me, Melly said, "This is probably a good time to reimburse Dietrich for the gas he's used and the wear and tear on his car."

"Oh, right," I said and penned in the generous amount of twenty dollars.

Dietrich accepted my check, but his face resumed its familiar doleful expression. "I wish I could tell you to forget this. There was a time when—"

"Don't mention it," I said. "It's not a personal sacrifice on my part."

Only when he found his automobile unscathed did Dietrich's face relax and the number of tics decline. Lamentably, though, it became our medical adviser's task to extract the Adjudicator from the bar across the street. A recalcitrant Mr. St. Cyr eventually permitted himself to be manhandled into the automobile. Moments later he seemed to be stewing with self-congratulatory fuel. "I ate the worm, Dietrich! I ate the worm!" he kept remarking on our long drive home. Or at least that's what I thought he said through his inebriated brume. "I bit down hard and masticated the crusty old thing. And then I . . . You have to finish the bottle to get to the worm. Today I pulverized the rascal between my teeth."

"Since when did you start drinking mezcal, Saint?" Dietrich asked reproachfully.

"What does he mean? About the worm?" Melly asked.

I thought "the worm" must be another way of saying the bottom of the barrel, which was what a dipsomaniac had to hit, according to my mother, before he could reform.

Dietrich ignored Melly's question because he was lambasting Mr. St. Cyr. "I'm warning you, Saint. Don't you dare croak, pass out, or throw up on my leather interior. Don't taint my lovely, chaste automobile with your addlepated condition."

In the month between Tesora's January and February appointments, we settled into a routine. Weekdays, while we attended our classes, Conchita devoted much of her attention to Tesora. By now the Four-Letter Four had achieved familiarity, even camaraderie and mutual trust, with the inhabitants of the migrant-worker camp. Only Twyla resisted our junkets, as she called them.

We didn't mind her disinterest until it interfered with our second return trip from Nogales. Melly had rigged her poncho to shelter Tesora, but when she, Sparky, and I entered the rec hall, Lizzie jumped up from the bedraggled couch. "Twyla says you can't go in our room right now. She says to stay with Sparky until she calls for you."

"But we need to go in for diapers and formula," I argued. "All kinds of stuff."

"Our books, for example," Melly said. "We *are* supposed to study once in a while. And I have a test."

"Twyla kicked me out of there about a half hour ago. She says she really needs privacy now. For my cooperation, she's gonna buy me new stirrups. And, oh yeah, she says she'll buy Tesora anythin' you want," Lizzie said.

"What's Twyla doing that's so private?" Sparky asked. "Dyeing her pubic hair?"

"Uh-uh," Lizzie said. "She's got a man in there."

"Really!" Sparky said with delight. "It isn't Mr. Party Time, by any chance?"

"Heck no. *This* guy's hot-diggety handsome," Lizzie exclaimed.

I loitered in the rec hall for over twenty minutes before I could no longer endure the suspense. I knocked first, of course, but I didn't allow Twyla time to say "go away" before opening the door.

If anyone had asked me to speculate on the identity of

Twyla's guest, I would have chosen Al Mandell conferring with her about further expenditures. But the man sitting on her bed was not the rumpled, world-weary, dispassionate person I had come to believe comprised all detectives who weren't my mother. This man appeared to be no more than ten years older than Twyla, in the prime of his life. And his tan, his neatly manicured fingernails, the elegant cut of his suit and his hair implied a life of summering on yachts and wintering in cities renowned for their men's shops. Obviously one of the scions of the aristocracy Twyla had dated, he must have traced her whereabouts to present a proposal of marriage. Complimenting myself on my powers of deduction, I cheerily said, "Hello!"

"Fleur," Twyla announced with a prideful yet jubilant curl of her lips, "I want you to meet my father."

I laughed at the preposterous notion, but I felt distressed by Twyla's patrilineal obsession.

"There's nothing funny about it," Twyla spoke sternly. "My father has been searching for me for years. And finally, no thanks whatsoever to Al Mandell—after all the money I've paid him—my father located me on his own."

"Great to meet you, Daddy-o," I said in an attempt to let them both know I couldn't be hoodwinked.

Twyla appeared to seethe, but before she could say anything, the gentleman stood up and graciously reached out to shake my hand. "I only discovered my darling's whereabouts a few days ago. And although I considered making our reunion a birthday surprise, I simply couldn't wait." He spoke with a slight accent vaguely reminiscent of Cary Grant's.

"Pleased to meet you," I said. "But come on, who are you really?"

"Stop it, Fleur. You're embarrassing me terribly," Twyla complained.

The gentleman interrupted Twyla, telling her to breathe deeply and let her lungs deflate while she counted to ten. Then he turned to me and said soberly and convincingly, "In all honesty, Fleur, I *am* Twyla's father. My name is Gordon Denver."

Contrite and sheepish, I hardly knew what to say. "Denver? Spelled like the city?" I spluttered.

"I hope so," he said, reseating himself on Twyla's bed and crossing his knees just so. "Denver itself was named after my great-grandfather. Silver lured him to Colorado, and silver kept my family there."

"Oh," I said, picturing a baby in sumptuous chambers on a bed of silver spoons. "Do you live there now?"

"No, no, I needed bigger horizons, entrepreneurially speaking. I've moved around quite a bit, which is probably why Twyla's detective couldn't locate me. I'm developing a chunk of Texas right now."

"I don't know anything about Texas," I confessed.

"You will, you will. Twyla will invite you to see our magnificent new manse," Mr. Denver said.

"Yes," Twyla exclaimed. "Everything is as I envisioned it. Father has enticed me to live with him in Oreal, Texas. It's a gorgeous new suburb of Austin. Don't you just love the sound of Oreal?"

"That's my girl," Mr. Denver said proudly. "Isn't she beautiful? Isn't she the perfect daughter? All right, Twyla.

Whatsay you start packing right now. I'll return for you in what, one? Two hours? We'll dine tonight at my luxury resort hotel in the beautiful hills. Then tomorrow we'll fly home to Oreal."

"Home." Twyla repeated the word in a dulcet tone.

"Home?" I repeated, though the word chafed the walls of my throat. "Twyla, please, you can't. Not yet. Not with so much going on here. You'll miss out. Don't you want to see Tesora grow strong? And you won't finish the semester. You won't graduate."

"Finding my father is all the graduation I need," Twyla informed me.

When Mr. Denver left, Twyla beckoned Melly and Lizzie back into our room. The three of us sat around like deflated birthday balloons. Even though it was three weeks away, we'd already made reservations for a party in a private room at the Lobster and Loins Restaurant in downtown Tucson for Twyla's eighteenth. For dessert Sparky had planned to whip up an Oreo Snow Swirl cake straight from the pages of *Life* magazine. Now, however, we could only watch Twyla arrange for the first day of what she termed her new, *genuine* life.

"Your leaving school is going to put an end to the Four-Letter Four," Sparky reminded Twyla.

"So be it," she said.

We lugged Twyla's trunks from the cleaning closet and tried to help her pack, but even after she gave away the less loved artifacts from her wardrobe, folding and compressing all her belongings defeated us.

"Wait a minute!" Twyla's voice rang out. "Father indicated

we're in a luxury hotel, did he not? All we have to do is cram everything into these trunks. At the hotel I can ask housekeeping to pack them properly. They'll do a professional job, stuffing the toes of my shoes so they don't get squashed and layering my sweaters with scented tissue paper. Thanks to my mother, I know how to finesse the staff in fine hotels, how to use the concierge as a personal assistant, and so forth."

"How?" Melly asked.

"On your arrival, you make a point of giving everyone who might be useful a moderate tip. It encourages them to do anything you request, no matter how arduous. You know why? Because they're assuming you'll be Lady Bountiful with the gratuities when you check out," Twyla elaborated as we stowed clothes and perfumes and souvenirs into the drawers of the trunks.

"So you don't tip them when you leave?" Melly asked.

"Moderation is the byword," Twyla said.

The disquieting thoughts I had about Mr. Denver muffled Twyla's tips on tipping. Why couldn't I trust the man? Without Charmian to script the indisputable need for handcuffs on his elegant wrists, I had no answers.

While I played, of all things, horsey in an effort to amuse Tesora, Twyla crammed French underwear into a trunk and enlightened me further about the man I'd just met. "Dad is so simpatico, don't you think? He's going to throw a huge party for my birthday at his country club. And he promises he won't for a minute let Mother horn in on my inheritance. We're going to set up some joint accounts at his bank and stock brokerage. Dad knows ways of hiding my assets and keeping my taxes at a minimum."

"Is he making it a joint account so he can add money to it?" I asked, thinking of my own bottomless checking account.

"I don't have time to explain it right now," Twyla brushed me off.

"And aren't you calling him Dad awfully soon?"

"*Dad*," Twyla enunciated, "said that taxes are the scourge of the rich."

"Well, my father says he's proud to pay taxes," I felt compelled to mention. "Maurice says that the heft of their taxes proves that he and my mother have made weighty contributions to the world."

"But Maurice and Charmian are *nouveaux riches*," Twyla said. "The *vieux riches* loathe taxes."

Then I heard myself ask a question that could have hailed directly from Charmian on *The Radio Mystery Half Hour*. "You didn't happen to ask for his . . . credentials? That is to say, did Gordon Denver give you any actual proof that he's related to you by blood?"

"Oh, Fleur, you're such a sheep. Everything to you is a mystery plot. I'm amazed you're not insinuating that Dad is a murderer, too."

"That's just it—you don't know anything about him," I burst out.

"I've seen him. I've sized him up. He's pure Anglo-Saxon, thank God. He had ancestors on the *Mayflower*. Gordon Denver is exactly what I need right now," Twyla said adamantly. "Now, if I can just get Dirk to take my trunks to the hotel."

Four taxis were enlisted to ferry my friend, her new father, and all her luggage to the hotel. At the last moment Twyla bestowed a kiss on each girl's cheeks, making it a French farewell. "Fleur, you don't mind if I take this with me, do you? I've been reading it and it's great." She displayed the copy of *Noblesse Oblige* that I had found in the library on my first night at school. Before I could protest, Twyla hugged and kissed me melodramatically. (If only Odiline had been present to restrain Twyla's theatrics.) Twyla made it abundantly clear that her heart and soul had already migrated to the wide-open spaces of Texas.

XVI

HOME ECONOMICS

"Please hurry," Mrs. Prail exhorted me. "There's an urgent call for you. It's from Hollywood," she added excitedly once she'd extracted me from my classroom.

My mother, in order to prevent delays, regularly alerted secretaries that her calls to their bosses were urgent. And only she would be phoning from Hollywood. When I picked up the receiver, I said, "Hello, Charmian."

"How did you guess that it was . . . *c'est moi?*"

"I didn't guess. I extrapolated," I said, quoting an oft-used line of dialogue from her show.

Eager to get to the purpose of her call, Charmian ignored the allusion. "*Ooh la la, ma petite* Fleur, I have news," she said. "Fortuitous circumstances have come my way. But what I'm about to tell you is very hush-hush. Can you keep a secret?"

"Depends," I toyed with her.

"I'm sure you're aware that the featured celebrity guests of shows on the little screen, such as *This Is Your Life*, aren't supposed to know ahead of time that they're about to be profiled."

"I'm not a slave of TV the way you are," I sassed.

"Well, your father—the dear boy—has clandestinely arranged for me to be . . . lionized on *Celebrity Surprise*. Isn't that *merveilleux*? They'll be doing an hour-long—how shall I call it—present-day biography of yours truly."

"That should be interesting," I said, noticing that I'd wrapped the phone cord around my arm so many times it looked like a sleeve.

"It should and will be. And your participation is required."

"Like what?" I asked, my stomach suddenly queasy.

"The producers will contact you to confirm a date," Charmian said. "I forget their names, but they'll identify themselves. You'll have to feign astonishment when they call. Promise me right now that you won't overact. And don't mention this to your schoolmates, either—not until closer to the shooting date. I did consider suppressing the information that I had a child, but Maurice said your birth is one of public record. Imagine! Being in the public eye has cost me my privacy."

"So when's the show?" I asked. "Are they going to fly me to L.A.? Will I have to say asinine things from behind a curtain until you recognize my voice?"

"*Celebrity Surprise* doesn't use that format," Charmian

informed me. "Not at all. They won't be introducing an aged relative, my first-grade teacher, or any other gorgons from my past, thank god! They work in the present. They'll interview you on your campus and then do a cinematic montage of the grounds. That's it, *chérie*, I'll let the producer tell you the rest. I'm off *à toutes jambes* to get my hair permed. I suggest you do the same."

"Charmian, haven't you listened to one word I've been telling you about Rancho Cambridge West?"

"Call here the minute you've heard from the producer," she said. Charmian let the dial tone say *au revoir.* Quietly I freed my arm from the telephone cord and placed the receiver in the cradle. "Good-bye, Mrs. Prail," I called as I left her apartment.

The implications of a visit from *Celebrity Surprise* fogged my concentration during afternoon classes. Perseus had saved his mother, Danae, from a fate worse than death (marriage to King Polydectes), but, I wished to ask an oracle, did I have a filial duty to rescue Charmian?

Twyla's birthday had come and gone and we'd heard nothing. So on the Sunday morning preceding our eleventh visit to the migrant-worker camp, I had high hopes when summoned to the telephone.

Jerry Golblatz from *Celebrity Surprise* began explaining his shooting schedule. "I'm giving you fair warning in case you need a trip to the beauty parlor," he said. "We'll be in Tucson three weeks from tomorrow."

"Should I expect to be interviewed?" I asked.

"Absolutely. People around the country are extremely curious about the life of a movie star's daughter."

"Mr. Golblatz, do they really consider Charmian a movie star? Do you?"

"Yes, well, Charmian Leigh is someone who is *in* movies," the producer equivocated. "That makes her plenty interesting to *our* audience."

"What questions will I have to answer?" I asked.

"I'm sure you've been asked all of them before," he said, with what I thought was a sigh.

"I'm very flattered that you've asked me to participate," I said diplomatically, "but I don't think my school is ready for . . . Hollywood. The disruption of cameras and crew would be unwelcome here."

"Not at all, not at all. I checked it out. The headmaster's wife was telling me that her husband is an accomplished actor, so we've agreed to interview him, too. And the owner is gung ho. Publicity is publicity, even in the education industry. We're giving the school airtime, kiddo, you see what I mean?"

"I see," I told the producer, and we said good-bye.

While I readied myself to leave for the migrant-worker camp, I told Melly, "If this school is shown on national television, my parents' names will be mud from coast to coast. But how am I going to convince them of this?"

"Let it be. Let the chips fall where they may. Let sleeping dogs lie. Let the trees in the forest fall unheard. Let slip the dogs of war. Let them eat cake . . ." Melly, though she seemed tired, recited a brief compendium of *Bartlett's Familiar Quotations*. She had lost all tolerance for my parents' deficiencies.

"I know, but somehow I feel sorry for them," I said.

"Anything that happens to them in connection to this school serves them right," Melly said.

"I basically agree with you, but I'm still thinking. Maybe seeing the workers will clear my head."

"Speaking of them, I'm not sure what to do," Melly said. "Dr. Martinez upped Tesora's dosage yesterday, and she's kind of punky today. But seeing her parents and siblings is probably the be-all, end-all remedy for any child. And what will her parents think?"

"If you think Tesora should stay home, well, she should. Missing one week with her parents can't hurt her too much—I think I can explain it to them. And a rest would be good for you, too," I said.

"If I stay here, Dr. Prail will say I've shirked my responsibility. He'll penalize me by adding extra Sundays. What I really should do is let Lizzie take care of Tesora and go on out there with the rest of you."

"Be honest, Melly. After today there are only two more Sundays in our three months of Sundays. When it's over, you aren't going to stop visiting the migrant camp. You'll be going until they move on. I know you will."

"Yeah, I guess you're right."

* * *

As the weeks had progressed, other students had joined our Sunday community service. We'd sardined ourselves in the station wagon, but now this Sunday Dirk had to roll out the rust-streaked, slightly listing school bus.

"What made you decide to join us?" I asked the new volunteers.

"Nothing else to do," said Dena.

"Supposedly the camp kids are worse off than us. This I gotta see," Cuyler said.

Some of my friends in Beverly Hills had spent a summer in Israel to experience "dedication and hard work." Could the migrant camp be considered a poor man's kibbutz?

When we'd all boarded and seated ourselves, the bus leaned severely to the left. "Okay, Cuyler and Eddie, on the double, get your fannies into right-side seats," Dirk hollered to the tallest and heaviest of the boys.

Cuyler moved across the aisle, but Eddie refused. Eddie, under the impression that Dirk didn't know one student from another, called out, "I *am* sitting on the right." I could see his shoulders bouncing with laughter a few rows in front of me on the left.

"It ain't possible," Dirk muttered as he grudgingly trudged down the aisle. "Okay, okay," he said on spotting Eddie. "You want to gull me—fine! I got all the time in the world." Dirk then returned to the driver's seat, dropped into it, crossed his legs, and leaned his head back into the palms of his hands. His Stetson covered his face.

Cuyler stood up and sat down again quickly, and Eddie did the same. This caused the bus to lurch, sag, and rock. "Hey, Roller Derby!" someone yelled while other students delightedly joined the boys in testing the shock absorbers. "Wanna bet we can tip this buggy over?" someone else gaily recommended. Dirk didn't move a muscle.

Only when boredom began nibbling away at the edges of the fun did Brian stand up. As though traversing a swaying bridge over a jungle abyss, he staggered to the front of the bus. "Okay, okay, shut up a minute," Brian shouted. "If you're on this bus because you decided to make some little kid's life nice for a couple of hours, you better get with it. The longer we mess around here, the less time the kids are going to have . . . to have a good time."

Taking his message to heart, several of the students arose and, with the humor of participants in a game of musical chairs, tried out various seating arrangements to see if they could balance the bus.

Seated alone by a window during the boys' shenanigans, I hadn't expected Brian to slide in next to me. "There we go," Brian called to Dirk. "We're in perfect balance now."

"Hey, what about me?" Lionel called to Brian.

"Try to take care of yourself for a few minutes, will you?" Brian told him, sounding sweet and annoyed at the same time. Everyone turned to see what the two were talking about. I liked being noticed in Brian's company.

"Um. I don't know if I ever mentioned that you cutting my nails that time was the best thing anyone's ever done for me," Brian said as soon as the bus sallied forth.

He *had* thanked me frequently, so I assumed he was using the subject as an icebreaker. "I noticed that you've been keeping them short on your own," I ventured.

"I file them down. It really keeps me from scratching. And since I can't scratch, and the itches realize it, they seem to give up itching for a while."

"Thanks for thanking me," I said, wishing he'd take hold of my own smooth hand, and wondering if the fact that he didn't meant he cared less for me than I'd like.

At the encampment, I made the usual pilgrimage to Tesora's parents' hut and, with Becillia's help, endeavored to account for the absence of Melly and Tesora. They understood and treated me kindly, and then Tesora's mother shyly handed me a large, ill-shaped clod of dried wheat or grass covered by a flour sack. Only after I'd turned it over several times did I recognize it as a pitiful replica of a doll. A lumpy doll made by a lumpen people, Charmian would have said.

"*Muchas gracias, voy a darle a Tesora,*" I said, thrilled to use the simple Spanish I'd learned.

While I'd been quasi-communicating with Tesora's family, Brian had taken the children out onto the now parched lake bed, strung netting lower than the norm between poles, and chiseled the lines of a volleyball court into the dehydrated mud. Where he'd found a relatively clean, fully inflated volleyball, I couldn't imagine.

With a patience that no teacher at Rancho Cambridge West had exhibited, Brian strove to teach not only the migrant children but his fellow students the rules and finesse of the game. If the ball actually made it over the net on a serve and was returned, both teams deemed it a victory. "Hey, that's great, you're doing swell," Brian would tell first one child and then another. And whether or not they could understand his English, his tone of voice made them beam with pride.

With the check I'd given her, Sparky had bought refreshments. Enthusiastic about being our purchasing agent, she'd begun keeping a ledger. Sparky now spoke earnestly about the economy of such new products as Tang and Carnation instant milk (with magic crystals). Preparing refreshments, mixing the powders into containers of water (fresh from the taps at school), she proudly announced, "Tang comes to around five cents a serving, but Carnation costs only two and a half cents."

"Then why doesn't Tang taste twice as good as Carnation?" I asked.

The children slurped the beverages gluttonously, then gathered around a large cardboard box Melly had sent along. In it they found the fusty, forgotten books from the library/canteen. I had assumed reading to the boys and girls would be futile because the books were in English, the helpers poor readers, and, as I'd been told, most of the children had never been to school. But, sitting on the dry, sticky soil with their thin paper cups of chemicals, the little ones appeared mesmerized by the sound of the words and the print on the pages.

"Wouldn't it be great if we could raise enough money to buy them real reading books, like *Dick and Jane*, so they could learn English?" Sparky asked.

"I'll write you a check when we get back to school."

"Wow, you must be loaded," she exclaimed.

"Maybe I am. I plan to keep spending until I find out," I confided. "So long as it's for a good cause."

During the bus ride home, Brian sat with me again. He must like my company, I reflected, and made my right hand available by placing it on the seat between us. Charmian wouldn't have stopped with so subtle a gesture. She would have feigned an inspection of Brian's fingernails; she would have stroked his palms. But my mother's methodology with men embarrassed me. Brian and I bounced along silently, except for the creaking of the bus and the chatter of the other students, for what seemed like eons.

"Brian, do you have a wife or something at home?" I asked shamelessly. It was a line from one of Charmian's movies.

He laughed. "A wife? I'm sixteen years old."

"Well, it's possible. If you were from India, it would be probable."

"What makes you ask?" he said slyly.

As we talked, we had faced forward, but now I turned to him. "I was just wondering why you don't want to hold hands."

Brian scrunched his forehead. "I want to," he said. "It's just that, um, I didn't think you'd want to."

"Why wouldn't I?" I asked.

"Because . . . because my skin's so disgusting."

"No, it isn't."

"It is. It's all rashy and rough."

"But I saw your hands before. I held them, remember? You didn't pull them away then. And I wasn't disgusted."

"Because you were playing nurse."

"Oh, okay, so pretend I'm playing nurse now."

And then Brian did a remarkable thing. He took my hand in both of his, as though it were a precious object. Laughing, he said, "You play nurse. I'll play doctor."

I felt thrilled to the point of giddiness. Someone I cared for cared for me in return! Significantly, I had asked for something I wanted and received it.

On our return to school, I headed toward the pay phone. "Before I start this conversation, I want Maurice to get on the extension," I told Charmian.

"No can do," Charmian said in her hard-boiled detective manner.

"Is Maurice home?"

"Barely."

"Then yes can do. Tell him that if he doesn't come to the phone this minute, I swear I will say the most spiteful, venomous things about you on *Celebrity Surprise.*"

"Fleur de dear, of course you won't," Charmian said, clucking at the preposterousness of my statement. However, she towed my father to the downstairs extension in record time.

"Charmian, Maurice," I began, "I know it isn't your habit to listen to me or take—"

"Get to the point," Maurice interjected.

"—my advice," I bravely continued. "But I'm telling you that if you don't ban the cameras from Rancho Cambridge West, you will become the laughingstocks of fan magazines and, for that matter, *The Hollywood Reporter* and *Variety*. For your own good, you must prevent that TV company from coming here. If you don't, you will never forgive yourselves."

I spoke brusquely, but I had their welfare at heart. Hadn't they spent all the years I'd known them striving to sand, smooth, and polish all surfaces of their lives into a slick, gleaming veneer? One zoom of a camera lens into the heart of Rancho Cambridge West, and no publicist, no matter how high-powered, would be able to undo the image. The work, the fabrications, the falsifications, the canards of my parents' lives would have been for naught.

"What on earth are you talking about?" Charmian asked.

Ha, I thought, *my impertinence has paid off.* I'd captured my mother's attention at last. "Charmian, Maurice, I've told you all you need to know. I have nothing further to say." Then, not unlike my mother, I rudely replaced the receiver on the cradle without saying good-bye.

Four days passed during which Tesora slept all day and cried all night. We tried to mollify her with the doll from home, the rattle, a new stuffed bear and rabbit. We sang. We walked her. We pleaded. By this point, none of the girls in the dorm could sleep. I blamed the medication; Melly believed the tears were caused by teething. Lizzie said, "If Tesora was a horse, you'd know she had stomach trouble."

"We've got to call Dietrich, or even Dr. Martinez," I implored Melly. "Tesora could die, do you realize that, all because we didn't do anything. Why did we separate her from her family? Because we thought we could do a better job. We have to do *something*."

"You're sounding panicky," Melly said.

Without question or complaint, Dietrich made a house call in the middle of the night. After a thorough examination during which the patient actually smiled, the doctor sat down on Melly's bed. "I've got news for you. This baby is a lot healthier now. And although I know nothing about children—never had any, never will—I've been dipping into *Dr. Spock*. A brilliant pediatrician, on paper, at any rate. I think he'd say that the crying you've reported to me is a case of the baby's clock being turned around."

"The Case of the Turned-Around Clock." I could hear my mother saying it as she concocted a story of mayhem, espionage, and insomnia.

"Now, here's what you do. No matter how sleepy Tesora is during the day, you must must must stimulate and entertain her, anything to keep her awake. At night you make the room as still as can be, and if she cries, you do nothing. Do not mollycoddle her. Wear earplugs if need be, but do not react. She has to learn to calm down and put herself back to sleep."

"This sounds like a job for Perseus," I said. "Not for ordinary mortals."

* * *

In order to "stimulate" Tesora during daylight hours, Melly, Sparky, Lizzie, and I took shifts dashing about the campus between classes to track down our baby and her custodian. On finding Conchita as she swept and swabbed the school, I'd whoop it up singing my own rendition of Paul Anka's "Tonight My Love, Tonight" as I tried to subliminally suggest to Tesora that the night was meant for slumber. I also made funny faces and turned cartwheels until dizziness set in. Then I'd dash back to class.

When classes finished at three o'clock, the full force of the Four-Letter Four (we'd invited Lizzie to replace Twyla) applied supreme dynamism and ingenuity to keep Tesora awake. For the moment Sparky and I were simulating a walk. I held Tesora under the arms, letting her body sway while Sparky lay on the floor controlling her feet as though the baby were a puppet with missing strings.

Over our cheers of encouragement and Tesora's own exhilarated squeals, we could hear a commotion of girls' shrieks and applause somewhere close to the canteen. Before it quieted down, Lizzie skulked in, the heels of her boots clunking on the tiles as usual.

"What's going on?" we asked.

"Beats me," Lizzie said. "The kids are acting like a herd of jackdaws just because someone famous walked in."

"What's a jackdaw?" I asked.

"Dunno," Lizzie said. "It's something my parents say."

"What someone famous?" Melly asked.

"Nobody I recognize. She's—"

"Do you think it's your mother?" Melly asked me.

"My mother was a radio star. Not many people outside of Los Angeles—"

Before I could finish my sentence, Melly had tossed Tesora on the bed and run from the room. By accident, my roommate had struck upon what became Tesora's favorite game, one that would keep her awake for many days. Our baby began butting her head forward repeatedly until I finally understood she wished to be bounced on the bed again. I'd picked up and dropped the giggling Tesora four-teen times before Melly, now breathing hard, returned.

"Get ready," Melly warned me. "When she's through giving autographs, she'll be coming this way."

"Autographs? Charmian? I can't believe she came."

"The kids are going ape," Melly said.

"But they've never heard of her."

"But they've seen her on-screen. They recognize her."

"Oh, shoot. And what about Tesora?"

"Quick, give her to me. I'll take her to Sparky's room," Melly said and instantaneously spirited Tesora away.

I could hear the tumult of Charmian and her newfound retinue echoing through the rec hall. Boisterous questions and wisecracks bombarded my mother before she flounced into my room. The slamming of the door behind her spoiled Charmian's customary majestic entrance somewhat. But then she had only Lizzie and me to serve as her audience.

"Darling Fleur de," my mother addressed me, as she often did, as though I were John Q. Public. "Here I am. I've come to see my little girl."

Charmian didn't deign to grant me a hug—not that I expected one—so it took me only a moment to heed her odd attire. She had on a pearly pink short-sleeve blouse, the tails of which, rather than being tucked in, were tied together in a knot to expose her midriff. And yes, the climate in Tucson had turned hotter, but in my estimation, that didn't absolve Charmian from wearing shorts so short as to be vulgar.

Another rather pitiful element added to my mother's impropriety. She had always taken pride in her long Lloyd's of London–insured legs, but she must have recently discovered some sign of corrugation or other deterioration: under her shorts, cladding her thighs and calves, she had on flesh-colored ballet tights.

Charmian panned the room quickly with a critical eye. In a breathy voice, she sibilated, *"Sacrebleu!"*

Lizzie took Charmian's pronouncement as a greeting and said, "Nice to meet you, too, ma'am." This was Lizzie at her zenith of courtesy.

"I can see I'm heaven-sent," Charmian replied.

The door opened a crack—amplifying the shouts and their echoes in the rec hall—so that Melly could slip through. "Hello, Mrs. Leigh, I'm Melly," she said. "So nice of you to come. I've heard so much about you."

"You have?" my mother asked. She sounded sincerely bewildered, but it may have been because she'd just noticed the piles of diapers and baby toys that cluttered our room. "What *is* this? What is going on?"

Melly stepped forward. "Oh, that! *That?* Are you talking

about the baby stuff?" she asked with an inculpable giggle. "All of it's mine. For a report that's due . . . in home-ec class."

"Homek class? I've never heard of it," Charmian said.

"Home economics. How to run a home," Melly said with a sly grin. She no doubt remembered my mentioning Charmian's aversion to learning domestic skills.

"A home with babies in it?" Charmian said, involuntarily clutching her throat.

"Exactly," Melly said.

Despite the heat that had forced her into shorts and a bare midriff, Charmian sent forth a polar wind. "Fleur, it's time for you to get your things together and get the hell out of here."

"Why?" I asked warily. Right then I couldn't imagine leaving Tesora, not even for a single night.

"You'll stay at my hotel until I can secure an airplane ticket for you. Despite the fact that there were banshees impeding my every step, I've seen quite enough. My mind was made up incontrovertibly when I passed that cesspool the brochure depicted as suitable for Olympic swimming meets. To think I considered letting television people come down here to film," Charmian said. "I plan to ask for a return of the tuition. I think I should sue."

My roommates gaped at me with a combination of envy and melancholy. And I must have been sending them signals of anguish and indecision.

"Well, Fleur, this is what you've wanted from the first day," Melly said resignedly. "Better take advantage."

"If your mom would let Gwendolyn come along, I'd go with her lickety-split," Lizzie said generously.

"Where's your luggage?" my mother asked nonchalantly, as though it didn't occur to her that I had emotions with which to contend.

"Don't think about it. Just go," Melly instructed me. "For one thing, you'll get an education in Beverly Hills. You'll be better off in every way. You know you will."

"Do I?" I asked, trying to dam my tears.

XVII

A One-Woman Show

My mother, whose credo maintained that she stay at five-star hotels, could find no such accommodations in Tucson proper. Her travel agent had instead selected a resort far out of town "in the fingertips of the Catalina Mountains." Consequently, Charmian steered the rental Cadillac well away from the main highway, and suddenly only a quaint white fence separated us from vast verdant meadows. The entirety of a lake from some minor northern state must have been piped in to green the grasses. The placement of trees laden with apples and the dozen or so placidly grazing cows suggested Gainsborough's touch. Even the most remote signs of desert had been obliterated with a creditable facsimile of Switzerland.

"This is more like it," Charmian voiced her approval. With its Tyrolean chalets, the resort reminded me of Hollywood. I felt right at home.

Charmian napped until cocktail time. "There won't be anyone in the bar worth seeing or being seen by," she said. "So call room service. And do order a glass of wine for yourself. I don't want my martini feeling lonely."

"I'm underage," I reminded her.

"You're with an adult who gives permission. A drink might loosen you up."

"If I'm not loose, it's because I don't like the decisions you're making for me." In fact, since Thanksgiving, I'd had no appetite for liquor of any kind. But to prove I wasn't a boa constrictor, which is what Charmian implied, I requested the following from room service: "One martini, very dry, with a single drop of vermouth and one . . . white glove, if you please."

Sometime later Charmian's eyes widened with delight when the waiter, dressed in lederhosen and a feathered cap, entered our room shouldering a large silver tray with our drinks and a bowl of unshelled pistachios.

"Nice touch," Charmian said, raising her eyebrows to indicate the pistachios or, possibly, the waiter's bare knees. Soon she snuggled on the couch in the anteroom and lifted her glass, indicating I should do the same. "Here's to getting you out of a jam," she toasted me.

I took a few sips of my white glove and, relishing the syrupy farrago that did its best to combat any implication of alcohol, mentally tipped my hat to Al Mandell. Then I said, "I'm not in a jam. You are. You're the Celebrity Surprise. I'm just a student you yanked out of one high school and now another. All for your own purposes, not mine. You haven't even asked what I'd like to do."

Charmian partook of her beverage thoughtfully, as though she hadn't heard what I'd said. Then she asked, "Are you hungry? The people you'd want to meet never go to dinner this early. But I suppose here, in this town, restaurants don't stay open much later."

The hotel restaurant resembled an alpine forest. Columns were encased in a barklike substance to simulate tree trunks, and limbs of artificial fir reached out. I could have sworn I saw the maître d', who was leading a brisk pace to our woodland table, brush a branch out of our path.

Unwilling to chance a stain on her better clothes, Charmian had arrayed herself in an outdated and outré orange chiffon cocktail dress, the hem of which seemed to levitate near the middle of her thighs. It had been fashioned by Edith Head for a Doris Day movie, *Lifeboat for Two*, that had never been produced. I slunk behind my mother in the sheath I'd worn on my first day of school. I planned to make our dinner as contentious as possible.

Charmian didn't keep step with the maitre d'. She minced some distance behind him, giving every patron of the restaurant the opportunity to register her presence and appearance. And indeed I heard a few whispered remarks: "Isn't that . . . ?" "Dozens of movies." "Her name was—" "Leigh someone?" "Look there!" "Where?" "The lady detective from radio." "Didn't we see her in . . ?" "Queen of the B's." "A queen bee?"

Just before we arrived at our table, Charmian came to such an abrupt halt that I almost collided with her. "Royzy!" she called out. "Knock me down with an ostrich feather! What are you doing here?"

Three men whom I certainly hadn't expected to see—Royzy, Dietrich, and Mr. St. Cyr—arose in a kind of bent-kneed bow.

"Sit down, please, sit down. I don't want to detain you from your scrumptious-looking aperitifs," Charmian announced in her most beguiling manner. But while Royzy introduced his friends, the three remained in their half-squats, politely hinting for Charmian to mosey on.

"Dietrich Stanhope? *Dr.* Dietrich Stanhope?" Charmian asked archly, shooting an angry glance his way and stiffening into her detective persona. "I'd heard you'd given up your practice. I certainly hope my information is correct."

"Dietrich retired a few years back. He has nothing, *nada, niet, rien,* to do with medicine anymore," the Adjudicator assured Charmian.

"And what do you do, sir?" Charmian asked, goggling at Mr. St. Cyr's velveteen cloak.

"Most people would say I'm retired, too," Mr. St. Cyr said. The air passing through his nose indicated a laugh.

"What would you say?" Charmian grilled him.

Giving me one of his famous cinematic winks, Royzy interrupted what seemed to be the commencement of an inquisition. "Aren't you going to introduce the little one, Charmian?" No wonder Royzy received accolades for his acting: his wink confirmed that my secrets were safe with him; at the same time it cautioned me to hold my tongue.

"Oh, I forgot, this is Fleur de Leigh, my little daughter."

"Pleased to meet you," the three men said in their various manners of speech.

Lest my expression betray our association, I interrupted. "Charmian, the maître d' is waiting for us. He's found a table with a view."

"For the moment I prefer the view right here," Charmian called to our guide through the pinewood forest of tables. To Royzy she said, "I must confess, my curiosity has gotten the best of me. Might I sit here a moment or two and inquire what all of you are doing in a town like Tucson?"

"They're not producers," I whispered to my mother. "It's not as though they can further your career."

"Never mind," she said and aimed her heart-shaped backside at the small space beside Royzy.

Accordingly, the Adjudicator slid closer to Dietrich to give me room.

"Finding you here in this enchanting restaurant, without . . . your womenfolk, is a *coup de bonheur*," Charmian began her razzamatazz.

Mr. St. Cyr pulled his cloak tight around his chest and neck as though to suffocate any errant thoughts. "We're the lucky ones," he said with as much geniality as I'd ever seen him display. "Miss Leigh, you must tell us, what brings you to town? A play? A movie? Television? We don't have actresses of your caliber in Tucson every day."

My mother's countenance betrayed her quandary for only a second. Telling the truth would be tantamount to televising Rancho Cambridge West on *Celebrity Surprise*. "You won't believe what's happened," Charmian said. In town only a few hours and already she'd begun to manufacture a plot. "My little daughter is in school here. For her health, you see. She'd be completely incapacitated if she couldn't live in this arid clime. Well, the school we ultimately chose for her came with the most exceptionable endorsements. It has the highest scholastic achievement west of . . . the Euphrates. And Fleur is learning . . . calculus, physics, Latin, and Greek, and she's only twelve years old. I just couldn't be more pleased."

"*Twelve*, is she?" the Adjudicator interjected, obviously recalling my actual age of fifteen.

"Charmian forgot to mention that mythology is my favorite class," I said for Mr. St. Cyr's gratification.

"But recently the owner of the school wrote to me," Charmian continued. "A more awe-inspiring letter you couldn't imagine. I told him he should be in Hollywood, writing scripts with his unparalleled prose. The gist of his letter was this: in order to continue to attract teachers with Ph.D.'s from . . . Harvard and Oxford and . . . the French Academy, in order to maintain the beautiful grounds— Monet's garden pales beside them—the school is going to have to abolish its scholarship program. But if it does, and really, the administration is too kind-hearted to cut it out completely, the owner knows he will lose some of their most promising students to the mean streets of . . . Cleveland and . . . Springfield."

"There is nothing so wasteful as squandering a genius to Springfield," Royzy said.

"Hear hear," said Dietrich and Mr. St. Cyr in unison.

"Well, there you are. What could I do? I have come to their rescue," Charmian announced, lifting her chin high in the air and chewing the scenery, as she herself would have put it. "I'm lending my name and throwing in my talent, modest though it is, for a fund-raiser."

The three men passed an amused glance among them. Then Royzy, slippery as wet shoes, said, "A scholarship program at a fine school—what could be more humanitarian? I also want to keep those promising students off the mean streets. How would you like me to throw in my modest talent, too?"

Charmian's jaw drooped, but not for long. "Oh my, yes indeed. What could be better than adding your famous name to the bill? I'd love us to do something together," she said coquettishly. "But sad to say, I'm, eh, I'm . . . I've already done my bit. My act. I regaled them with a one-woman show just this afternoon."

"And I missed it," Royzy said, his face twisted with pain.

"Don't leave us out in the cold. Tell us what you did," Mr. St. Cyr urged her.

I saw Charmian's eyes flitting about as though danger lurked in every response. *"Eh bien,"* she said at last. "They wanted a historical figure, so I played Marie Antoinette. But you know"—and here she laughed—"without my costume and my grand seven-pound wig, I can't remember a word of the script."

I had to admire my mother's talent for improvisation. Evidently so did our companions, because they made no protest when Charmian proposed that we dine together. "If you don't mind," she said after she ordered lamb chops with mint jelly, "I've been holed up with Marie Antoinette for a month. I'd prefer to talk about you."

* * *

All night and all morning, while awaiting Charmian's awakening, I endeavored to compose a convincing argument for my return to Rancho Cambridge West. But when the wheels of the Cadillac at last began to roll, Charmian seized the reins of conversation: "What Royzy sees in that awful doctor and that strange saint, I can't understand. Some people say that Royzy is a fairy, but I really don't think so. He was squeezing my thigh adroitly under the table, and he's asked to 'see' me upon our return to civilization. A fairy would never seek a tête-à-tête with someone of my bottomless femininity."

"What makes you hate the doctor?" I asked.

"*Hate* is too mild a word. The cad was the premier surgeon in Beverly Hills a few years back, about the time I was signed to star in *Where the Ocean Meets the Sky*. That picture would have been my one big break in Hollywood," Charmian said.

"You never made *Where the Ocean Meets the Sky*."

"No kidding! Just before production began, the producer, who had a very minor problem with his spleen, was slaughtered on the operating table by none other than Dr. Stanhope. Later, an investigation proved that the surgeon had been drinking before and during the operation. Drinking! What kind of doctor is that? What kind of a human being is that? And when he killed my producer, he killed the movie along with my career," Charmian vituperated.

I wished to recount the manner in which Dietrich was making amends for his sin, saving Tesora's life and trying to salvage Mr. St. Cyr's. Instead I commended my mother. "It was good of you not to bring up the subject."

"It was either that—and you can't imagine how I wanted to tongue-lash the man—or cement my relationship with Royzy. If Royzy weren't such a stunner, I would have run Dr. Stanhope through the wringer."

We were well away from the chalet now, on a highway stretched over sand and lined with telephone poles that, I believed, led directly to the airport. The time had come to speak up. I took a breath. "Charmian, I'm glad that you have seen for yourself what a junk pile my school is. I've been wanting to come home more than anything, but—"

"Did I mention I called your father last night?" Charmian interrupted. "And unpleasant as it is, we agreed it's for the best if you remained at Rancho Cambridge West. What a pretentious name! But after all, you have only nine weeks left—we counted them up—until the end of the semester. We'd never get our tuition back, and if you came home now, your schooling would get out of whack."

I'd revved up my arguing engine and found it difficult to shift into reverse. "Gee . . . I'm glad you see things my way for a change," I said, unable to hide my astonishment. "It makes me feel that you actually listen to me on occasion."

"*Mais oui*, of course I listen to you," Charmian said.

"So what are you going to do about *Celebrity Surprise*?"

"Maurice is taking care of it. He'll phone Mr. Golblatz on Monday and explain that you aren't well. That you've had a relapse or something."

"A relapse? Of what?"

"Well, we don't want to be mendacious, so he plans to be terribly vague."

"So there really is nothing wrong with me?"

"Of course there isn't."

"If Maurice is vague, people will think the worst. Rumors will spread that I have beriberi or something."

"That's very cute," Charmian complimented me.

"I'd rather you didn't say I'm sick when I'm not. I have a future, too, you know."

"But your future is, well, in the future. When it comes, no one will remember what has been said today."

"*I* will. I wish I *could* forget what you say, but I seem to remember every word you've ever uttered. So I think it's best if I do the phoning. I will simply, politely, decline Mr. Golblatz's request for an interview. If he persists, I can say something sweeping, like not wanting to air dirty laundry in public."

"No! No mention of dirty laundry! It's too plebian. And I don't want my audiences thinking I have a negative child."

"Charmian, teenagers *are* negative. They're supposed to be."

"Well, I can't have that. I'm an actress, with a reputation for gaiety and optimism. My spirits must always be buoyed. No matter what you do, you must never drag me down. In public or privately, is that understood?"

"I've always understood," I said, giving the line an exceedingly theatrical reading.

* * *

Charmian dismissed me from the Cadillac near the Rancho Cambridge West sign. "No point in my surveying the campus again. I've had my fill. I'll be seeing you in a couple of months," she said. "Ta ta for now."

It being Saturday, the campus had been abandoned, every student evidently having qualified for a pass to town. Melly most likely had taken Tesora for a walk. I felt as though I'd entered a ghost town or the Hollywood equivalent thereof. By summer, Rancho Cambridge West *would* be a ghost town. Swinging my suitcase as I traipsed down the cement path, its cracks as familiar as the students, I pledged to myself that I would make these last months count.

"Hi," Brian said glumly. He'd been sitting, obscured by a shrub at the side of the pool, and I hadn't noticed. He didn't seem particularly pleased to see me.

"What's wrong?" I asked.

"It's the storm after the silver lining."

"Bri . . . Are you sad because you think I'm leaving school?" I asked a little too jubilantly. "Well, I'm not going, so you can cheer up."

"That's great," he said, but he still sounded dejected.

"What else?" I asked.

"The same old thing. So go on, tell me, I've got it easy. Tell me about the kids in wheelchairs or the ones in iron lungs," he said, looking ashamed. "My mother's given me that lecture about a thousand times. But she's my mother—she doesn't notice the mess I am. My skin . . ."

Brian stopped himself. "I guess I sound like some idiot girl."

"Your skin's not nearly as bad as you think," I told him.

"How would you know?" he asked angrily. "I keep it covered."

"I see your hands every day. I saw your arms that once."

"*Just* my arms," Brian said bitterly.

"Okay, then, why don't you show me the rest?" I dared him.

"I'm not in a mood to kid around."

"I'm not kidding. Not one bit. Take off your clothes and let me look. It's chancy for me, too, you know. Because maybe your skin is worse than Medusa's hair. Maybe one eensy glimpse of you will turn me to stone. But I'm betting it won't," I said.

Brian looked at me in a manner I couldn't readily interpret. Perhaps he was attempting to read my mind. Or did I detect some glint of appreciation in his eyes? He put his arm around my shoulders, big-brother-like. "You're not serious?" he asked.

"Yes, I am," I said emphatically, hearing somewhere in my head my mother adding, *you big lummox.*

He remained silent but didn't remove his arm from around my shoulders. His wholesome masculinity made me feel immensely secure, cherished even.

"Okay, we can go to my room. There's no one in the dorm right now. They're all at the movies," he said lightly, now challenging me. He expected me to bolt, but I slipped my arm around his waist and matched his stride.

A profound quiet saturated the boys' dorm, but it didn't—how could it—eliminate the foul smell of the beleaguered gym socks of twenty boys. I raised my hand to pinch my nose but quickly decided that Brian might misinterpret the gesture.

"Sit down, I guess," Brian said.

I set my suitcase near the door and looked for a chair. There being none, I seated myself gingerly at the foot of the bed.

Brian drew the shades loosely without obstructing all the sunlight. "You're sure you want to go through with this?" he asked, no doubt hoping I'd renege.

"*I* dared *you*," I reminded him.

Standing before me, a bit brazenly it seemed, Brian began unbuttoning his shirt. Starting at the collar and painstakingly moving downward, Brian turned into a butterfingers. When he understood I did not intend to leave, his fingers began to tremble. His shirt seemed to have an inordinate number of buttons.

Keeping his eyes on me, waiting no doubt for me to shield mine, Brian slid the shirt off his shoulders and away from his T-shirt, exposing only the here-red, there-grainy rash on his arms. There were no blood-blotched scratches running the length of them. I said nothing and continued to watch as impassively as I could. Brian bit his lip and then bashfully untucked his T-shirt from his jeans. After he pulled it over his head, exposing his mottled chest, he giggled. "It would be much more fun if you were stripping for me," he said.

I didn't answer. I believed that if I moved a single muscle, it would break the spell. However, Brian didn't resume his ecdysiastic exercise until I said, "I'm with you."

He smiled a little then, or maybe it was a smirk, as he kicked off his shoes and pulled down his jeans in a single swoop. His shorts hung low on his hips, hardly touching his indented abdomen. He wore boxers, I theorized, because jockey shorts would have exposed more of his flesh. I did notice that the rash had not neglected his legs. A furfuraceous coating delineated his knees.

"Go on," I encouraged him softly, keeping my gaze steady and as emotionless as possible.

Brian closed his own eyes, allowing me once again to admire his long lashes. Shyly, more like a girl than a boy, he lowered his undershorts. I had forgotten that men, too, grow pubic hair, and the thick dark grove around his penis startled me. But his penis surprised me more, because it had grown stiff. Then Brian did something frivolous and endearing—he pirouetted twice so that I caught a glimpse of his small, firm buttocks. They were oddly untouched by his ailment. Well, almost.

But I really wasn't seeing his skin anymore. Maybe the sloping light from the blinds was kind to him, but his physique interested me so very much more than his epidermis. Brian possessed perfect proportions. His deltoid and pectoral and gluteal muscles, and all the others whose names I'd neglected to memorize in biology class, were not the exaggerated bulges forced into life by dumbbells and weights. Brian's were naturally firm, compact, and gracefully shaped, the apples of his youth, the envy of any grown man.

In our living room at home, my mother kept a small bronze statue she had christened the Sleekèd Boy. And though he decidedly belonged to her, all through childhood I had gloried in his nakedness, admiring his perfect shape and speculating about his genitals on a daily basis.

Now it was as though I had received a gift from Aphrodite herself, my very own breathing, talking, feeling Sleekèd Boy. I felt a warmth, a compassion, a fascination for Brian that I'd never felt for anyone else, not even the statuette.

"So I guess you're revolted, right?" he asked.

"By only one thing," I responded while continuing to admire the whole of him.

"Oh yeah? What?"

"Your socks. They spoil the ambience."

Brian knelt to pull them off and then straightened again. I saw him frown at me, as if to say, *Now what?*

I, most assuredly, had not made any plans beyond this point. Brian had been a good sport, and by now, I believed, I had made my point that his rashes and bumps didn't repel me. I hoped he would intuit that other girls, or women, would react just as I had. Hesitantly, clumsily, and amazing even myself, I held out my arms.

Genuinely astonished, he stepped close, and his arms encircled me. It didn't take him nearly so long to undress me as it had to undress himself. It didn't even occur to me that his fingers were touching me in places I had hardly ever touched myself. But I had no wish to stop him. We squirmed and kissed and giggled and kissed again. Certainly I could feel the crusting on his skin, the *eschar*, as Melly's medical encyclopedia called it, that felt like a scattering of uncooked oatmeal. But I could also feel Brian's internal warmth and gratitude.

Perhaps due to his scaly skin, Brian became for me one of those mythological dolphins carrying me into an undiscovered sea. Though as he swam into the aquatic depths of myself, it seemed that he was the ichthyologist and I the rare fish.

If I felt pain, I endured it with the belief that every great adventure requires discomfort. Charmian had always intimated as much. Only too late did I remember my mother's caution that girls weren't physically ready for intercourse until they were over twenty-five years of age. I hadn't believed her at the time she'd parceled out such information, and now I felt that if it *was* true, Brian's welfare rested on my taking that risk.

Moments later, it didn't matter whether or not all the physical machinations that women were supposed to undergo in sexual liaisons happened to me. I felt thoroughly satisfied. I believed Brian and I were perfectly mated.

XVIII

Taking a Bath

After classes had finished for the day, I opened our dorm-room door, took a step, and tripped over a small bundle. "Wow," I said, hoisting Tesora to my lips. "Look at you. You're crawling!"

Tesora must have understood my pleasure in her achievement, because a prideful grin crinkled her face. It didn't erase my vexation with Conchita, who had left the baby alone.

"I'm sorry," a dreamy but distinct voice said. It emanated from Twyla's bed. Since she'd left school, her cot had evolved into a changing table and a repository for our growing inventory of baby supplies. Now someone had crawled under its covers. "I told Conchita she could leave. I told her I'd take care of the baby. And then I must have fallen asleep. I'm so dreadfully weary," Twyla said.

"Twyla? Is it really you?" I asked, sounding like a character in one of Charmian's melodramas. My emotions were divided between rapture that Twyla had returned and aggravation that she'd shirked responsibility. Nonetheless, with Tesora straddling my hip, I bounded to Twyla's side. Before I smothered her with questions—how did you? where were you? what happened? why didn't you stay?—I threw my arms around her. I'd missed my old friend terribly.

Twyla wrestled her body to a sitting position, and I observed her unkempt hair. Her complexion appeared blotched, lusterless; she hadn't been taking care of herself. And an unfamiliar appreciative tone crept into her voice when she said, "You have no idea how much the knowledge that I'd find you still here has bolstered what little spirit I have left."

"Oh dear. What happened?"

"Not to change the subject, but did I leave any bubble-bath powder behind?" she asked, sounding like the old Twyla and the older Daisy. "If so or if not, fill the tub, will you do that for me, please? I won't be coherent until I bathe."

It galled me to be taking orders from her, but sensing that she'd suffered another emotional cataclysm, I did my utmost.

Once Twyla had situated herself beneath the blanket of bubbles, she sighed and said, "Ah, this feels as purifying as baptismal waters."

While she basked, I undressed Tesora and, placing a

mound of towels under her, sat her at the other end of the tub. The baby stroked the bubbles and laughed at their fragility. She lifted handfuls of suds high in the air and let them slither down her arms with such enchantment that tears came to my eyes.

"Does she have to be in my bath?" Twyla complained. "That baby is sick, her lineage is absurd, and I've had as much misfortune as I can possibly stand."

"Tesora is the one with misfortune," I said indignantly, but the baby belied my statement by shrieking with joy at the globules of foam.

Twyla cringed.

"All right, I can take Tesora out and dry her, but she'll cry. Then I'll have to amuse her someplace else. Or I can keep her here, totally occupied with the bubbles, and catch up with you." As much as Twyla's return had piqued my curiosity, the baby's welfare came first.

"Leave her in the tub, then."

I knelt and leaned against the tub's rim. If Tesora slipped, I would be sure to grab her.

My old friend's countenance sagged with exhaustion, or dejection, as she attempted to relate her recent escapades. "At dinner in the hotel the night I left RCW, I would have told you my future looked as promising as . . . I don't know. A wedding cake? No, they get sliced up and devoured. In any event, Dad made everything about Texas seem fresh and glamorous. A sweet, ripe casaba melon, he said Texas was, ready for the plucking. It sounds tacky now, but at the time I was thoroughly smitten.

"No sooner had our plane touched down in Austin than Dad spirited me about fifty miles away from the airport to the highest mountaintop. That's not to say that there are many mountaintops in the vicinity, or that they're very high."

"Texas is flat as a pancake, isn't it?" I asked.

"More like a crepe," Twyla said. "There are hillocks here and there. And on one particular, well, hilltop, Dad proudly gave me a tour of a spanking-new mansion with a spanking-new guesthouse and pool, so new, in fact, that construction hadn't been completed. Walking through curlicues of lumber and dunes of sawdust, Dad gallantly introduced me to the workers. You saw what elegant manners he has. They called him Mr. Denver and me Miss Denver, which I quite liked. Several of the men noted our conspicuous resemblance. Dad and I toured the wine cellar, the ballroom, the projection and billiard rooms, the master bedroom and bath. There were unhindered prairie views everywhere—it was going to be sensational. Though Dad hadn't mentioned one, I thought it belonged to his boss."

"What does your father do?" I asked.

"Let me tell this my way, please," Twyla said. "Eventually Dad steered me into an immense chamber on the second floor with a private bath and sauna. 'Would you be happy living in this room?' he asked. 'You mean this house is *yours*?' I practically screamed with glee, thinking of my torn-down home in B.H. 'Or perhaps you'd prefer the guesthouse. A girl—a *woman*—of your age, I want you to have whatever your heart desires. But you'll have to be a wee bit patient. With luck, though one never knows with contractors, our home will be completed before your birthday on the ides of March.' People betray themselves by the language they speak, Fleur, but I didn't absorb the obvious. You remember 'Beware the ides of March.'"

"When they bumped off Julius Caesar?"

"In the next breath, Dad told me, 'I was going to save this particular tidbit as a birthday surprise, but I'm too excited to wait. I'm petitioning the city to name the road that leads up to our little fiefdom Twyla Lane.'"

I heard a shout from the bedroom. "I can't believe it," Melly said, bursting into the bathroom. "Twyla, I never dreamed I'd see you again. What brought you back? Ah"— Melly spied Tesora, whose cheeks were covered with bubbles—"look at our little darling."

Twyla appeared bewildered and uncomfortable.

"Oh, are you having a private conference?" Melly asked.

Twyla shrugged. "It doesn't matter. You might as well hear. I have nothing to hide anymore. I guess you could say I've lost my pride."

"Maybe that's for the best," Melly said, seating herself on the toilet lid.

We filled Melly in up to that point, and Twyla continued. "Dad explained that because he'd been offered an astronomical price for his previous house, with a swift thirty-day escrow, he'd had to move out in haste. His furniture, his good clothes, all his art and valuable *objets* were in storage. 'I'm temporarily bivouacked in a trailer, living the rustic life, a regular Thoreau, and loving it. You will, too, until our manse is in move-in condition,'" Twyla quoted her father.

"It *was* fun at first. We had plenty of water, a chemical toilet, butane gas, and a terrific camp stove on which Dad cooked a different gourmet meal every night. A life member of the Food and Wine Society, he taught me about food and all its 'historical vicissitudes,'" Twyla said fondly, forgetting for the moment whatever had transpired later. "So I learned to make sukiyaki served with heated saki—very romantic and impressive—and, listen to this, I can sauté octopus in its own ink."

"I'm not sure I'd like that," Melly said.

"Nor I," I agreed.

"We went to the best market, best butcher, best florist, et cetera, et cetera, and I discovered that Dad loves to shop. And though I didn't have much to do during the day while he went to the office, every evening he took me over to view our castle, one day closer to completion. Dad is so companionable. Try to understand—I truly believed that at last I'd found my emotional twin, a genuine blood relative with whom I shared an absurdist's view of the universe. For several weeks I couldn't have been more content or full of anticipation."

Tesora, excited by the cheerier tone in Twyla's voice, began splashing and laughing at the bubbles that glided toward Twyla.

"Will you make her stop?" Twyla asked sharply. She waited until I coaxed Tesora into playing a very soft patty-cake.

"So why didn't you call me when you were bored?" I asked.

"We didn't *have* a telephone, and when I asked about getting one, Dad laughingly said that he'd parked the trailer illegally, so he couldn't apply for any utilities. He took all his calls at his office, he said, and at night he truly enjoyed the solitude. He reminded me that it was only a temporary inconvenience, but if I really wanted one . . . Of course I said I didn't."

"What about letters?" Melly asked. "You could have written."

"Without a return address? I was embarrassed."

"Did you have a car? How did you get around?" I asked, California native that I was.

"Dad's passenger car, a year-old Bentley, was in the shop, he said. Parts had to be shipped from England, but the right ones never came. So he temporarily drove a pickup truck!" Twyla abruptly stopped talking when she heard the thwonk of Lizzie's boots.

"What the hay?" Lizzie said, poking her head into the bathroom.

I wondered if our roommate's presence might put a damper on Twyla's confessional, but when Lizzie asked, "What're you doin' here?," Twyla said simply, "Taking a bath. I'm also telling the story of the last two months of my life. Have a seat. You might as well get an earful direct from the horse's mouth."

"Don't mind if I do. Hello, Baby Tesora," Lizzie said as she collapsed her limbs on the bath rug. "Look at our big girl in the tub."

"Even though Dad could recite whole pages of

Faulkner, Auden, and Machiavelli from memory—so beautifully it broke my heart—after about a month I got antsy. My good clothes remained layered in their trunks, just as the hotel housekeeper in Tucson had packed them. Dad's one-burner meals lost gastronomic verve. I was lonely, so I started pressing Dad about meeting his friends. Why hadn't they invited us over, I asked.

"Embarrassed, apologetic, he confessed that he'd kept my existence secret. None of his illustrious friends, none of the eligible bachelors at his club, none of his fellow entrepreneurs yet knew that Gordon Denver had a gorgeous daughter, he said. Then he outlined his plans for my debut ball, which included a sit-down dinner and a symphony orchestra. 'The moment the house is finished,' he said."

"I wish you'd written to me about this," I couldn't help but say.

"I wrote a thousand letters in my head. But put any of this on paper? Why? So you, Miss Daughter of a phony private eye, could, like that baby, burst my bubble? I guess in my heart of hearts, I knew something sounded off the mark. But, Fleur and Melly and Lizzie, if you'd have been with me, if you had listened to his spellbinding projections . . . He made everything sound so thrillingly imminent. Even when the house wasn't ready on my eighteenth birthday, he took me to a resplendent restaurant where a violinist played whatever I requested for the duration of a spectacular eight-course meal. Though I did hope we'd run into some of his friends . . ."

"Twyla, you're the most sophisticated person I know.

Didn't you think— Weren't you just a little skeptical?"

"No. He's such a terrific companion. He's so attractive, and we had so much fun. He brought me flowers. Perfume. He made me laugh. He is a brilliant raconteur with a wealth of witticisms, though now I can't think of a single one."

"Does this end with me riding down to Texas and clobbering his brains out?" Lizzie asked.

"The day after my birthday, we had lunch with his banker, James Ashmund, and set in motion the transfer of my money to the United States. Dad said we needed to invest it immediately in some high-dividend blue-chip stocks that would increase my wealth tenfold. He used words like *tenfold* liberally, and I thought it lovely. But here's where life with Father got sticky. When Mr. Quincy, my guardian at the Credit Suisse Banque, heard about the requisition, he balked. In fact, he stalled the transfer.

"For the first time since we'd met, Dad saw red, and I felt a little frightened. Then a secretary from the Austin bank drove all the way out to the trailer to deliver a special-delivery letter to me. She said something rather telling, too: 'I would have given this to your father, but I wanted to be sure you received it.' Mr. Quincy had written seven pages single-spaced to tell me I was making a terrible mistake, that I was jeopardizing my entire estate, which was perfectly safe, making excellent interest, where it was!

"Mr. Quincy's message shook me," Twyla said. "I fired back a ten-page letter describing my father's virtues and my fortuitous circumstances. Then I hitchhiked into the city to mail it. I only wish I'd kept carbon copies."

I wished she had, too, but I could imagine a bespectacled Mr. Quincy squinting with anguish at Twyla's onionskin paper and complaining of eyestrain as Mr. Prail so often did.

"I neglected to tell Mr. Quincy that we were living in a trailer," Twyla continued. "What did it matter, since Dad and I had begun choosing carpeting and drapes for our permanent home. I simply plunged in and described what didn't fully exist. I planned to send photographs to my distinguished trustee as soon as we moved in.

"Mr. Quincy's next letter implored me to telephone him collect in Switzerland, but the time element—eight hours' difference—made it almost impossible. Meanwhile, Dad wasn't exactly *pressuring*, just kind of *pressing* me to insist on the transfer. And finally Dad and Mr. Ashmund wrote a letter to the president of the Credit Suisse Banque, alerting him to the illegality of withholding my funds. They— well, *we* because *I* signed it—demanded that my money be transferred immediately. And that day Dad put in a hundred dollars so we could open a joint checking account.

"I don't know why, but while Dad and Mr. Ashmund were talking in another office, I picked up a phone and called Al Mandell. I told him everything, and Al said, 'He's a con artist, Twy. Maybe he's your biological father and maybe he's not, but I bet he has a dozen aliases—which would account for why I couldn't find him—and a record.' But after we hung up, I asked myself why I should believe Al. He'd been a lousy detective."

"Hey, what do you know?" Sparky said. She stood in the doorway taking in the scene with amusement. "The Four-Letter Four reunited. Welcome back to the funhouse."

"We have to include Lizzie," I said. "It better be the Four-Letter Five."

"I'm no longer a worthy member," Twyla confessed. "So Lizzie can have my place."

"Oh, boy! What happened to you?" Sparky asked, sounding quite pleased.

"We'll dig the dirt later. Just let Twyla finish." Lizzie made her statement sound like a threat.

"But wait," Melly said. "Look at Tesora. Her hands are all pruney, and she's shivering."

"The water *is* getting terribly cold," Twyla said.

"Why didn't you say something?" I asked.

"Tesora was having so much fun, I didn't want to disturb her," Twyla explained.

"Wow," Melly said, as surprised as I by Twyla's new-found sensitivity.

Tesora shrieked as I pulled her out of the tub. In order to hear the rest of Twyla's story in peace, we had to heat the tub water and redeposit the baby in it.

"You're a water baby," Melly told Tesora.

"Al Mandell must have contacted my mother. She sent a special-delivery fifteen-page letter, care of the secretary at the bank, in her usual violet ink: *'I know you think I am after your MONEY, but I'd much rather YOU have it than that SNAKE who is NOW calling you HIS daughter. He'd take advantage of a QUADRIPLEGIC if an opportunity arose.*

Give that WORM ten seconds alone with your MONEY and, like the sleazy CIRCUS ACT that he is, he'll make it VANISH. It is my maternal DUTY to tell you of my FIRSTHAND combat. You're falling for the biggest SNOW JOB since snow began to fall! My advice is to SNEAK out of town ON THE DOUBLE.' She went on to say that though she had beauty, charm, wit, and talent, the only reason my father had married her was for her money. Now that I had the dough, he was pursuing me.

"That's basically what my mother wrote, but by then the mansion was, for all intents and purposes, finished. You see, I still wanted what he promised to come true. So I broached the subject that was uppermost in my mind: why not move in?

"'That will be hunky-dory, sweet pea. Any day now,' Dad kept saying. 'As soon as the marble people finish sanding. As soon as the terrazzo is polished. As soon as the appliances arrive.'" Twyla halted her commentary to burst into tears.

I looked around at the other girls. We all felt compassion. We all wanted to express it, but we also wanted Twyla to tell us the rest. "Is there anything we can do for you?" I asked, trying to cover up my impatience.

"One morning, fed up with being completely dependent on Dad, I took my new checkbook and hitchhiked into the city to a car dealership. Fleur, I bought myself something I've always wanted—a precious powder-blue convertible Mercedes 190 SL—and off I went. But being in the city, and I use the word loosely, I thought I would explore it. In less than an hour, I had exhausted the cultural attractions.

"So I tooled over to say hello to my banker. Mr. Ashmund was in Houston, but that nice secretary, abhoring trips made in vain, asked if she could help me balance my bank statement. 'What statement?' I asked her.

"Once she'd laid it out in front of me, I became hysterical. I saw that everyone—Mr. Quincy, Al Mandell, even my mother—was right. Out of the two hundred thousand seven hundred thirty-three dollars and seven cents that had been transferred to Texas from Switzerland, only"—and here she began to sob again—"approximately forty-three thousand remained. Subtract from that the price of my car. I had twelve thousand left."

"Twelve thousand dollars!" Melly exclaimed.

To Twyla, twelve thousand dollars was nothing; it precluded French frocks, soirees, and marriage to a baron. But twelve thousand would buy Melly the world she most wanted: college tuition and her family's relocation to Tucson. For a wild moment I considered writing a check to Melly Weisdorfler for that grand amount. Wouldn't Maurice be thunderstruck?

"The fact that my father would render me destitute was revealed to me four days ago. I felt so ashamed of my stupidity, but furious with Dad, too. I ordered the teller to hand over all the money I had left. I demanded it in cash, hoping it would put the bank out of business for a day or two. Then I climbed into my 190 SL and started driving."

"Oh, Twyla," I said. "I'm so sorry."

"Ohhhh," Tesora exclaimed.

* * *

"Here we are again—the catacombs," Twyla announced as we stepped into the living room of my parents' house.

"Not an apt description," I argued good-humoredly. "I'm glad to be here. The rooms are spacious, and there's no one dead in residence."

"I'm talking about the predominant mood," Twyla said.

"You're talking about your *own* mood."

Handbag dangling from her arm, high heels pitting the carpeting, Charmian gave us the high sign, then scooted past us toward a ringing telephone. We soon heard her pounce on Miss Dora of the Hollywood International Domestic Employment Agency. "You took your time about calling me back. The maid just quit and cleared out, the cook is on the verge, and I have guests coming tonight. You absolutely must send in a second-string lineup within half an hour. I am your foremost client, am I not?"

Twyla nudged me. "Does it ever stop? The hirings and firings? The quittings?"

"Evidently not. Even Odysseus had an old nanny left in his castle to recognize him. I have none."

Once she'd put down the receiver, Charmian turned to us. "What are you doing here? Weren't you going to drive across the country? I thought you were *days* away."

"We drove from Tucson to here," I explained. "It took about twelve hours."

"You didn't give me time to remove my things from your room. And Hattie is *not* going to want to feed you now."

"Charmian, we stopped for hamburgers three times, so we don't need food. We don't need a clean room, either. We're really tired. Twyla and I just want to hit the hay."

"Please," Charmian said, "no vulgarisms in my house."

Thanks to a capacious water heater in the hidden recesses under the house, Twyla was able to submerge in the tub while I showered. Since Christmas vacation I had yearned to wallow again in my own shower wherein five spigots on each yellow-tiled wall sprayed my entire body with warm, welcoming liquid.

Anxiously anticipating the end of my banishment from home, I hadn't allowed myself to absorb the grief of leaving my friends at Rancho Cambridge West. Now, surrounded by comforting hot vapor, I replayed the recent memory of restoring Tesora to her parents' custody. Healthy and smiley, the baby had been serene when Melly and I reluctantly placed her in her mother's arms. We'd brought along a suitcase of toys, the Mickey Mouse piñata I'd purchased in Nogales and, courtesy of Maurice, six months' supply of Isoniazid. With Becillia translating, we were able to exact a promise from Tesora's mother that the baby would visit Dr. Martinez whenever they returned to the area. We'd kissed them all, young and old, and, somewhat abashed, I'd handed out slips of paper with my Beverly Hills address. I needed to create the illusion that I would hear from them.

"I feel as though I've lost my sight or my hearing," I'd

told Melly as we boarded the rickety school bus for my last ride.

"Me, too. But doctors go through this all the time, whenever they lose a beloved patient to death or even a cure," Melly said. "I've read their accounts. Just remember, we were instrumental in healing Tesora. So if we start helping someone else right away, we can fill up the emptiness she's left."

Melly had no such advice about our parting. "We'll write, come hell or high water, once a week. We'll do it the rest of our lives. Your mailman will learn to hate me," she declared cheerfully. "Plus, California's not that far from Tucson, right? I'll come visit you. And you can call me anytime. At your father's expense. Agreed?"

"I heartily agree." I knew we'd see each again, and we did.

As for Brian, I had few misconceptions then. The day before our leave-taking, he had given me a sterling silver six-cornered star, a Jewish star about the size of a quarter, with a chain so it could be worn like a necklace. He'd bought it in Nogales, and the storekeeper hadn't bothered with polish. I vaguely understood that Brian had meant the keepsake to symbolize his love and acceptance of things about me I hadn't accepted myself. But the star defined me, trapped me within its rigid, six-pointed symmetry—I would have preferred a curvy heart. I wasn't ready for definition yet; I looked to the future for that. But I thanked him and pretended to cherish the memento even while envisioning the derision my parents would subject me to if they saw it.

I realized then that even if Brian could have moved to

my neck of the woods, our alliance would be ill-starred. Place him for a moment in my parents' company, and they would look askance at his skin. Two minutes later, they would gaze heavenward for an explanation of his provincial speech and limited vocabulary.

Brian, who lived in faraway Delaware, seemed to intuit this, too. "I'll keep the cards and letters coming, sure, but you're going to grow tired of me. I can't compete with Beverly Hills."

It was our physical connection, our coupledom, our corporeal habit, that made our farewell especially distressing. Perhaps this is what my mother referred to when she'd mentioned that at my age I lacked the maturity needed for intimate relations. We'd held each other one last time, skin to skin, and through my tears, I'd been able to say, "Someday I'm going to write about you." I meant it. I wanted to pay him tribute.

When Brian answered, "I'd write about you, too, if only I could," it didn't sound so corny.

Twyla and I were too exhausted to change the sheets. We simply closed the shutters to darken the room, smoothed out the rumpled linens, and climbed into bed.

"My whole body is tingling," I told Twyla. "Is it from the needles of shower water or the vibration of the car?"

"It's the scourge of sports cars," Twyla said. "I have the same sensation. Or maybe, now that we're here, it's fear in the raw."

"What are you afraid of?"

"I'm only eighteen and I'm entirely on my own."

"Oh, Twyla. It *is* scary. My heart goes out to you. I hope you know that I'll do anything to help you. Any thoughts on what you want to do?"

"Oh, most assuredly. First, I'm going to rent someone's guesthouse in Benedict Canyon."

"That'll be very expensive."

"Yes, but I was remembering as we drove that my grandmother left me six hundred thousand dollars. Only two hundred thousand wound up in Texas. Mr. Quincy obviously kept four hundred thousand of it in Switzerland—that's the kind of person he is. I'll call him, but I'm quite certain. So, as I was explaining, I plan to move as close to Odiline as I can get. You see, I have accepted the fact that—much as she infuriates me—Mother is an exquisite actress. And didn't I learn the hard way that my father is a convincing actor, too? I have to assume I've inherited my parents' acting genes. Twofold."

"You have more going for you than their genes," I said sincerely.

"That's why instead of going to college I'm going to study acting with Odiline. She says I have the adaptability and imagination and perseverance essential to stardom. She's promised to give me daily private instruction. And God knows she has plenty of contacts in Hollywood. Odiline is positive I will have an auspicious career."

"And you'll have a doting mother. It's wonderful, Twyla. You'll be terrific."

"And you? What are you going to do?" she asked.

"All year long I just wanted to come home. I wanted to attend a school where the people who run it aren't cuckoo, where the teachers are dependable and know their subjects. I missed my friends here who are interested in current events and actually read books for pleasure. They care about music and art. They think about college and careers and the meaning of life. I missed my parents' friends, too, their stories, their ideas. I missed the stimulation.

"But now that I've returned home I realize that all along I simply couldn't brook being rejected by my parents. Mr. St. Cyr called them negligent. They certainly aren't—what do you call it—nurturing, but whatever they are, and as unfortunate as it is, for now I need their acceptance."

"This summer?" Twyla asked. "What will you do?"

"Twyla," I exclaimed. "You're interested in me!"

"Haven't I always been?"

"Usually only when it comes to correcting my pronunciation and English usage," I said.

"But that should *prove* my interest."

"Which is exactly what Charmian would say. Incidentally, your rules about speech are preposterous."

"Fleur, they're in a book. I know you've seen it before." Twyla slipped out of bed and rooted through her purse. Finally, she pulled out the same little book I'd removed from the Rancho Cambridge West library on my first evening there: *Noblesse Oblige*.

"You kept this? You've got to be kidding," I said.

"It proved especially useful while I lived with Dad. I kept it in my handbag. Have you read it?" she asked.

"Some," I said. "Twyla, it's meant as a joke. The writers are *ridiculing* snobbism, not promoting it. Don't you understand?"

Twyla appeared baffled, then properly shamed. "I just wanted to fit into the right circles," she said.

"If you were merely nice to people, if you'd give up being prejudiced, you'd fit in anywhere." I didn't want to belabor my criticism, so I changed the subject. "But to answer your question about this summer, I plan to follow up on those volunteer opportunities they list in the newspaper. It may be trite, but one of the things, among many, I learned at RCW was that I truly take pleasure in helping those less fortunate than myself."

Twyla didn't respond. I heard her breathing soothe into the rhythm of sleep. Not for her the rigors of insomnia. I remembered Charmian commenting that the ability to doze anywhere, anytime, and therefore wake up refreshed, was a prerequisite for good acting. And then I heard the rustling of my mother's clothes.

"Are you looking for me?" I asked.

"No, my cigarettes," she whispered.

"But Charmian, there's a whole basket of cigarettes on the gueridon in the living room."

"Not my brand."

"Are you sure you didn't want to talk to me?"

"Well, if you're awake . . ."

"I am."

Charmian sat down on the side of the bed. "It must be a relief to be emancipated from that dreadful school," she said softly.

"It is, but I grew to love some of the kids, so it's bitter-sweet, too."

"Bittersweet, bittersweet," she mused. *"Bitter Sweet.* It was a brilliant play by Noël Coward. What memories I have of it. Did I ever tell you how I landed the starring role? Not in London, regrettably. Here in Los Angeles. I had to toil, let me tell you, over just the right English accent and brush up on . . ."

I'm back. I've really come home, I thought, and relaxed enough to fall asleep.

About the Author

Diane Leslie is the author of *Fleur de Leigh's Life of Crime*, a *Los Angeles Times* bestseller for twenty-eight weeks. She lives in Los Angeles, where for many years she has hosted author readings and led book groups at Dutton's Brentwood Bookstore.